HUGH GARNER

STORM BELOW

HUGH GARNER

STORM BELOW

PaperJacks

Markham, Ontario, Canada

A CANADIAN

PaperJacks

One of a series of Canadian books
by PaperJacks Ltd.

STORM BELOW

The Ryerson Press edition published in 1968
PaperJacks edition published 1983

ISBN 0-7701-0255-7
Copyright © 1949, 1968 by Hugh Garner
All rights reserved
Printed in Canada

The Canadian corvette, H.M.C.S. *Riverford*, which serves as the setting of this book, is fictitious only to the extent that it is a composite of many. The members of the crew are also fictitious, but, I hope, recognizable as human beings behind the hyperbole and distortion which is the privilege of the fiction writer.

It takes all kinds to make a world, and it also takes all kinds to make a war—or fight one after some of the others make it.

This is not the story of a ship, but the story of a few Canadian sailors who formed the ship's company of the *Riverford*, during six days at the tagend of an escort run in March of 1943. There is nothing much about them to inspire poetry, or a patriotic shiver of pride in the reader; that is not the object of this book. They are not even "typical" sailors, if such exist. All I can say to justify them, is that they are drawn in the image of hundreds who made up the Royal Canadian Navy. They do not need an apology —they were out there, and we won.

THE AUTHOR.

The dawn of March 9th, 1943 rose above the spinning earth. For the many it was without significance, except to herald the coming day, but to the few it was epochal, and filled with meaning. It was the first dawn for those who were born the night before, and the last for those who had to die.

They were to die in many ways on that fateful, yet undifferent day: In the gas chambers of Osweicim, on the spittle-caking roads of North Africa, in a birth-bed in the Queen Mary Marternity Hospital in Sheffield, before a Ustachi firing squad outside Sarajevo, of prostatic cancer in a hotel for indigent men near the corner of the Bowery and Houston Streets in New York City, at the wheel of a 1940 Buick at a level crossing near Buenos Aires, in the tail turret of a Halifax bomber over the German Ruhr, of pulmonary embolism in a sheep-herder's hut in Queensland, Australia . . .

The Canadian Flower Class corvette, H.M.C.S. *Riverford* was proceeding west-south-west at ten knots, part of the escort force of a merchant convoy, eleven days out of Londonderry, Nothern Ireland. She was adhering to an Admiralty specified zigzag on the port, forward anti-submarine sweep, abreast of the leading file of fifty-six assorted merchantmen returning to North America in ballast. They had rendezvoused in the Clyde from such scattered points as Tilbury, Murmansk, Birkenhead, Loch Ewe, South Shields, Bristol, Oran, Queenstown, Lisbon and Hull for the break across the North Atlantic. They ran the gamut of sea transportation from a twenty-two-thousand ton Norwegian whaling factory through Liberty Ships on Australian refrigerator ship, a Canadian lower laker, to a decrepit Greek coaster which trailed the others like a dirty-faced young brother on a hike. Also escorting them were a Canadian four-stacker destroyer, four more Canadian corvettes, and an English trawler on its way to the West Indies to take up mine-sweeping duties outside the port of Kingston, Jamaica.

The pre-dawn air was chill with the wind which swept off the blue-glass ice shelf of Greenland a few hundred miles to the north-west, and the cold black sea was raised into sullen, turgid ridges, its fringe of white petit-point blown away with each gust of wind.

Ordinary Seaman Clark, nineteen years old, Royal Canadian Naval Volunteer Reserve, stepped quickly through the sliding door of the wheel-house, shutting it behind him, and stood in the darkness on the narrow platform staring out at the noisy, heaving sea. He looked up into the darkened sky, catching a glimpse now and again of a patch of star-studded heaven as it dipped and curtsied behind and between the wider ceiling of scudding clouds. The whole cosmos revolved around an axis formed by the jutting bow and fo'castlehead of the small ship, and the whistle of the wind through the struts and halyards accompanied the pirouette of the fading night.

As he stood still, fastening the top toggle of his woollen duffle coat against the wind, he became aware of the dark, dreadful loneliness of the sea. He was suddenly afraid, and he tuned his ears to the more familiar sounds of the ship and his fellows. From below him came the clatter of pans in the galley as the assistant cook, who had been baking his nightly batch of bread, cleaned up before his mate arrived to prepare breakfast. Up ahead the four-inch gun strained at its lashings with every rise and fall of the gun deck, and the shells clanked mournfully in their racks. There was the sound of feet being stamped on the boards above his head as the port look-out changed his position on the wing of the bridge. The noises from aft were swept away with the wind.

The sounds of the ship only accentuated the noisy quietude of the limitless expanse of the sea, so that the boy shivered, and his hands gripped the railing beside him. Suddenly he was afraid of losing his grip on this heaving thing which was his only connection with security, and he feared to be cast away into the sea which hissed and foamed as it reached with white-nailed fingers upon the free-board below.

Standing there he realized that the sea cannot be loved; it is an enemy upon which men sail their puny craft—an alien thing armed with a multitude of claws ready to pull them beneath it with scarcely a ripple or a trace. It is too vast and too black and too uncomprehending to be loved. It gives neither succour nor hope nor life to those who must depend upon it. It is beautiful and terrifying, and gigantic and insatiable; a desert of water over which men travel through necessity.

He no longer thought of submarines and torpedoes, for now his fears were those which have followed men from the dawn of time; the primeval fears of the elements: of wind, of lightning, of the sea.

He strained his eyes aft to try to catch a glimpse of the look-out on the ack-ack platform; to find another human being with whom to share his terror; but the man could not be seen; he was alone. He fought with himself against the dread which rose through his fibres like a scream. With a desperate urgency he stumbled down the steep steps of the ladder, his heavy coat buckling around his thighs and his hands sliding down the wet railings, not allowing himself to look at the water, his eyes fixed on the swiftly falling stern of the ship. Half-way to the bottom his rubber sea-boot slipped from the serrated step, and his hands lost their grip upon the rails. With a soft thud, and an imperceptible swoosh of clothing, he fell the remainder of the way to the steel deck, and lay there, one arm doubled behind him, and his terrified eyes hidden behind their curtained lids. To his unhearing ears came the slap of the stoical sea as the tips of its tentacles caressed him through the drains along the scuppers.

CHAPTER 1

Lieut.-Commander Joseph Frigsby, D.S.C., R.C.N.R. stood on the bridge of his ship, leaning forward over the dodger. Now and again he glanced back at the boiling wake, running white in the green water, and murmured steering instructions down the voice pipe to the seaman at the wheel.

He was a short, thin man with sharp features beneath the visor of his cap. He was attired in a roll-necked woollen sweater, over which he wore a shabby officer's uniform jacket from the sleeves of which the pair of lieutenant's chain-linked stripes had been torn. His cap was regulation, but upon its front was fastened a soggy green replica of a naval officer's gold badge. On his feet he wore a pair of turned-down rubber boots, and covering everything but the boots and cap hung a long khaki-coloured sheepskin coat.

His thin jaws worked methodically as he chewed a peppermint drop. He was thinking that no matter how often he crossed the ocean he could not get away from the feeling that when the ship was running a northerly course it seemed as though it was running uphill, and when it was travelling south, it was running down again. Of course it is ridiculous, he argued with himself, just one of those ridiculous little thoughts which people use to amuse themselves, especially ships' captains whose life is much more introverted than those of others on the ship. He thought, it is the fault of the Mercator's Projection which hangs on the Wardroom bulkhead to show the U-Boat dispositions.

But regardless of the fantasy of such thoughts, you could not get away from the fact that as soon as your course became southerly, somewhere west of Iceland, a new feeling gripped everybody aboard; and when you drew the new line on the wardroom chart it looked for all the world as though you were coasting downhill to Newfoundland a few hundred miles ahead.

You knew that it affected others the same way because you had seen the steward's face light up each time he had noticed the new change in course on every crossing. The junior officers became a little more boisterous, and the men showed their feelings in a hundred ways: more singing and shouting, more laundry being done, a general relaxation from the tenseness which had gripped them all since the beginning of the trip . . .

He sighed and stepped back from his position at the voice pipes and took a turn around the asdic cabin, which housed the submarine detection gear, motioning to Lieutenant Harris, the officer on watch, to take over.

Dawn was breaking, the slow zigzag pattern of the ship's course swinging the rising sun along the port side from the bow almost to the quarter. Mechanically he glanced at the look-outs on the bridge wings to see that they were keeping an eye out.

As he stepped to the watertight door opening into the radar cabin he met the Leading Steward coming up the ladder with a teapot and cups in his hands. He reached out and took a cup while the steward poured it full of hot black tea. "Thanks, Roberts," he said. "What's on for breakfast this morning?"

"W-w-w-w-w-w-eggs, sir," the steward answered.

"Thank you," said the Captain, walking away. It was a damnable affliction, stammering. He wished that Roberts could be drafted. A bloody embarrassing thing to have to listen to. Eggs, but what kind of eggs? It was impossible to ask Roberts.

He drank the cup of scalding tea with a smacking of lips, feeling the heat of it warm him under his sheepskin coat. Placing the empty cup on the starboard Oerlikon-gun platform, he made his way once more to the radar cabin and looked inside. The operator, a middle-aged Scotsman, named Wright, was sitting with his back against the bulk-head, his eyes on the screen in front of him. "How are the ships showing up?" asked the Captain.

"They're nae bad, sirr; it's been guid ever since I came on watch."

12

"Do you get a pip from the *Milverton*?"

"Where's she, sirr?"

"Let's see, she should be on the port beam. Around four thousand yards."

As the operator began manipulating his wheel, the door flew open, and the face of Sub-Lieutenant Peter Smith-Rawleigh looked in. He was excited, and his pudgy countenance was filled with the momentousness of the occasion. He was freshly shaved, as he always was since he had found that his sparse beard was an object of levity among the men. He was the only man aboard who shaved every day at sea. He said, "Sir, there's been an accident to one of the seamen. He's pretty badly hurt."

The Captain asked, "Did you get the Sick Berth Attendant?"

"No sir. That is, I've sent for him, sir."

"Tell him to report to me as soon as the man is made comfortable."

The Sub-Lieutenant made his way down the ladder again, his oversized feet gripping the rungs carefully in his descent.

He's rushed off to get the Sick Bay Tiffy himself, the Captain thought. Caught with his pants down. Bloody little snob. How did a Canadian get a hyphenated name? It was as ersatz as his Vancouver Island English accent.

"I've got the *Milverton*, sir," Wright said.

"Eh? Oh good! Good work!" said the Captain, glancing at the screen.

He took another turn around the bridge, standing for a minute or two in the shelter of the splinter shield, gazing to starboard where the serried rows of freighters bobbed up and down in the middle distance. Beneath their high-riding plimsolls the red oxide of their bottom plates showed momentarily above the whitecaps. The little Greek coaster trailed a soggy tassel of black smoke along her wake.

Leading Seaman Hector McCaffrey lounged on the Captain's couch in the wheel-house and puffed dreamily on a cigarette. In his hand rested a red-covered, lurid romance entitled *The Fleshpots Of Sin*.

He was a heavy young man who was on the sixth year of his first seven-year hitch in the regular navy. Because of his three or four year seniority over most of the other members of the crew he was inclined to be a little distant with them, and he could not forget that for the first three years of his enlistment he had hardly dared open his mouth. Since the advent of so many civilians—"plough jockeys" he called them—he had come into his own, and now that it was his turn to rule the roost he resented the lack of feeling for his position which the new entries showed him. Along with their ignorance of naval protocol was an easygoing camaraderie which they were forever trying to force upon him, a leading seaman. With the exception of the Captain and the Navigating Officer who were ex-Merchant Navy men he had nothing but contempt for the officers, whom he grouped together, regardless of civilian occupation, under the opprobrious term of "bank tellers".

He settled himself more comfortably on the couch, placing his feet against the wooden foot of the bunk. He was using his duffle coat as a cover, and his lifebelt as a pillow. Over a suit of dungarees he wore a blue denim smock.

"You wanna watch out, McCaffrey," the seaman at the wheel said, covering the voice pipe with the palm of his hand. "You know what the Old Man'll say if he knows somebody down here's smoking. He's up top, you know."

"He can't smell this fag from here."

"He can smell 'em a mile."

"Is he on the blower now?"

"No, it's Harris."

"Quit worrying." He went back to his book, waiting until nobody was looking before surreptitiously stamping out his cigarette.

The wheel-house was quiet again except for the da-da-da-dit, da-dit from the wireless room which was separated from it by a door, and the quartermaster's answers to the officer on the bridge, "Steady on two-one-oh."

McCaffrey was immersed in the chapter of his book in which the white girl had been bought at auction by the Bey of Tunis, and was being led away bathed in tears to a fate worse, even, than she had experienced at home at the hands of her erstwhile boss, Karl Tarbish.

The starboard door opened noisily, automatically plunging the wheel-house into darkness, and a hand pushed aside the blackout curtain and shut the door, turning on the lights again. A seaman entered, the Bosun's Mate, who had been sent down to the galley by McCaffrey to scrounge a cup of coffee and a sandwich. "Hey, Mac, young Knobby's hurt pretty bad! They got him layin' on the mess-deck table!"

McCaffrey laid the book down and jumped to his feet. "What happened?"

"He fell down the ladder right outside here."

"When?"

"I guess it was about an hour ago when you sent him forward to wake the hands."

"Is the tiffy there?"

"Yeah."

"You notify the officer of the watch?"

"The subby is in there now."

"Okay. Go and report it to the Old Man —"

"The subby's gone."

"All right, get these blackout screens down and let some air in here. You relieve Wilson on the bridge and tell him to go aft." His indolence had disappeared with the coming of the Bosun's Mate and the news of Knobby's accident. Now he was fully awake, his senses tuned to the emergency. There would be a man short on the next red watch. They would have to get the injured man's hammock slung somewhere out of the way where he could have a little quiet and privacy. The Coxswain would have to be notified. If they were going to keep a man in the crow's-nest today it would make them still another man short. Have to get the Coxswain to take the extra man from the radar people . . .

With a parting word to the man on the wheel he pulled on his duffle coat, picked up his lifebelt, and pushed his way out into the now lightened day. When he reached the deck he made his way forward under the break of the fo'castle to the seamen's mess.

Just forward of the depth-charge rails at the stern was the Chiefs and Petty Officers' Washroom, which opened from the upper deck, and stood at the head of the companion-way which led below to the quarters of the Chiefs and P.O.s. It contained a toilet-bowl, a wash-bowl, and a shower around which hung a grimy white curtain. It was utilitarian, and had the appearance of being placed aboard

15

as an afterthought by a naval architect who had been under the impression that any ranks below commissioned should excrete over the side. It was much too small to contain more than one person at a time, unless the second person stood in the shower, and showers were disallowed at sea.

Its occupant, Stoker Petty Officer Jimmy Collet, washed his face and neck with hot water preparatory to shaving. About a month before, he had experienced an accident involving a broken tube of shaving cream and a new tailor-made suit of blue officer's serge which had come in contact, one with the other, in his bag. Since then he had shaved with face soap.

He was a slight young man of medium height, with the arms and hands of a manual worker. His face, even under the quick ministrations of soap and water, showed the black pits which were the result of his trade, as though the pores had absorbed their quota of oil and grit from long association. He wore a pair of oil-dulled issue boots, above which hung from his spare hips a pair of stiffened, brass-riveted dungaree pants. He was naked from the waist-up, and the white, almost feminine, skin of his arms was covered from wrist to shoulder with various inked mementos of the tattooist's art.

His face felt good after its eleven-day holiday from the razor. He figured out mentally that he had about two more days to go. He wouldn't shave again until they entered the gates of St. Johns, Newfoundland. Then a real clean up, with a bath, and up to the canteen on Water Street, dressed in his second-best "drinking" suit—there to absorb a dozen or so bottles of ale to wash away the taste of the cook's smoked fillets.

The P.O.'s messman, a stoker, came through the hatch from the quarter-deck and leaned his body inside the wash-room door. "One of the seamen is knocked cold," he said.

Collet turned from the mirror, half his face camouflaged with soap suds. "Who?" he asked disinterestedly.

"One of the new kids we picked up this trip."

"Oh. Hurt bad?"

"They got him in the mess deck; on a table."

"How'd he do it?" he asked, slicing carefully down the right side of his jaw with the safety razor.

"Fell down the wheel-house ladder."

"Mmm! What's on for breakfast?"

"Shirred eggs, the cook says," answered the other, brought back to the realization of his duties by the question.

"What the hell's shirred eggs?"

"You know, done in the oven, in a bake-tin like."

"Okay. You woke the watch yet?" asked Collet, as though to end the conversation.

"I'm going to as soon as I get this coffee down below." The messman turned from the doorway, and gripping the hot handle of the coffee-pot through the thickness of a handful of cloth waste, he manoeuvred himself down the heaving steps to the mess where the engine-room watch-keepers and the ship's Coxswain were sitting at the table awaiting breakfast.

As he finished shaving and wiped his face on a bath towel Jimmy Collet was thinking of the news he had just received. It was tough on the kid, getting hurt on his first trip. Seemed to be a nice kid too, not a Jack-Me-Hearty like some of the punks they were getting these days. Probably wasn't hurt very bad.

He cheered himself with the thought that in a couple of days they would be in port, and making ready to proceed to Canada for a refit. The thought of a refit made everything, including the seaman's hurts, seem very inconsequential. As he rubbed his face vigorously with the rough towel he contemplated the good times waiting for him on twenty-eight days' leave at home in Hamilton.

He thought, it will be around the end of March when the first half of the ship's company take leave, and around the end of April before they come back. If I wait for the second shift, it will get me home in May for the warm weather. I'll go down to the plant and see the boys, and maybe take a bottle of hard stuff with me. After that I'll go up to the Delight Café and see Daisy—that is, if she's not in war work at the Canadian Car or Westinghouse. Anyway, I'll go and make the round of the hotels, and see who is still around . . . He began to whistle as he gathered up his things, and made ready to go below for his portion of shirred eggs.

The ship's Sick Berth Attendant swung gently in peaceful slumber in his hammock, on the port side of the communications mess, which was reserved for the miscellaneous ratings: cooks, stewards, supply assistant, and himself.

He was dreaming that he was berry-picking in a heavy wooded copse that lay about a half-mile behind his father's farm in Nova Scotia's Annapolis Valley. Somehow or other he was accompanied by his old school teacher, Mrs. Gregory, and she was shouting to him to move along the raspberry patch, for the berries he was picking were blue ones, when they should have been red . . .

"Hey, Tiffy!" somebody was shouting as they grabbed him by the shoulder.

"W-w-what!" he yelled, automatically grabbing for the deck-head pipe which he used for a trapeze in getting in and out of his hammock.

"Come on up top, somebody's hurt!"

"Hey?" Wiping the sleep from his eyes, he looked over the side of the hammock at the face of a seaman who was standing on one of the lockers beneath.

"Come on, one of the new kid's hurt himself. They've got him on a table in the seamen's mess!"

"Okay," he said, as the reality took precedence over the dream. He swung himself over the side of the hammock and dropped in his stocking feet upon the deck.

"Are you coming right away?" asked the seaman, whom he now recognized as the Bosun's Mate of the watch.

He shook the last vestiges of sleep from his eyes. "Sure. Let me get my boots on first. How bad is he hurt?"

"I guess his arm's broke, and he's unconscious."

He pulled on his sea-boots and unslung his first-aid bag from its hook on the bulkhead. Then he followed the seaman up the ladder.

CHAPTER 2

Ransome Shelley Bodley — to give him his complete name, although he never gave it to himself except when sheer necessity compelled — was twenty-two years old, a retail clerk in civilian life, who had joined the Navy as a Sick Berth Attendant under the mistaken impression that he would be employed solely in hospitals ashore. It was to his credit that when he had found out the fallacy of such reasoning he had not attempted to back out of going to sea, but had accepted the draft to the *Riverford* with a sang-froid which was as brave as it was pretentious. Now that he had been a member of the ship's crew for a year he was glad that things had happened as they had. The mere thought of serving as a pot-juggler in a hospital had now lost its allure, and the only time he wanted to visit a hospital was on his infrequent trips to Halifax when he could call on some of his old classmates and let them see what a real sailor looked like.

He was a very handsome young man, was Shelley, with straight white teeth, a mother's boy complexion, and black oily hair which he arranged in a series of waves by a deft, practised chop of the heel of his hand. He was not effeminate, although some of the more rough-and-ready members of the crew were under the impression that all sick-bay tiffies were.

On the morning when he was so rudely awakened by the Bosun's Mate he was attired in his regular sea-going night clothing consisting of two-weeks'-old underdrawers, a pair of regulation heavy serge trousers, a once-white collarless shirt, a hand-knitted blue sleeveless sweater (a donation by the Imperial Order Daughters Of The Empire of Quebec

19

City) and a pair of black cotton-and-wool socks. It was his boast that the action station bell would never catch him unprepared, and his affairs were so arranged that it was only necessary to step into his boots and pull his duffle coat over him before he raced for the upper deck.

He followed the Bosun's Mate up the slightly weaving ladder, and they crossed the narrow space which lay between the wooden safety door at the top of the companionway, and the steel bulkhead, behind which was the small canteen. They went to starboard, passing the forward food stores, and climbed across the foot-high coping beneath the heavy watertight door which gave access to the seamen's mess deck. Immediately inside the door was the ship's refrigerator, and as they passed it they looked inside where the Supply Rating was struggling with a welter of piled-up meat, trying to retrieve a cellophane-wrapped cottage-roll. The Bosun's Mate could not resist the opportunity to make a remark about the supposed state of putrefaction of· the food which the ice-box contained. "Phew!" he exclaimed, so that the Supply Rating could hear him. "What the hell you got in there!"

"It smells like a bag shanty," commented the Sick Berth Attendant, playing along with the joke despite his eagerness to get to his patient.

They pushed past the open door of the ice-box and entered the mess deck. It was a chamber stretching across the width of the ship at their point of entry, and narrowing towards the bow, where it ended at a watertight door opening on a paint locker. The low deckhead was a maze of pipes, air ducts, and hammock bars sprayed with a cork solution to keep it from sweating. This, however, was hidden at the moment by a false ceiling of undulating hammocks which covered every available inch of space, and narrowed the head room beneath to about five feet. The dead-lights were battened down over the port-holes, and the only light came from two or three sixty-watt bulbs which tried vainly to shed their light through the close-knit hammocks beneath. The furniture consisted of a pair of wooden cupboards containing some enamel dinnerware, three salt-shakers and a pepper-shaker, an inadequate amount of cutlery, the remains of a soggy pound of butter, two opened tins of evaporated milk, and a cannister of tea-stained sugar. Against the after-

20

bulkhead, between the port and starboard doors, was a heavy, wooden, cattle-stall affair which served while in port as a receptacle for the rolled-up hammocks of the seamen. At the moment it was doing duty as the sleeping place for two men who had been unable to find room to sling their hammocks above. There were three tables bolted to the deck, which served as the eating places for the thirty men who lived there, and along their sides were three narrow benches, also bolted down. Around the sides of the chamber were a tight-packed series of wooden lockers, the tops of which formed a wide shelf upon which was stored accumulated duffle such as bags, boxes, head-gear, mitts, photographs in frames, good shoes, dirty socks, and such miscellaneous possessions as could not be safely stored elsewhere. Beneath this shelf, but jutting out from it, were the tops of the clothes-lockers which formed a long seat continuing down both sides of the mess. This was covered by a number of long leather cushions used by other members of the crew for sleeping accommodation due to the over-crowding.

The Sick Berth Attendant pushed his way through the small knot of seamen and stokers to where Ordinary Seaman "Knobby" Clark lay upon a table, still attired in boots and duffle coat, his face white and strained under its tan. One of his arms was folded on his chest, while the other lay loose and twisted beside him.

"Clear a gangway there!" shouted the young Sub-Lieutenant, whom Bodley now noticed for the first time standing at the head of the table. He placed his first-aid bag on the deck, and said, "Let's get his boots and coat off, fellows." Two of the seamen pulled at the injured man's boots which they threw on one of the lockers. The Sub-Lieutenant and another eased Knobby out of his coat.

Bodley leaned over the table and began feeling the arm which lay along the injured boy's side. As his fingers followed the bones he was conscious that the others were watching him in silence, showing the respect and awe for medical knowledge which the layman usually does. When his fingers felt the rough, gritty fracture below the elbow he took his hand away and said, "There it is."

He looked up to find them staring at him, and he thought, what the hell, any of them could have done the same! But the fact that none of them were aware of it gave him a feeling of power, and for the first time in his life he basked in the importance which comes with the respect of one's fellows.

He was about to open his bag and take out the bandages and splints it contained, when suddenly the surgeon's instructions during his course returned to him. "Never believe that a patient's only injuries are the obvious ones." Trying not to show his indecision, he straightened up again and felt the pulse of the injured man's good arm. Then he passed his hand over the patient forehead. "Take everything off him," he said to those standing around. It was good to be able to give orders which the Sub-Lieutenant could not countermand. "Get his blankets out of his hammock and cover him well." As they began doing this he ran down below to the small medicine cabinet over his locker and returned with a bottle of aromatic spirits of ammonia.

When the patient was undressed and under the blankets he passed the bottle of ammonia under Knobby's nose. There was no response. He pulled the blankets down and looked the man over for other injuries, but none were apparent. The crowd in the mess, reinforced now as the next watch-keepers were awakened, were beginning to grumble impatiently. To show them that he knew his job he took out the wooden splints and bandage and with a dexterity he had not known he possessed he pulled the arm into position and applied them. Taking a piece of unbleached cotton from the bag he fashioned a sling and tied it behind the patient's neck.

"How do you think he is, Bodley?" asked the Sub-Lieutenant.

"I can't say, sir. His arm is okay for now, but there may be internal injuries." It elated him to mention such things, although he was ashamed of his elation as soon as he had felt it. Knobby was his first real patient in a year with the exception of several gonorrhoea cases, a stoker who almost severed a finger in the heavy washroom door, and ten survivors whom they had picked up off Iceland the previous summer.

The survivors had been a disappointment. They had been floating high and dry in a sea boat for only a few hours, and they had drunk the rum from the first-aid kit, so that they came aboard in a happy state singing "Roll Out The Barrel".

22

The only medication they had required was a spoonful of bicarbonate the morning after their rescue.

It seemed that sailors only became gravely ill in port, and except for *mal de mer,* of which there was plenty on a corvette — especially among the new men the first day out — there was not enough sickness among his charges to let him earn his passage.

The voice of the Sub-Lieutenant interrupted his thoughts. "Can you find out whether he has any internal injuries?"

"No, sir. We should get a surgeon to look at him."

"Will you leave him here?"

"There's nowhere else, except in one of the officer's cabins."

Sub-Lieutenant Smith-Rawleigh blanched as he suddenly remembered that he, as junior officer, would be the one who would be asked to give up his berth and sleep on the wardroom settee. (This had happened when they took aboard the newspaper correspondent for the trip from Gibraltar to Londonderry before Christmas.)

Several of the bystanders snickered when they realized that it would be the subby's cabin which would become the sick-room. To cover his retreat from such insubordination Smith-Rawleigh barked, "You fellows see that he doesn't fall off the table," pointing to the injured man. Then he said to Bodley, "The Captain wants you to report to him immediately."

Bodley followed the officer under the blackout curtains and along the deck to the ladder leading to the bridge.

The sky which now stretched overhead was a deep blue, and the clouds which had scudded across the sun following the dawn had melted into the horizon where they lay like a low pile of slate-grey dough. The wind had dropped, and with it the sea had ceased to run so wildly as during the night. The waves were longer and greasier, and their white tops no longer blew from crest to crest, but melted into the green with every falling motion.

The *Riverford* was passing close to the convoy as it made a bow sweep. The first file of merchantmen lay to starboard a quarter of a mile away. Members of the closest ship, an empty British tanker, were standing alongside the forward structure watching the movements of the little corvette, while on its poop the gun's crew were cleaning the gun, stopping now and again in their labours to point at the smaller ship.

As the Sub-Lieutenant and the Sick Bay Tiffy reached the bridge they found the Captain working on a chart in the asdic cabin. He motioned them inside. "How is the lad?" he asked, addressing Bodley.

Smith-Rawleigh began, "He's got a broken — "

"That's all for now," said the Captain crisply, dismissing the officer with a nod. Then he turned to the other.

"Well, sir, his right arm is broken below the elbow, but I'm afraid that there is more wrong with him than that. I don't like his pulse, and he's unconscious."

"Traumatic shock?"

"Beg pardon?—oh yes, probably, sir." It was remarkable how much a ship's Captain could know about another's job.

"Is he warm and fairly comfortable?"

"Yes, sir," Bodley answered. He looked around him at the asdic operator, who lolled on his stool and held an earphone to his ear. There was the steady, rhythmic "p-i-ing" of the submarine detection gear as it sent back its echoes through the earphones.

"We'll leave him where he is, then, until after the watches are changed. You stay with him and try to bring him around. If he is still the same we'll move him down to one of the officer's bunks."

"Yes, sir," Bodley answered, wondering whether to salute or not. He suddenly remembered that they were under cover so, desisting, he turned on his heel and went below again.

"Butch" Jenkins, Ordinary Seaman, R.C.N.V.R., leaned his back against the mast, and from his lofty position in the crow's-nest surveyed the gently pitching expanse of ocean clove by the dipping bows of the *Riverford*.

To starboard the nearest file of plodding freighters seemed stationary, but for the small white bones they bore in their teeth. The Coxswain had told him that they were carrying nothing but a ballast of sand and shale in their holds, the tankers weighted down with water ballast. He could see the crew of a ship standing in the lee of a deck-house as they watched the corvette passing before them. He hoped that they noticed his woollen-helmeted form as he stood there doing his part to protect them. It made him feel proud and—part of things, to be one of those doing his bit out here. The sight of the merchant sailors was the first real intimation that the convoy was not only formed of the shapes of ships, but also contained human beings, who, like him, formed a close-knit fraternity arrayed against the U-Boats. He wondered how many people were represented by the ships stretching over ten square miles of ocean. He thought, I'll give them at least seventy-five men to a ship. There are fifty-six merchant packets and seven escorts, counting the trawler. That makes sixty-three ships at seventy-five men apiece—almost five thousand men out here. The thought of being only one of the so many suddenly raised his chances of survival.

As he watched the merchantmen, they began a flaghoist, first one and then the other along their ranks bending the pendants to their halyards as they answered the Convoy Commodore's signals. The gaily coloured bunting reminded him that this was the culmination of everything he had trained and hoped for since leaving high school the year before. He had been afraid that the war would end before he had a chance to get into it, and at night he had lain awake dreaming that if God was willing to keep it going a few more years he would probably end up in London on the Horse Guards Parade while the King placed on his chest the wine-coloured ribbon of the Victoria Cross . . .

He happened to glance below and caught Lieutenant Harris staring up at him. Suddenly he was all eyes for U-Boats. Turning from the convoy side he regarded the empty sea stretching a thousand, no, ten thousand! miles to the south—stretching to the barren ice of Antarctica, with nothing between. It was hard to believe that out there beyond the horizon, or closer even, under the ripple of the chop, were the submarines lying in wait for their slow-moving target. It seemed impossible that there could be anything else on the surface, or under it, of this peaceful sea.

This was his first trip on a corvette, and he had been pleasantly surprised to find that there was no apprenticeship. They had left Londonberry behind, and as soon as they were running down the swiftly moving River Foyle to the sea he had been shown the Watch and Quarter Bill, and the Coxswain had said, "Read it and remember your stations. You will be on ack-ack ammunition supply at action stations, you'll take to No. 5 carley float if we abandon ship, and you'll eat at the port table in the seamen's mess. You're in the red watch, and you go on watch in the second dog."

It had been exciting, and a little scary too, when the Coxswain had mentioned taking a carley float when the ship was abandoned. He had found the leading hand of the watch, a fellow called McCaffrey, and had asked him what time he had to go on. "Six o'clock," the leading hand had answered. "You'll eat when they pipe 'Second Dog-watchman to Supper'."

And so he had learned what he had to know. He had found that a dog watch is two hours long, and that the second one began at six o'clock. After that the watches were four hours long until the next afternoon at four, when the First Dog began. Through using his head and ears he had discovered during the last eleven days (except for the second and third when he was too sea-sick to get out of his hammock) what some of the terms meant, and those which he heard, yet could not fathom, he had enquired about.

Now he looked upon himself as a sailor, a veteran of the Battle of the Atlantic. He had been in an encounter with German submarines five days out from the United Kingdom, and the convoy had lost one ship, while another had been damaged and had gone to Reykjavik, Iceland, for repairs. To the older hands in the crew it had been but an incident, but to him it was the epitome of death and destruction.

Everybody aboard knew that the ship was due for a refit this trip, and he was glad. He would go home to Verdun with something more to talk about this time than barrack-room tales. He could picture himself and Knobby Clark, who had promised to accompany him on leave, arriving in Bonaventure Station.

They would get off the train, and conscious that they were combat veterans, walk down the dusty platform towards the ugly red-brick waiting-room. Over their shoulders would be slung the gas-masks which were the mark of the overseas man. His mother would be standing there, and as she saw him she would nudge his sister Shirley before beginning her run towards him on shoes that were just a little too tight for a lady of her build and age.

He would kiss them both before introducing Knobby. "Ma, this is Knobby Clark, a shipmate of mine from

26

Medicine Hat, Alberta. He's going to stay here for part of his leave." Then he would turn to Knobby and say, "And this is my kid sister Shirley."

After the introductions were over and they were seated in the taxi, he would be asked, "What does it feel like to be on land again?" by a mother who wanted the taxi driver to share with her the knowledge that her son was a sea-going man.

Later, after a supper that consisted of real, honest-to-God roast beef and Yorkshire pudding, they would go for a walk, he and Knobby, and stop in at Beaulieu's Tavern at the corner for a quick one. Mr. Beaulieu would look at them, mentally gauging their ages, then, seeing their uniforms, would shrug and place the sweating glasses of ale before them.

They would talk of the English pubs, not too loudly, but loud enough to let the civilians hear, and after a few to "give them an edge on" they would take a trolley down-town to St. Catherine Street and see what they could do in the way of picking up a couple of girls . . .

When the watches changed at eight o'clock Butch eased himself gingerly over the side of the crow's-nest and scrambled down the mast to the bridge. Two of the officers were talking and laughing together as they stood against the voice pipes. One of them was Mr. Bowers, the First Lieutenant, and the other was the Jewish-looking one, Harris. They stepped aside absentmindedly as he passed them.

He hurried to the mess, realizing that if he was late most of the issue would be eaten, and that he would have to make a trip to the galley with his plate. This was a fool-hardy undertaking while the leading cook was there. It was better to go hungry or fill up with bread and butter rather than have this martinet give out with a blast about young ordinary seamen who came for second helpings just because the weather was calm.

As he entered the mess he became aware of the aura of quiet where usually at this time of day there was noise and laughter. He peeled off his coat and cap and threw them over the hammock rack. Instead of the debris of plates and cutlery the table usually contained, there was a person

27

lying asleep. He thought, with a feeling of alarm, "Oh God, I'm either too early or too late this morning!"

He moved closer, holding with one hand to a stanchion, and peered into the face of Knobby. "Well, you old son-of-a-gun!" he cried, happy to find that it was his friend who lay there. "Get up, we want to eat!"

"Stow it, dough-head!" a voice called from across the mess.

"What's the matter? I can wake Knobby up, can't I?"

"Leave him alone; can't you see he's hurt?"

He stared at the figure on the table. "Hurt?" he asked bewilderedly.

"He's got a broken arm. Come on over here and eat."

Poor Knobby! He had looked forward so much to his visiting with him in Montreal. Now they would be sure to take him off in Newfoundland and send him to hospital. He brightened suddenly. And yet that didn't mean that he would be unable to go. By the time they got their leave Knobby's arm would be healed and he could come back to the ship. Sure, what was he worrying about!

He moved over behind the table and sat down on the locker. Maybe Knobby would like a cup of tea, he thought. He began shaking him by the shoulder to awaken him. Knobby's eyelids fluttered and he turned his head, but did not awaken.

"Hey, Jenkins, here's your grub over here," Leading Seaman McCaffrey yelled through a mouthful of food. "Come and get it while it's warm."

"I don't want any. I'll sit here with Knobby until he wakes up."

"Suit yourself," answered McCaffrey. Butch could hear him asking which of the others wanted an extra egg.

He and Knobby had gone through training class together. They had been inseparable on the liner going over to Scotland, and in the barracks there they had been together every time they got the chance. When the draft came for two men to proceed to Londonderry for the *Riverford* they had asked for it and, miracle of miracles, they had been sent together.

He was a year younger than Knobby, but between them was the bond which joins the last two entries into a mess, or the two youngest members of a group, anywhere. During

28

the incubation period, before a man proves himself to his fellows, he is lonely and hurt at their misunderstanding. He wants them to know him as he really is, but is prevented from showing them by the fact that he cannot hurry up the process without being brash and forward, and thus defeating his purpose. Knobby had been a fellow-sufferer upon whom he had leaned for the companionship denied him by the others. To remain alone was unthinkable.

Low, so that the others could not hear him, he whispered, "Knobby!" There was no movement to reward his plea. He pushed his way under the hammocks and went below to the sick-bay, the euphemism given to a small cupboard screwed on the bulkhead in a corner of the communications mess. The Sick Berth Attendant was eating his breakfast by himself. He looked up as Jenkins descended the ladder. "What do you want?" he asked.

"It's about Knobby."

"What about him?"

"He looks pretty sick."

"Do you want me to hold his hand?" asked Bodley sarcastically. The remark was not meant to show a lack of feeling toward the injured man, but was a protective mechanism thrown up by a person who knows that something is beyond his limitations.

"I want you to do something for him," cried Butch angrily.

"Listen, mate, I've done everything I can, so far. After breakfast we might move him into one of the officers' bunks, and I think that the Old Man is going to get the M.O. over from the *St. Helens,*" Bodley said, his impatience gone now as he saw the genuine distress upon the other's face.

"Oh," said Butch, mollified. He was glad to learn that others were also trying to do something for Knobby. "Okay, thanks!"

He hurried up the ladder and took his place again beside the table upon which Knobby was lying. He straightened out the blanket covering the boy, being careful not to move the injured arm. After this was done he sat staring silently at the face of his friend.

From across the mess could be heard the subdued laughter and talk of the other seamen. A stoker came through the hatch from below and took a look at Knobby. He asked an unspoken question of Butch, who shook his head.

After a few minutes Knobby seemed to rally. His head twisted on the rolled-up duffle coat serving as a pillow, and his legs stretched as though feeling for the bottom of a bed.

"That-a-boy, Knobby!" Jenkins said. "You've got it beat, kid. Wake up, fella, this is Butch here."

"How's he doing?" McCaffrey asked from the other table.

"He's coming round."

"Sure, he'll be all right."

Butch lifted Knobby's head and cradled it in his arm. The boy lifted his eyelids and stared uncomprehendingly at the low ceiling of hammocks above his face. Then he turned his eyes and looked at Jenkins. His good arm moved from beneath the blanket and gripped Butch by the front of his shirt.

"That's the stuff, Knobby. Relax, kid, and I'll get you a cup of tea," said Butch happily.

The hand gripping his shirt twisted itself into the denim, and Knobby's eyes fluttered wildly before rolling back into their sockets. His breath was expelled in a long, low snarl, and from his nose and ears the too-red blood flowed down in slow, limpid streams upon the shoulder of his friend.

"Hey!" yelled Jenkins, panic-stricken at the sight. "Hey, get the tiffy quick! Knobby's bleeding!"

Two or three ran over from the other table. Jenkins saw it all in slow motion, even to one of the seamen dropping a cup he was wiping into the wash-bowl. He saw their eyes, which were staring his way, slowly turn from disbelief, to compassion, to horror as they gazed at the boy cradled in his arms. And without looking down again he knew that Knobby was dead.

He tried to back away and remove his arm from beneath the other's neck, but the death grip on his shirt held him fast. It held him while the blood of the other rolled slowly down across Knobby's cheek and spread in a small pool on his own shirt. "Get him off!" he screamed. "Somebody get him off!"

"Shut up!" shouted a voice in his ear, and the heavy hand of McCaffrey slapped the panic from his face. The leading seaman unclenched the fingers of the dead boy and

placed the limp arm beneath the blanket. Two of the ⌐
lifted the almost fainting Butch from the locker and ⌐
him across the mess.

McCaffrey said, "Williams, you go and get the tiffy.
Manders, go down to the wardroom and tell the Old Man
that Clark is dead. You—you there with the dish-cloth—
get something else and wipe this blood up outa here before
it washes under the lockers."

CHAPTER 3

In the *Riverford's* wardroom the stewards cleared away the breakfast things, except for those lying at the Captain's end of the table. At a small desk in a corner, Lieutenant Harris, who had finished his breakfast after being relieved on the bridge, was going over some new anti-submarine procedures before placing them between the covers of a weighted book.

As usual the Captain had waited until the officers had eaten before taking his place at the table. This, like some of his other habits, he had brought with him from the Merchant Service. If he had been asked why he preferred to eat alone, he would have replied, "Well, it's hard to say. It's not snobbishness exactly—although I'd have a hard time proving it to the others—but it is something which I believe is necessary for the discipline of a ship. I may be wrong, but I believe it because I was brought up to believe it."

If pressed further he might have continued, "You know, what people fail to realize is that I am the chief sufferer from my self-imposed anti-gregariousness. Suppose, now, that I were sitting here with the other officers, and they were skylarking and having a good time—which they certainly would not, were I here—and in order not be a boor I joined in the fun. Do you know what would happen? Well, I'll tell you: there would be an immediate rise in their friendliness towards me, but a distinct slackening in their respect. In order to keep their respect—which I believe is vitally necessary out here—I will forego their deeper friendship. Hence I dine alone while aboard."

He buttered his second slice of toast and rang for some marmalade. When the steward placed it before him he spread it on his bread with studied deliberation. "What is our bread ration these days, Roberts?" he asked.

"Th-th-th-two loaves, s-sir, n-n-n-ow that we're b-baking our own."

"Does it do us?"

"Not al-al-al—no, sir."

"Where does the extra come from?"

"F-f-f-from the c-c-cooks, sir."

"The next time we're short, break out the biscuits; we're on general messing the same as anybody else aboard."

"Y-yes, sir. W-w-w-will your have some more c-coffee, sir?"

"Yes, please, Roberts. Not so much milk this trip."

When the steward had gone for the coffee, he turned and looked over at Lieutenant Harris. "Did you hear about the seaman who was injured?" he asked.

Harris swung around quickly in his chair and faced him. "Yes, sir, I did. It's hard lines."

There was something a little distasteful about Harris using such Anglicisms, thought the Captain. Hard lines! Still, the language was free. God knows there weren't many things free to a Jew these days—in Europe, of course. "I think we should get the surgeon over from the *St. Helen*," said the Captain. "Would you go up to the bridge and have Mr. Bowers request that he come over. Tell them that we will leave our position if given permission, or to send instructions as to how they wish to make the transfer."

"Yes, sir," said Harris, reaching for his cap as he left the room.

The steward brought a fresh cup of coffee, and the Captain stirred some raw, brown sugar into it. He pondered upon Harris. Inscrutable like all Jews. Could not seem to get behind his façade somehow. Wonder what he was in private life? Lawyer perhaps, or in business. Hard to tell what sort of business a Jew was in these days. Used to be old clothes and pawn shops, but now it could be anything.

His thoughts soon skipped from Lieutenant Harris to the letter he had received in the last mail before leaving Derry. Ever since the trip had begun, his thoughts had not wandered very far from it. He had read it so often that it was imprinted

33

on his memory, and he no longer had to take it from the locked drawer of his desk, as he had done many times during the first few days out.

Dear Joe:—

Ronald and I are both well. We received a letter from your mother last week. She is fine, and is expecting you to call on her as soon as you reach England again. Burford-on-Keys has been blitzed. Imagine! It seems that Jerry dropped two or three fire bombs in the market place, and of course the whole town has been in a turmoil ever since. You'll probably have visited her before you get my mail anyhow. I don't know where you have been running the past few months, but I can guess from your letters. Things seem to be going well in Africa. Do you know anything about it? That is just a subtle woman's way to find out where you are. I'm sure that wherever you are, that you are enjoying yourself more than I am at this moment. You see, dear, I have a confession to make to you.

Do you remember when you were commissioning your ship in Quebec, and we took that walk along the promenade outside the Chateau? We spoke then of our personal lives, and how nothing we could do to each other would destroy the feelings we had, one for the other, then. Dear Joe, that was only two years ago. I don't know what your life has been like when you have been away from me, and I don't want to. We promised that if we kissed, we would not tell. But darling, what I have to tell is more than that. You see, I am in love with another man.

If that hurts you, dear, it hurts me just as much to have to tell you, believe me. This feeling I have for Reggie is so overpowering that I can't fight it.

I met him at a party at the Burroughs'. He is an R.A.F. Squadron Leader who is stationed in Montreal with the Ferry Command. It was a case of I met him, and I'd had it.

(Damn it all, she was using R.A.F. lingo already!)

Dear Joe, will you give me a divorce? I know that things are far more complicated than that, what with Ronnie and everything, but please will you talk it over *with me in your letters, and when you get back to this side, we'll have the whole thing out?*

I don't deserve it, but please don't think too bad of me.

Joyce.

It was like a bloody sixpenny novel, even to the other fellow's name. Reggie! Christ!

That was the way it was; a man and woman lived together for fifteen years as man and wife, with not even a flirtation coming between them. They grew dulled to each other by the knowledge that there could never be anything as juvenile as a love affair with somebody else, cropping up. Then a war came along and they were separated a little longer than usual, and this

Even before the war, when he had been sailing to the West Indies and South America on the tankers, and she had lived alone with their son in Montreal, there had never been cause for the slightest breath of suspicion.

"Please give me a divorce!" Couldn't she see that it was impossible? Did she think he was going to let her take his son to be raised by a bloody desk wallah called Reggie? It was fortunate that they were being refitted this trip. He would go home immediately and find out how much truth there was in what she had written. He felt sure that a marriage such as theirs could not be broken up by somebody else if he were only there to stop it. The thought that he was on his way home, sliding south to St. Johns, as it were, made things a little easier to bear.

Lieutenant Harris came down the companion-way and entered the door. "The First Lieutenant is having your signal sent, sir," he said.

"Good. Where is the *St. Helens*?"

"She's doing a search between the convoy ranks, sir."

"Can she receive our flashing?"

"Yes, sir. She's answering."

"Thank you. Oh, by the way, have you read the stuff on the new German torpedo?"

"The sonic one, sir?" Harris asked, knowing that the Captain only wanted to know by his mention of it whether he knew what he meant.

"Yes. Very clever, don't you think? It'll probably come

35

shooting up our oscillator beam. Great thing for Allison to pick up on his asdic."

"I thought that it was attracted by the noise of our screw, sir?"

"It's one or the other. We'll find out before the war is much older, no doubt."

"Yes, sir," said Harris, taking his chair again at the small table. The Captain picked up a sheaf of wireless signals from the top of the bookcase. He was reading through them when there was a knock against the door frame, and he looked up to see a seaman, cap in hand, standing there.

"Yes, Manders?" he asked.

"Sir, I was sent down here by Leading Seaman McCaffrey. Ordinary Seaman Clark is dead, sir," he said.

"Dead!" cried Harris, swinging around.

The Captain put down the signals and dismissed the seaman. "That puts a new light on things," he said. He opened the bookcase and pulled out the heavy volume of *King's Regulations & Admiralty Instructions,* and began thumbing through the close-packed pages.

CHAPTER 4

Stoker petty officer Jim Collet stood on the deck-plates of the forward boiler-room, and instructed Second Class Stoker "Frenchy" Turgeon in the changing of a broken water-gauge glass. In his hand he was holding a gland nut, and was showing Frenchy how to fit new packing rings.

"Dis kid, he broke 'is arm, eh?" Frenchy asked.

"Yeah."

"Dat's de firs' time I ever know somebody to die wit' dis."

"He didn't die of a broken arm, stupid."

"What 'e die of, den?"

"Old age," said Jimmy, fitting the new glass.

Whenever there is an emergency upon a ship of war, there are men detailed to take care of it, and except for these men, the other members of the crew carry on with their normal routine. The job that Collet and Turgeon were doing this morning, down below in the boiler-room, was a small one, and yet it was important to the lives of every man aboard.

A ship crossing the ocean in wartime, except in cases of dire necessity, cannot stop. The pulse of the engines is so vital, and so necessary, that the men begin to believe nothing can ever happen which will break down that inexorable forward thrust, which is so much a part of their lives afloat. Were the engines to stop, the ship immediately ceases to be a fighting unit, and becomes a floating hulk, prey to enemy action, and prey also to the vast seething sea lying beneath it, ever ready to boil and froth and suck this saucy thing of steel and wood and human bodies into its vortex.

Frenchy put some tools away before he said, "Dis kid was but—*un jeune garçon*—young boy. 'Ow could 'e die of old age?"

"Okay, make an argument out of it," answered Jimmy.

"I don't unnerstan'?"

"Neither does anybody else."

Jimmy climbed up the vertical ladders from the stoke-hold and took the gauntlets from his hands in order to wipe the sweat from his forehead. He stood for a minute or two framed in the hatch, watching the approach of the destroyer *St. Helens,* as she came sliding up on the port side.

From beneath him he could hear the clang of the engine-room telegraph, and the sound of Frenchy answering the voice pipe in the stokehold. Frenchy's voice had an argu-mentative ring, with its French-Canadian accent and the Gallic inflections on the word endings. It wafted up through the hot air from the boilers, "Sure, wat you t'ink? Je' Chris'! I shut him off ten minute ago!"

Poor Frenchy! He was the only one of his kind among seventy-seven jeering French-baiters. From morn until night he listened to the talk about the "pea-soupers" and the Quebec draft-dodgers. The crew kidded him, laughed at his accent, and drove him almost to madness, yet there wasn't a man aboard who wouldn't have given him his shirt. And when they talked about the anti-war sentiment in Quebec (without quite knowing what it was all about) they made an exception of Frenchy.

Jim turned around, and lowering his head inside the hatch, yelled, "Quiet, you pea-souper, they can't hear them-selves on the bridge."

Frenchy made an uncomplimentary remark about what they could do on the bridge if they didn't like it.

Collet crossed to the railing around the engine-room fiddley and leaned there watching the activity of the crew aboard the destroyer. They were lowering a boat from the davits, and with the ship still under way they were being careful that it did not capsize when it hit the water.

With a small cloud of spray, and some mad scrambling by its crew to get rid of the lines, it was cast off, and the crew began pulling towards the *Riverford.* In the stern sheets sat two officers, one of them the surgeon and the other the officer in charge of the boat.

Jim let his eyes take in the destroyer crew who were lined along the weather deck. Standing abaft the torpedo tubes was a friend of his, a chief stoker, and he tried to get his attention by making motions as though he were hoisting a glass of beer. The other would not look in his direction, but centred his gaze on the boat.

It was a lot of use to send the M.O. aboard now, after the kid was dead. Why did the Old Man want to have the doctor come and tell him what everybody knew? It must be a formality or something, he thought.

Peebles, the leading cook, climbed up the ladder and stood beside him, his face glistening in the cold air. "Is this the M.O. coming aboard?" he asked.

"Yeah," answered Jimmy curtly. He resented having to give Peebles a civil answer, who never to his knowledge had spoken civilly to anybody in his galley.

"It's about time."

"Yeah."

"That kid died of internal haemorrhages," Peebles said. "The tiffy should have known what to do."

"How would he know?"

"He could have found out."

"Oh, balls; he's not a doctor! A person can't know everything. For instance, you can't bake bread," he said, getting in his sting.

"I don't see you chucking it over the side."

"You don't see me eating it either."

They were quiet as the boat was made fast to the corvette's side. A ladder was lowered and the surgeon, trying to appear accustomed to climbing out of small boats in the middle of the Atlantic, came inboard.

He was a tall, gangling young man of uncertain age, wearing glasses. He carried his head high with a hauteur which could have been due to his rank, or may have been caused by astigmatism. The First Lieutenant met him and led him through the hatch to the Captain's flats. The doctor's demeanour was a study in the effect of lieutenant's stripes on a bedside manner. It looked as though he wanted to appear officious and businesslike, but was prevented by his professional charm.

"He looks as though he's going to deliver a baby," said Peebles.

"It looks to me as though he's just had one," answered Jimmy.

The telegraph rang and the ship got under way again.

When the Captain entered his cabin from the bridge, after seeing to the transfer of the surgeon, the doctor jumped to his feet, but was waved down again. The First Lieutenant said, "This is Lieutenant-Commander Frigsby. Sir, may I present Surgeon Lieutenant Craddock?"

The Captain shook his hand. "It's getting cold out," he offered by way of greeting.

"Yes, sir, it is," Craddock answered. He had noticed the D.S.C. ribbon on the Captain's uniform which was hanging in the closet. Not a very prepossessing man, he thought. Short and thin, very English. Not altogether "old school tie", but a damn good facsimile. Merchant Navy type. Probably not as much spit and polish as some, but everything in damn good working order.

"Your boat will pick you up at eleven hundred," the Captain said.

"Yes, sir."

"Probably a bore riding with us until then, but we've got to regain our position with the other ships."

"I understand, sir."

"You know, of course, that your patient is dead?"

"I wasn't aware of it, sir," answered Craddock without showing his surprise.

"He died about an hour ago."

Craddock looked at him, as though asking why, then, he had been summoned.

The Captain surmised his thoughts. "I'd like you to take a look at the body," he said. "We have to know the cause of death and things of that sort." He thought, this man hasn't been a doctor very long. Probably a medical school graduate who is doing his internship in the Navy.

Craddock rose from the chair in which he had been sitting and followed the blue-sweatered form of the Captain up forward to the seamen's mess. Some of the men jumped to their feet at the entrance of the officers, but the Captain murmured, "Carry on," and they sat down again.

The doctor pulled the sheet from the body of Knobby, and looked him up and down, flexing the unbroken arm, and looking into the eyes. The Captain whispered a few words to the First Lieutenant who left the mess, reappearing again a moment later followed by the Sick Berth Attendant.

When the doctor looked up and saw the red cross on the sleeve of the tiffy's jacket, he asked officiously, "When did you first see this man?"

"As soon as they got me up, sir, about seven o'clock. Maybe a little before that."

"What was his state then?"

"Unconscious, sir."

"Where was he?"

"Lying here on the table, sir."

"What did you do?"

"I had him undressed, and applied splints to his broken arm."

"Did you notice anything else?"

"I took his pulse. It was slow and erratic."

"Was his coma prolonged?"

"He never woke up, sir."

"What was your diagnosis? I mean after you noticed his pulse?"

"I had none. I notified the Captain that I was afraid there was more wrong with him than a broken arm."

"Were you not aware that he was suffering from a fractured skull?"

The Captain answered before Bodley. "There was no haemorrhage then. The Sick Berth Attendant wrapped him up, and mentioned to me that we should call on you. I believe that this is the standard practice in cases of this kind. If he had been aware that the man's skull was fractured he could have done nothing more than keep the patient warm and apply cold cloths."

"Quite so," the doctor answered. He thought, this bird is tough, and he sticks up for his men.

"Are you finished with Bodley?" the Captain asked, pointing at the tiffy.

"Yes. Oh, of course."

"Carry on, Bodley," said the Captain.

Later on in the wardroom the Captain gave Craddock a drink of rum and Coke. When the M.O. had made a

41

tentative sip at his drink, the Captain asked, "How long will a body keep, Doctor?"

"It depends of course o nthe temperature, and the state of injury or cause of death."

They are like lawyers, the Captain thought, never give a straight answer for fear it is the wrong one. Hedge and wander around a question like a child licking an ice-cream cone. "How long will that lad's body keep aboard a ship? One, two—maybe three days?"

"I think so."

"The reason I'm asking is that I'd like to take him into St. Johns and have him buried ashore. Some day, after the war, his parents might like to visit his grave. That sort of thing means a lot to a parent."

The doctor thought, I like him; he's hard, and he doesn't like me, but I like him. He answered, "I think you could carry the body that long."

"Good. Where do you suggest we put him?"

"Somewhere cool. On the upper deck, or the ice-box."

"No, not the upper deck, and I'm afraid that the ice-box is out too."

"Anywhere that is reasonably cool."

The Captain called, "Steward!"

"Yes, sir," the steward said, appearing like a genie from the pantry where he had been eavesdropping.

"Get the Coxswain and the Chief E.R.A."

In a few minutes the two chiefs appeared outside the wardroom. The Coxswain, a short, bandy-legged Great Lakes sailor with a heavy set of black whiskers, was nervously twirling his cap in his hand. The Chief E.R.A. was a much older man than any of the others aboard, a Merchant Marine reservist who had spent thirty-five years on Grand Banks trawlers. A pair of solid legs held up a gigantic belly. His face was round and red-mottled behind its three-day beard.

"Come in, please," said the Captain. He introduced them to the Surgeon Lieutenant.

"We have a problem on our hands," he said. "We have decided to carry the body of Ordinary Seaman Clark to St. Johns for burial ashore. Can either of you suggest where we can place it for the next two or three days?"

The Coxswain said, "How about the ice-box, sir? There

42

isn't much meat and stuff in there now, and we could—"

"No, the ice-box is out. I don't want a mutiny aboard."

The Coxswain laughed self-consciously.

"How about you, Chief?" asked the Captain, facing the C.E.R.A.

"Well, sir, you could put him down in my stores. It's cool down there—well below the water line—and—it's private."

"Good! That's an excellent suggestion." He looked at the Coxswain, who was thirstily staring at the doctor's half-finished rum. "Now, Coxswain, I want you to take three or four of the older men, Wright and McCaffrey and one or two others, and get the sail-maker to sew the boy up in a hammock. I don't want him to be made ready for a sea burial or anything like that, but fastened so that the body will be protected until we can put it ashore. The Chief will have his men ready the stores, and you'll place the lad down there, making sure that he is wrapped securely, and—properly stowed. Any questions? Good. That's all."

After they had left, the Captain rang for the steward and told him to bring the doctor another rum. "I wonder if you'd have a look at another patient while you are here?" he asked.

"Why yes, sir, what is wrong with him?"

"The usual. He is a signalman who is currently suffering from an occupational disease common to young sailors, picked up, I believe, in a bistro called the Silver Harp in Belfast. The Sick Berth Attendant has been feeding him sulpha pills, but I thought that it wouldn't hurt if you had a look at him."

"A case of the quick and the dead," the doctor said as the rum began to warm him.

"Not quick enough I'm afraid," answered the Captain with a short laugh as he let himself down, tiredly, on to the settee.

Chief Petty Officer Frank Cartwright, the Coxswain of the *Riverford*, entered the seamen's mess, took off his cap, and called across to the hammock which held Leading Seaman McCaffrey. "Hey Mac, I've got a job for you."

McCaffrey pushed himself up on one elbow and, hanging on to the hammock next to his own, asked, "What?"

43

"Get up and I'll tell you."

"Oh Jesus, Frank! Let me get my head down. I've been up during the morning watch, you know."

"I know, but this is orders from the Old Man."

He could hear McCaffrey sitting up somewhere across the expanse of swaying hammocks, then his legs came into view as he pulled on his socks over his dirty feet. McCaffrey jumped down to the deck and found his sea-boots under the lockers and pulled them on. When he came out from beneath the hammocks he was rubbing his eyes, which were bloodshot and bright against the dark, ten-day stubble of beard.

"What the hell is it now, Frank? Can't you get any of the other leading hands for a change?"

"The Old Man told me to get *you*," the Coxswain replied, sitting down on one of the benches and ducking his head under a low-slung hammock. He gave a critical glance across the deck at the pool of black water with its flotsam of cigarette packages and bread crusts that was slopping to and fro under the lockers with every movement of the ship.

"What does the Old Man want? Two hands to paint the subby's cabin?" asked McCaffrey sarcastically.

"We've got to stow the kid here for the rest of the trip," the Coxswain answered, pointing behind him at the still form on the table.

"Stow him!"

"Yeah, we're taking him with us to Newfy."

"Oh good God! Why?"

"I don't know. The Old Man and the doc from the *St. Helens* had me and the Chief down in the wardroom. They asked us where was the best place to stow the body until we got in."

"We can't carry a stiff that far. How many more days does he think it'll take?"

"Two or three, I guess."

McCaffrey shrugged, pursing his lips distastefully. "Where will we put him? In the tiller flats?"

"No, in the Engineer's stores."

"Thank God for that!"

"Get Pearson to sew him up in his 'mick. You know, just so he's covered decently. After that's done the Old

44

Man wants you and Wright and a couple of other old hands to get him down below. I guess Pearson'll do for one, and maybe Newfy Powers could be the other."

"Okay."

About an hour later, after the remains of Knobby Clark had been sewn into his hammock, the carrying party tied him into a basket stretcher. They each grabbed a sling and set off down the starboard side of the ship to the engineroom hatch. A few men who were off watch were huddled behind the funnel getting some air. "Why the hell don't they bury the kid at sea?" shouted one of them.

The Coxswain thought, it didn't take long for the news to get around. "Pack that stuff up!" he shouted, looking up and trying to see who it was that had spoken. The faces looking down were all blank.

With much heaving and tugging they lowered the body into the engine-room, and through the door to the stores. "Where'll we put him, Frank?" McCaffrey asked.

"I don't know. How about lashing him on to this bench?"

"This affair is nae guid, Cox'n," said Wright. "We carried a woman once frae Penang tae Singypore when I was on the cruise ships afore the war. We haed naught but trouble wi' her. She died a' stoppage o' the bowel. We had a typhoon in the Malacca Strait on account a' her. Ye all may think I'm daft, but it's nae guid the same."

"Okay, Wright, stow that kind of crap," the Coxswain said sharply. "The first thing you know you'll have all the kids aboard believing you. Whether it's right or wrong, it's orders. The Old Man must have something in the back of his mind."

"Wright's saying what we're all thinking, Frank," McCaffrey said. "I don't believe anything about the bad luck or things like that, but I think that the kid would have liked it better if we'd have given him a real sea burial. This was his first trip, and he only had eleven days seatime, but they meant a lot to him. He figured, and rightly too, that he was a sailor; and he should have been buried like one, not taken to a cemetery in Newfy so that a bunch of rum-dums and their tarts could use his grave for a bag shanty every night."

"What do you think, Pearson?" the Coxswain asked, wanting to gauge the feelings of the others before he committed himself.

"I guess it don't make much difference to the kid, *where* he's buried."

"You, Powers, what do you think?"

The Newfoundlander licked his lips before replying. He was a short, gnarled figure with an oarsman's shoulders. His face was salt-lined, and his eyes seemed to be wearing a perpetual squint. His neck was etched with weather-creases, deep ones, from the hair-line to a point beneath his roll-necked sweater. "I figure it don't make much diff'-runce to a body where we'll be buried, but I agrees wit' Scotty that it's bad luck for a vessel that's carryin' a corpse——"

"Oh, to hell with the bad luck!" the Coxswain shouted in exasperation. "It's only two days, and the Old Man wants it this way. Powers, lash him to the top of this bench."

They wrapped a light length of signals halyard around the head and feet of the stretcher, and Powers with his small-boatman's skill tied it secure so that the stretcher could not move. When the job was done they filed through the dor and up the engine-room ladder.

The E.R.A. on duty stared at the small procession, before going over and peeking through the door into the stores. As he went back to his position near the throttle he was shaking his head in bewilderment.

CHAPTER 5

The Captain sat in his cabin reading some signals. It was mid-afternoon, and the convoy pushed ahead through the oily sea. There had been a rain squall about an hour before, which had turned to sleet, and now the lines and shrouds had taken on a gloss, and the steel decks were slippery underfoot. The barometer had fallen since morning, and the weather had closed in, so that at times the convoy was invisible from the bridge.

The Captain could hear an argument ensuing in the galley which lay abaft his cabin. From what he could make out, one of the cooks and the supply rating were arguing over what constituted a man's ration of tinned pears.

"I don't care what the ration is," the cook was saying, "I'm the guy who has to stand here and take all the guff from the crew. If any of the chronic beefers, like McCaffrey, Dunderfield or Henderson comes back tonight I'm going to send him down to you. Okay?"

"Sure, send them down. I eat the same grub as anybody else aboard. I'll show them *my* ration of pears too. Some of those punks try to make a whole meal of the duff. You'd think that the dessert was the main course the way they squawk. I've seen 'em ashore: they get into Halifax or some place, and all they think of is going to a restaurant and buying ice-cream sundaes——"

The Captain shut his ears to any further gastronomical titbits emanating from the galley, and went on with his reading. He tossed aside signals dealing with Japanese Hospital Ships, or Corrected Procedure re Fueling Seniority at Haifa, and concentrated on those which were of importance to his own ship. He read over the weather report, noting the changes since the day before of the low-pressure area centred over Baffin Land and Northern Greenland. Three days behind them, a wind of hurricane force was boiling up the seas off Iceland and was expected to reach the outer Hebrides by evening. That's something we missed anyhow, he thought.

He read over the fuel report given to him earlier by the Chief E.R.A. No need to worry about fuel yet.

When he cleared his desk of papers, and had called one of the Coders to take the stuff away, he rang for the steward and asked him to get all the gear belonging to Ordinary Seaman Clark, and bring it to his cabin. As an afterthought he called the officer of the day, and sent him along also to make sure they would get it all.

They returned, the steward pulling the dead man's sea-bag behind him, and the officer carrying Clark's small case, hatbox, and an armful of clothing. "Thank you," the Captain said. "Just leave it there on the deck." When they had gone he pulled the small case on to his desk and opened it.

The first thing which caught his eye was a clean blue collar such as seamen wear. It had been washed in Javel Water to make it "salty", taking the deep blue from it, so that now it was a bleached, or Mediterranean, blue.

He held it in his hand, puzzling over the psychology which caused these boys to bleach their collars, so they would appear to be wearing one which had been washed a hundred times. It was a natural human trait; everybody at some time or another pretended that they were more than they were. He remembered the first ship he had boarded as an officer. How he had wanted the crew to look upon him as an old hand. That was the *Saoma*, a collier which plied between the Tyne and Hamburg and Kiel. Looking back, he could see how transparent his artifices had been; there wasn't a man aboard who had not known that it was the first ship in which he had sailed, wearing a stripe on his sleeve.

He placed the collar on the desk and turned over a large cardboard-backed photograph. The picture of a young pretty girl stared back at him. She would be about seventeen; cheap, a salesgirl or a waitress. But was she? During the past few years girls had striven, through wearing good imitations, to confuse the average male as to their social status or their wealth. And this, in itself, was good. It was part and parcel of the revolution which was taking place around them. A revolution which depended not so much on the Hitlers and Stalins, but on the small, insidious changes in thought and behaviour which were bound to make the world different at the end of the war to what it had been in 1939.

He stared hard at the photograph of the girl, apologizing to her for his first impression. "You could be a waitress," he said, "but you are not tawdry or cheap. You are not common, except inasmuch as we all are common. You are a young seventeen-year-old girl who has changed over-night from a child to a young woman, the sweetheart of a sailor who is dead. Will you mind his passing?" he asked the photograph. "Did you also swear undying fealty?"

He read the scrawled inscription on the bottom of the portrait. "Wayne, I love you," it said. Why had she written that? Was it because she wanted him to know? Was it in the hope that this reminder would keep him true to her memory? Was it magnanimity or carelessness or daring? He tried to reconstruct the meeting of these two in his mind.

Her name would be Peggy or Alma or Pat. She would be standing near the ticket booth in a small dance-hall in Medicine Hat or Vancouver or Toronto. From a small group of training-school sailors one of them would walk across the floor to her, rolling himself in an imitation of how he thought a sailor should walk. He would ask her to dance, and she would consent because he was young and good-looking, and he had the narrow hips and grace of the young male dancer.

They would fox-trot or jitter-bug to the music, feeling the nearness of each other through their clothing, aware that they were male and female, and that if they wished, this could be the beginning of a love affair and a sub-sequent marriage. They would talk of little things: the music, the heat of the hall, "Do you come here often?" "I very seldom come here, it's rather cheap, but my girl friend brought me." She would be a little shy, and her reticence would be a feather in her crown, the catnip which would help to lure him on.

"What's your name?" "Peggy Taylor, and yours?" "Wayne—Wayne Clark." "It's a nice name, Clark." "Do you think so?" "Why yes, don't you?" "Where do you live, in the East End?" "Am I supposed to live there?" "No, but I thought you might . . ."

His breath would smell of two glasses of beer, but it would not be this small amount of Dutch courage which would prompt him to take her home. He would suddenly realize that she was a *nice* girl, and he would say quickly, before she was lost to him forever, "May I walk home with you, Peggy?" "I'm afraid that it's too far for walking." "I didn't mean it that way, what I meant was, can I take you home?" "Why me? There's lots of other girls here." "But it's you I like." "You must say this to all the girls you meet?" "No, only to the good-looking ones."

They would go together for a month, dancing twice a week, once a week to the movies. He would meet her parents and her brothers. They would be very nice to him, but they would show also that they hoped Peggy would marry someone she had known longer, one of the boys from the neighbourhood. They would say to her, "He seems like a nice boy, but you know what they say about sailors." They would console themselves with the thought that in a short while he would be gone anyway.

He would write to his mother and tell her about Peggy. She would write back to him warning him that sometimes first impressions were not always the best. She would ask, "What religion is she? What does her father do? What's wrong with the girls back here at home?"

When he received his draft for the coast Peggy would give him her photograph, and because she was not sure of him, and in her secret heart knew that they would probably never meet again, she would sign it, "I love you . . ."

He laid the photograph down and tilted back in the chair, staring at the bulkhead upon which was affixed with adhesive tape a picture of his wife and son.

He had met his wife during the Whitsun holidays on a pier at Brighton. She had been employed as a "companion" to a maiden lady at Hythe; really another name for a domestic. Her association with this lady had given her airs, so that it was months after they were married before he found out that her father was a porter in a large Birmingham greengrocer's shop.

He remembered the walk along the sands, and the tuppenny boat ride they had enjoyed. Afterwards they had stood and listened at the Pierrots, and he, with the generosity of a moon-struck young fool, had dropped a tanner in the proffered hat.

She had not let him accompany her home to the boarding-house where she was staying, but had pretended that she was living at one of the better hotels. He had bid her good night (with a gay salute, he thought bitterly) on the High Street, and they had gone their separate ways with a promise to meet at the Pier on the morrow.

The affair had rushed to a climax that week, until on the following Sunday night (he was to rejoin his ship on the Monday) they had gone for a long walk into the country, stopping for tea at a quaint little teashop whose prices were more than he could afford. Later on they had walked along a lane leading past the wrought-iron fence surrounding a large country house.

When it became dark they sat together on the grass, and he, with the impetuousness of the moment, after an uneventful week of one-sided courtship, had become very amorous. She had broken into tears, calling him a "beast" and "a person who takes an advantage of a young girl". It was not until the following year, during an early married squabble, that he found she had not been a virgin on their first meeting.

He let the front legs of the heavy chair thud against the deck as he straightened up again. "Damn her!" he said to himself. He looked again at her photograph and knew that the oath had been directed, not at her, but at himself. I still love her, he thought. Even now, after getting her letter, I still love her.

His reverie was interrupted by a knock at the wooden door. "Come in," he commanded, straightening up and busying himself again with the dead boy's possessions.

Sub-Lieutenant Smith-Rawleigh brought him some flimsies.

"Anything important?" asked the Captain.

"Apparently we're running into five subs which were

51

sighted by the Air Force dead ahead, about four hours away, sir."

"Mmm! What is the Commodore doing?"

"They're raising a flag-hoist now. I think that it'll be an emergency turn."

"Right. I'll be up directly." He noticed the Sub-Lieutenant staring at the photograph of the girl which lay face up on the desk. "This is a photograph of Ordinary Seaman Clark's friend," he said. "How does she strike you, Smith?" He always avoided the hyphen.

"She's very pretty, sir."

"She is indeed."

The Sub-Lieutenant made for the door.

"See if the L.T.O. has those other depth charges hoisted into the racks yet, will you?" the Captain ordered. "I'm going to put you back on the ack-ack platform in future. If we have any more action this trip, that'll be your position."

"Yes, sir!" exclaimed the Sub-Lieutenant enthusiastically.

"Oh, and by the way, Smith, let the Supply Assistant and Williams have their heads with the guns. They've been with me a long time; they know how to handle them."

"Yes, sir," answered Smith-Rawleigh with considerably less enthusiasm.

CHAPTER 6

The weather, which had closed in several times during the day, finally shut in completely with the setting of the watery sun. The convoy moved ahead quietly through the shrouding mantle of darkness, the parabolas of its three-score wakes lit with the phosphorescence of the icy sea.

Those upon the bridge took hold of something steady and stared into the murk. The Captain and Mr. Allison, the navigating officer, stood together conversing in low voices, their coat collars turned up against the freezing wind. "If they're waiting for us, we should be abeam of them before long," said the Captain.

"I think so, sir. Of course, they may have lost us since it began to blow."

"They might." They stood together in silence, staring into the darkness.

There was a camaraderie between these two, which while not overly apparent to the casual observer, held them together, to the exclusion of the other officers. Being former Merchant Navy men they had more in common than did the others, who had followed many professions, and they had an equal respect for each other's knowledge and seamanship.

"How is Moody making out on the asdic plot?" asked the Captain. Moody was one of the coders, whose job during action was to help Allison on the plotting table where the maze of anti-submarine runs were charted, so that the position of the submarine, in relation to the ship, was always known.

"He's a good boy. He's learning fast," answered Allison.

53

The Captain walked across to the port side of the bridge and stood behind the look-out, staring into the darkness. The sea ran past the ship at express speed, the corvette's fourteen knots being magnified by the illusion of the tumbling water.

He turned around and glanced for a moment at a small group of figures standing in the lee of the funnel. He thought, some of the crew have anticipated action stations tonight. It was remarkable how the news got around the ship. Probably the telegraphists and coders spread it—or, more than likely, the stewards. Farther aft, on the quarter-deck, three or four seamen were struggling with a depth charge which they were hoisting into one of the stern rails.

There was no noise save the wind brushing through the ship's upper works and the faint hum of the engines from below. The voices of those standing around the funnel were driven across the stern by the wind.

He felt his way again to the starboard side and paused there, able now to hear the dit-da-da-dit-dit of the telegraph keys from the wireless cabin below. The starboard look-out and the signalman on watch were standing together, hands deep in pockets, their faces half turned from the searing wind.

The Captain walked forward again, skirting the Oerlikon platform, and rejoined the navigating officer against the forward dodger. He glanced at the compass needle before turning his face to stare out into the darkness.

He thought, it is a silent war out here. A war of ambush and shooting fish in a barrel. Jerry lies out here somewhere, knowing that we are approaching him; able to hear us with his sound-gear. He sits just above the surface of the water, his tubes trained on a ship in the convoy, and he waits until he can't miss, before he fires his torpedoes. We in turn try to pick him up on our radar, or sight him; then we attack, with gun-fire if he is above water, and with depth charges if he is below. If he dives we follow him with the asdic, and we plot all his turns and evasions. The hunter becomes the fox, and his manoeuverability is limited by the element in which he must hide. We, in turn, are being plotted by him, and he knows where we are lying also. He can hear our screw churning up the water above his head, while we can tell where he is lying or moving by the magic of a detection gear which sends us his position as though we were probing for him with a pole.

His job is completed when he has fired his torpedoes, and all he wants to do then is hide. But our job is only starting and we follow him, if we can, relentlessly, as though he were a cockroach running evasive action beneath a human boot. When we find ourselves above him we drop our charges and hope that he will be destroyed.

There is no human element in submarine warfare. It is submarine against ship, then ship against submarine. It is a fourteen charge pattern of depth charges, each containing three hundred and fifty pounds of high explosive, being dropped in the area in which the submarine is believed to be lying. It is the explosive war-head of a torpedo ripping to shreds the boiler-room or the fo'castle of a plodding ship.

It is only after the battle that the human element is apparent at all. It is only when the stunned, frozen and oil-smeared survivors are lifted from the boats and rafts; only when the sullen, deafened Jerry prisoners are hoisted aboard in their lifebelts that the thought occurs that there were men on these steel things which were fighting one with the other.

It is a war of strangers, friend and foe alike. A mile to starboard lay the convoy. There are men aboard all the ships, and they have been travelling with us for eleven days, and yet they are perfect strangers to us. Just as much strangers as are the men who are lying in wait in the submarines somewhere ahead.

It was a mean, sneaking way to wage a war. Indian warfare carried from the forest into the width and depth of the ocean; no preliminary barrages, no attacks over the top of a trench, no infiltration. It was a war of deceit and deception; a battle of the sharpest eyesight, both human and mechanical.

If it belongs to the enemy, sink it without warning. Blow the guts out of it. Kill every man aboard with hot steel and concussion; with the caress of live steam from his blown-up boilers; with the slow strangulation of the Atlantic; with the zut-zu-ut of small-arms fire as he tries to surface and swim for his life. Ram him if he is smaller than you are; cut him in half.

If a handful of Laskar seamen scramble into a floating raft, shoot them like vermin for the glory of the Third Reich. If fifty men are floating on the surface in their life jackets and a submarine is hiding beneath them, fire your charges and sink him, even though it means the death and rupturing of the fifty swimmers above. Even though it means the tremendous shock of sea-water through every pore and orifice of their bodies, and they scream to you to pick them up . . .

"There it goes, sir!" cried Allison, pointing to a flash of flame to starboard. A dull thud floated across the water, followed almost immediately by a long, low, frightened hoot of a ship's whistle.

Before Allison had finished speaking, the Captain had his thumb jammed down on the button of the Action Station bell.

Frenchy Turgeon stood on the deckplates in No. 1 stokehold, engaged in a shouted conversation with his watch-keeping mate, First Class Stoker Wally Crabbe, in the No. 2 boiler-room.

Beneath the bright electric bulbs on the bulkhead, the valve wheels, pumps, gauge glasses and oil feed pipes were a devil's workshop which supplied the steam to run the engines of the *Riverford*. The fuel was pumped from tanks, situated below decks throughout the ship, and was carried by means of fuel lines, through pumps, into the fire-boxes beneath the boilers. It ignited, and sent its thermal power above to heat the water in the boiler tubes. This was boiled into steam, which in turn passed back through lines to the reciprocating engine, where it pushed the pistons, turning the shaft, which spun the propeller.

Through the open, watertight door between the two boiler-rooms, Frenchy caught occasional glimpses of Wally as he went about his work. Above him, the boiler face sloped toward the bulkhead at his back, as though ready to topple forward, and cut him off forever from the air and night sky which lay hidden in the higher gloom, beyond the stokehold hatch. It seemed to Frenchy that the stokehold was a vibrating steel cavern, into which he had been lowered to do penance for his sins. Now and again he glanced into the white, shimmering heat of the fires, turning his face away quickly from their searing blast. The voice of the other stoker was distorted and magnified, as it reverberated in the confined, steel-lined space.

During the past three or four days, since the convoy had left the warm waters of the Gulf Stream, the boiler-room had cooled, and the temperature on the deck, differing from that higher up the ladders, was cool enough to warrant the wearing of a shirt or sweater.

The oddly distorted echo of Crabbe, singing one of his ribald songs, bounced from the steel plates.

> *"The French . . . a funny race, parley voo,*
> *The French they . . . race, parley voo;*
> *The French they . . . a funny race,*
> *They fight with their feet . . . with their FACE,*
> *Inky, dinky . . . ley VOO!"*

"You shut your mout', you *maudit* baskerd!" Frenchy shouted back. His voice reverberated above the roar of the fires, and the vibrations of the ship.

"What . . . you say?" came back the question from Wally.

"You watch dem fire, dat's all you can do. You t'ink you smart fella wit' your song. You make a noise like a *cochon*—like a beeg pork!"

"Work! Who don't work?" asked the other, purposely misconstruing Frenchy's last sally.

Frenchy ignored him and wiped his hands on some waste, and sat down on an oil-stained butter box which served as a bench. He glanced at his gauges before taking a package of cigarettes from his back pocket and extracting a smoke. His hand left black fingerprints on the clean whiteness of the paper.

Back home in Montmagny the maple sap would be running soon, and the Young Peoples Society at the church would be organizing sugar parties into the maple woods south of town. The night shift would be at work in the foundry, and M. Revillon, the foreman of the plate shop, would be shouting at Chasson or Jean-Claude Boucher to stop their chatter and get on with their work. His girl friend Gabrielle would be sitting in Mme. Robichaud's *Chez Cecille* toying with a Coca-Cola, while she read his last airgraph letter to her friends.

He grew sad when he thought of Gabrielle. Though she had not mentioned it outright, several times during the last few months there had been half-concealed hints that Paul Gregoire, who had found a job as a provincial motorcycle policeman, had asked her to go out with him. When he pictured the tall, moustached figure of Gregoire, and remembered how far *he* was away from Gabrielle, he wished sometimes that he had stayed on at the stove company and got his draft deferments like the others.

How far away was he now, he wondered? Geography was not one of his strong points, and the Atlantic Ocean to him was a square body of water, eleven to fourteen days' sailing time across, in which were scattered such exotic places as Newfoundland, Ireland, Gibraltar, Iceland and the Azores. The Azores was the only place he had visited which seemed to him to be islands. Though they said that the other places were also islands, with the exception of Gibraltar, he did not believe them. An island to Frenchy was a piece of land lying in the water, both ends of which could be seen from a few miles distance.

"Frenchy!" rumbled the voice of Wally.

"W'at you want?" he shouted back.

"Nothing. I thought . . . dead, that's all."

Frenchy's reply was halted in his throat by a noise which sounded like the ship's bottom being struck by a gigantic padded hammer. It was followed immediately by the clamour of the Action Station gong. He jumped to his feet and ran to the connecting doorway between the stokeholds.

The vibrations on the deck-plates were suddenly increased, and from the engine-room came the accelerant shug-shug of the steam through the pistons as the engine was revved up. The ship heeled to port, and there was the clatter of small gear on the plates as everything movable shifted with centrifugal force. He grasped at the bulkhead for support, and shouted to the other stoker, who was making his way across the canting deck, "What is it, a dep' charge?"

The face that Wally turned to him was chalk white beneath its streaks of oil, and he shouted back above the incessant ringing of the bell, "That was no depth charge . . . torpedo . . . something's been fished!"

He turned from the doorway, fighting back the panic which gripped him at the other's words. There was the noise of heavy boots on metal, and he looked above him to see the weaving form of Stoker Petty Officer Collet coming down the ladder.

Since he had come off the morning watch to find Knobby lying on the table in the mess, Butch Jenkins had felt lonelier than at any time since joining the Navy. When the terrible import of his friend's death had overcome him he had been led to his hammock where he had lain awake staring at the welter of pipes above his head.

The death of Knobby had hurt him with its suddenness and the void it had left, but more than this it had impressed upon him the fact that death was imminent, and that it could happen to one even as young as he. The zest for his job, and the eagerness he had felt for his coming leave, had gone, and he had been left defeated and frightened. While he lay in his hammock he was certain that nothing lay between his life and the forces of destruction around the ship but a fragile three-eighths-inch thickness of steel, as easily pierced by the war-head of a torpedo as is a sardine can by the point of a can opener.

With Knobby alive their indestructibility had seemed assured, and the fact that the ship might ever be struck and sent down into the cold, green sea was beyond his ken. But as he lay there in his aloneness this possibility of death was magnified by his fears until he found himself tense with the expectation of it. The noise of the ship slapping down upon a wave, the slightest deviation from its regular thrusting rhythm, an involuntary shout from one of his messmates, brought the sweat to the palms of his tightclenched hands, and the hot flush of fear to his face and neck.

Once, during the morning, the *Riverford* had thumped into a bigger wave than average—"hitting a mile-post", it was called by the men—and he had jerked himself upright with a half smothered cry, and had grabbed wildly at a covered steam pipe which crossed the deck-head above his hammock. When he had looked about him and seen the startled, upturned faces of those who were sitting around below he had been ashamed of himself and had lowered his body quickly out of sight again beneath his blankets.

He had heard them pipe "Up Spirits" before dinner, and had lain there listening to the reassuring talk and laughter of the crew as they lined up in the mess for their grog.

When it had been issued, and the Coxswain and the officer-of-the-day had gone, McCaffrey had shaken him by the shoulder and placed a cup in his trembling hand, containing McCaffrey's own tot of rum. "Here, kid, drink this," he had said. "I know you feel tough about your winger dying like that, but don't let it get you down."

"I don't want it, Mac, thanks," Butch had answered. Not being old enough for an issue of spirits he had tasted rum only once before, on the first day at sea when he and Knobby had purchased tots from Newfy Powers and a telegraphist. It had made him elated and very manly until its effect had worn off and he had been forced to spew his dinner over the side.

"Drink it up," McCaffrey ordered, and not wanting to refuse such a generous offer of help, and hoping that it would serve to allay his fears, he had propped himself in his hammock and had tossed the raw liquor down his throat. After his gorge settled he had felt much better, and was no longer afraid. Later he had dropped off to sleep and had slept through dinner, though he had been half-conscious of somebody shaking him, and a voice saying, "Leave the kid alone, let him sleep."

He had stood his watch during the afternoon both as a bridge look-out and quartermaster. His trick at the wheel under McCaffrey's direction had forced him to concentrate on the compass needle, and had banished all thoughts of the body of Knobby lying down below. When he had been relieved, however, he had felt again the gnawing uncertainty and nervousness of the morning, and after eating a light supper he made his way to the boat deck where he had stood in the lee of the funnel watching feafully as the northern night crept down upon the convoy.

There were several others who had chosen to stay on the upper deck that evening, as though they felt a necessity to get away from the claustrophobic pressure below decks. Most of them had lain down on the hot plates above the boilers, wrapped in their coats, or else they had stood in a small group talking quietly, gaining from each other's proximity a lessening of their apprehension. For something was afoot, they knew. There had been rumours at supper time that action was expected that night, and a casual mention by a communications rating or a steward that five subs had been sighted dead ahead had passed from mouth to mouth with the speed of such things aboard a ship.

Butch had tried to go to sleep on the deck but the bitter wind had knifed through his clothing each time the ship changed course, and the talk of the small group near him had kept him awake. He had heard one of them say that they would have bad luck for the rest or the trip as long as the body of Knobby was stowed below, and none had tried to contradict the speaker. Out of loyalty to his friend he had wanted to protest, but he had desisted when he realized that Knobby's death had brought about the fear within himself. If it was true in his case, how could he argue that this fearful tension, this promise of ill luck, did not hold for everybody else aboard?

He had heard the rumour that action was expected, and he prayed that it was false as so many rumour were. He tried to reassure himself by a sight of the convoy with its few thousand other human beings, but when he looked in its direction he could see nothing at first but the dim shapes of nearby waves and the lighter mass which was the clouds above the sea.

As he looked he was rewarded with a sight that he had been fearing to see, and yet one which he would not have missed if a choice had been given him. There was a dull red flash to starboard which lit up momentarily the silhouette of a merchant ship, followed by the low, mournful hoot of the ship's whistle. It couldn't be true—but it was! Not a mile away from where he lay on the deck of the *Riverford* he had seen a ship torpedoed. He watched as the flash of the explosion rose from the water-line like a gigantic roman candle!

"Hey, did you see it!" he shouted, jumping up from the deck. He hardly heard the dull boom which followed the flash; before he had a chance to say any more the Action Stations gongs began their clatter, and the group of men who were standing nearby scattered to their stations as though slapped by a giant's paw. He hurried down the ladder to the port deck and raced along it to his position on the ship above the small-arms ammunition magazine. A hurrying rush of men pushed against him in the darkness as he heaved and tugged to get the hatch cover open. Some of the men, blinded by the night, cursed or laughed nervously as they tripped avore the manholes and other obstacles which projected above the deck. Some ran up the ladder to the bridge and wheel-house, while still others came sliding down to hurry to their stations on the throwers or the forward gun. In less than a minute everything was quiet again except for the depth-charge-thrower captains reporting their crews closed up.

From the forward gun deck came the voice of McCaffrey as he answered the voice pipe from the bridge. A small blue light was switched on in the wardroom pantry below the hatch and the face of Roberts the Leading Steward looked up at him. He smiled at Butch and pointed at his feet where two cases of Point-five Browning ammunition were ready to be passed to the guns if needed. Butch smiled back and waved his hand recklessly. He was no longer afraid.

Bodley, the Sick Berth Attendant, placed the jar back in his medicine cabinet and turned to his patient, First Class Signalman "Cowboy" Henderson. "Take three of these four times a day," he instructed, dropping a daily dozen of sulphanilamide tablets into the open pocket of Cowboy's shirt.

"How come I take twelve a day now?" asked the disconcerted Cowboy, loking askance at the formidable size of the disc-like pills.

"That's what it says here," Bodley answered, pointing to a scribbled prescription which the *St. Helens* doctor had left with him.

"That guy must be nuts," said Cowboy. "Even when I was only taking eight of them a day I could hardly do my trick on the bridge. These things make me sick. I must have eaten more than a pound of them since we left 'Derry."

"If they make you sick take one of these along with them, they'll help to settle your stomach." He poured four over-sized soda tablets into Cowboy's reluctant hand.

"Eating these must be sure saving the Navy grub," muttered Cowboy disconsolately.

"It's not my fault; you had your fun, now you've got to take your medicine."

"That's what hurts. I was too drunk to know whether

62

it was fun or not. Wait till I get back to the other side, those chippies in the Silver Harp'll be playing harps all right."

"We'll be going for a refit first," Bodley said, tasting each word as he spoke them, remembering that the trip would be over in two more days, and then home to Nova Scotia.

"Hey, Tiffy, do you think that I'll be all right by then?" asked Cowboy. "I just remembered, I'm supposed to be getting married next month."

"I wouldn't get married so soon if I were you," said Bodley, fixing the other with his best consultant's frown.

"What's the difference, if I'm cured by then? And if I'm not, all I can say is that this outfit needs better saw-bones than they got."

Bodley regarded him, thinking that Cowboy should be the last man on earth to ever contemplate marriage. He was twenty-seven years old, tall and slim, with the quizzical good looks which often accompany light wavy hair and a sprinkling of freckles. He had the arrogant lithesomeness and the banal brass of the likeable show-off. Because he had never lacked the attentions of women he treated them all with a good-natured contempt, and in return for his studied disregard for their virtue, and his trampling down of their cherished conventions, they hounded him to death wherever he went. His home was Toronto, but during the pre-war years he had knocked about all over Canada and the United States, working at a bewildering variety of jobs, never settling long in one place. The name "Cowboy" had been given him early in the war when as the result of a drunken party he had been seized with an uncontrollable urge to ride a milkman's horse through the Halifax dockyard.

"You should take it easy, Cowboy," said Bodley warningly.

"Take it easy—with all these pills to swallow every day! I'll be lucky if I'm not the second guy you bumped off this trip," the other answered. Then as he noticed the hurt look on Bodley's face he slapped him on the shoulder. "I'm only kidding, Tiffy. It wasn't your fault that the kid died. Forget it."

After Cowboy had turned in, Bodley moved across the

mess to the communications side to listen to the record player. This instrument was one which had been donated to the ship by the Town Council of Riverford, Manitoba, for which hamlet the ship was named. Due to the official misconception that only telegraphists were capable of changing a phonograph record, the machine had been placed in their mess. The music from the phonograph was piped into the other messes of the ship, and the denizens of these nether regions had the choice of either listening to the communications ratings' choice of music, or of turning off the speaker.

Bodley spread a liberal helping of plum jam on to a thick slice of bread and butter and sat back at his ease listening to the slightly bawdy lyric of "She Had To Go And Lose It At The Astor". He was buttering a second slice of bread when there was a heavy bump on the ship's bottom plates and the Action Station gong began its insistent "r-r-r-r-ring—ring—r-r-ring".

Almost instantly the place was alive with the figures of men dropping from their hammocks, and there was a hurried scramble for boots, duffle coats and lifebelts. Bodley made his way to his hammock, pulled on a wind-breaker, and grabbed his first-aid bag from the bulkhead. He had to wait impatiently at the foot of the ladder until the seaman and stokers who formed the ammunition party came down to the magazine which lay below the mess.

CHAPTER 7

After the crew had found their places in the darkness, and the jarring ring of the Action Station bell had ceased, the ship speeded quietly through the night. The fire party moved around shutting the watertight doors and readying the flood valves on the upper deck. They laid out lines of fire-hose and connected them with the hydrants. The crews of the four depth-charge throwers huddled silently at their stations; the anti-aircraft gunners fed the first rounds of their belts into the chambers of their guns, and at the stern the Leading Torpedo Operator, and a coder who assisted him, readied the charges in the rails. Except for the commands of McCaffrey on the four-inch gun platform, nothing could be heard but the hiss of the ship through the water and the sound of the wind as it whirred through the rigging.

Bodley began his rounds, peeking through the blackout curtains over the engine-room hatch. Far below him he could see the figures of the Chief E.R.A. and the watchkeeper as they tended the quick-pulsing engines. The oiler ran around the narrow catwalk of the top ends of the flashing reciprocating engine like a grubby gnome carrying a long-necked oilcan. There was the odour of oil and steam from below, like the smell of a washday kitchen at home.

Up on the anti-aircraft "bandstand" with its pair of twin-barrelled Brownings the Supply Assistant and a seaman manned their port and starboard guns. Leaning on the edge of the armoured, waist-high plate which surrounded the platform was the helmeted figure of Sub-Lieutenant Smith-Rawleigh staring into the outer darkness with a "hearts-of-oak" expression on his face.

Benny Peebles, the Leading Cook, held the lanyard of No. 3 heavy thrower in his hand, an ear pressed to the voice pipe, waiting for the setting command from the bridge.

Bodley clambered forward above the engine-room skylights toward the wheel-house, passing beside a seaman who held a stripped Lewis gun on his knees as he swung his legs against the side of the potato locker which was serving him as a seat. From below him on the port side, near the small-arms magazine hatch, came the whispered voice of Knobby Clark's chum, Ordinary Seaman Jenkins. He was braced against the side plates of the superstructure talking to somebody down below, huddled in his coat against the bitter wind.

The tiffy pushed his way into the wheel-house. When he shut the door behind him the lights flashed on again, and those who were there looked to see who had entered. The Coxswain stood at the wheel in a life-jacket and shirt-sleeves, answering the steering instructions from the voice pipe. Beside him stood a young seaman handling the engine-room telegraph and the revolution counter. Another seaman was sitting on the bunk, tense with the expectancy which comes of having nothing to do, and being shut off from all sight and contact with those outside. "Hello, Tiffy," he said, "what's happening out there? Have they got any contacts yet? Are they going to fire the gun?"

"It's pretty quiet. We seem to be heading somewhere awfully fast," answered Bodley.

The door to the wireless cabin was open, and the clickety-clack of the staccato morse filled the room. Two telegraphists were busy sending and receiving messages, which a coder placed in a container to be pulled to the bridge through a tube. "Anything hit yet?" asked Bodley of the coder.

"Yeah, one—the one we heard before the bell went."

"Hard aport!" came the terse order from the voice pipe.

The Coxswain repeated the order, and the ship yawed to port.

McCaffrey had reported the gun crew closed up, and they waited in the darkness, the layer and trainer standing at the training and elevating gear, the sight-setter at his dials, and the others standing or crouching around the serrated deck. McCaffrey stood against the ready-use locker, on his feet a pair of turned-down rubber hip-boots, around his waist a belt of priming cartridges, and his upper figure bulging under a Mae West jacket. Against the clouds, he appeared as the reincarnation of some long-forgotten English pirate, fighting again to hold the mastery of the Western Sea. Abaft the gun was a line strung through a block, which led below through an open hatch and into the communications mess. A stoker stood down there waiting to relay ammunition from the magazine below. Two seamen were in the magazine setting star shells. One of them shouted to the stoker, "Haul away!" as he placed two shells in the canvas buckets attached to a brass hook on the line. The stoker hoisted them clear of the hatch, disengaged the bags, and carried them across the mess where he hung them on the line leading to the gun.

"Tell them that those two are set long!" shouted a voice from the magazine. The stoker repeated the message to those up above on the platform.

"What?" came the querulous demand from the gun deck.

"Setting long—five thousand feet!"

"For God's sake speak up! We can't hear you!"

The stoker repeated his statement.

Another voice, sounding like McCaffrey's, came through the open hatch. "Turn off that God-damned record and we'll be able to hear you up here!" The stoker ran to the phonograph and removed the record, cutting short the tale of a young lady's loss of something at the Astor.

"Now, what did you say?" asked the voice from outside.

"Those two shells I just sent up are set long—five thousand feet."

"Okay. Tell Robinson to set the next two short, and to send up six cordite charges right away."

The Captain stood up forward on the bridge, his night glasses held to his eyes, searching the expanse of sea into which the corvette was knifing at sixteen knots. He was looking for an object which had been picked up on the radar screen, dead ahead at 4,200 yards. He swung his glasses in a narrow arc, covering the area.

Nothing showed up but the highly magnified crests of

the heaving sea. Astern of the ship, but towards the starboard quarter, the convoy moved ahead with almost bovine relentlessness, its numbers lessened by one as the torpedoed tanker settled by the bow, and was left behind.

Lieutenant-Commander Frigsby took the binoculars from his eyes, and let them fall to his chest, where they swung heavily at the end of a strap around his neck. "Anything else from the radar?" he asked Lieutenant Bowers, who stood beside him.

"Nothing else, sir; they've lost the pip."

"I think we'll give them a star shell or two," said the Captain calmly. "Bowers, fire a spread from red two-oh to green two-oh—setting long."

The First Lieutenant leaned across the dodger, dispensing with the use of the voice pipe. Cupping his hands, he yelled against the wind, "McCaffrey!"

"Yes, sir?" came back the voice of the gun captain.

"Starr shell—setting long—sweep red two-oh to green two-oh. Fire when ready!"

McCaffrey repeated the command, and the trainer swung the gun on the bearing while the sight-setter reported "Sights moving, sights set." There was the sound of a shell being slammed in the breech. A member of the gun crew placed a silk bag of cordite behind it; another rammed it home with a long-handled ramrod. There was the sound of the breech-block clanging shut. McCaffrey grasped the lanyard. "Gun ready. Fire!"

The gun cracked with a door-slamming noise against the empty night, accompanied by the pressurizing shouts of the gun crew. As the breech was reopened, the smell of burnt cordite wafted over the ship, followed by a small shower of smoke and charred paper. Those on the bridge: the Oerlikon gunners in their harness, the Yeoman of Signals, a Signalman, a seaman who served as the Captain's messenger, the Oerlikon ammunition numbers, the Captain, First Lieutenant, and Lieutenant Harris, closed their mouths again, as their ear drums dilated after the blast. Reports could again be heard from the gun deck. A second shell tore its way through the night.

All eyes were turned to watch the bursting of the shells. The first one flickered momentarily against the background of clouds, before it hung suspended on its parachute, a disappointing pin-prick of light which failed to illumine the sea beneath. The second one shimmered into a brilliant white radiance, beneath which the ocean lay black and naked, the whitecaps nodding from a thousand waves. In quick succession three more shells added their glare to the scene.

The Captain strained his eyes behind the lenses of his binoculars as he ranged the lighted area, searching for the tell-tale hump of a conning tower breaking the surface of the mottled sea. The starry glares swung slowly, until they fluttered into extinction in the water.

"He may have submerged," said the Captain to the First Lieutenant, unable to conceal his disappointment. They turned their eyes astern at the heavens lit up with the star-shell brilliance from the other ships of the escort. Well down on the port quarter could be seen the silhouette of their running mate, the corvette *Milverton*.

"Some damn fool has lighted him up," Lieutenant Harris said. As they watched, a heavy geyser of water spewed into the air astern of the other ship.

"He's dropped a shallow pattern," the Captain said, enviously.

There followed a long period during which the *Riverford* moved along through the darkness as it executed an acute, then an obtuse, sweep, searching with its radar eye and asdic ear for the U-Boats.

"We must have left them somewhere astern," said Lieutenant Bowers between periods of blowing on his hands.

After a time the Captain ordered his messenger, "Get me the position of the convoy from the radar operator." He gave a helm order through the voice pipe to the Coxswain below at the wheel, and the ship swung around in a long yaw to starboard. As it came abeam of the runnning sea a heavy wave broke over the fo'castle, drenching the gunners, and sending a small Niagara through the open hatch into the communications mess. There was the sound of spluttered curses from the gun crew, and a startled yell from someone standing in the illumination of the small blue light below the hatch.

Now and again the convoy crackled to life with shell-fire as it felt through the darkness for its harrying attackers.

Then the *Riverford* received an echo from its asdic gear . . .

Allison stood on widespread feet in the middle of the darkened asdic cabin, capless, a pair of earphones clamped to his head. Through the phones came the "pi-i-ing" of the echo. He tapped the H.S.D. rating on the shoulder, and this young man, a happy smile lighting his face, turned about on his stool and nodded excitedly.

Allison opened one of the shuttered windows and called to the Captain. "Echo bearing red four-oh, sir—range oh- two -oh!"

"Good work!" the Captain said. He turned his head and shouted down the voice pipe, "Port twenty—steady on south by west. One-four-oh revs!"

The stern settled deeper in the water as the ships' speed increased, and a fine spray settled on the forward gun crew, causing them to turn their already sodden backs to the knifing prow.

The Coxswain spun the wheel in his hand, his eyes on the liquid flow of the compass needle atop the binnacle. When the ship was steady on course he checked the revolution counter.

"Are we making an attack, 'Swain?" asked the young seaman at the revolution counter.

"We're not going to your Aunt Mabel's tea," he answered, trying to appear warlike beneath his beard.

"Maybe we'll sink it!" the boy exclaimed, his face lighting up with expectation.

His face became serious again as the Coxswain said, "Yeah, and maybe it'll sink us. Just hang on tight and pray like hell!"

Allison shouted, "Echo bearing dead ahead—range oh-one-oh. Target closing—moving slowly left!"

Down in the deep aloneness of the magazine Able Seaman Robinson felt the surge of speed, and knew what it meant, but he had no way of knowing whether the attack was going to be a surface one, a depth-charge, or a ramming attack. He said to his mate, "Let's get the hell out of here and stand in the flats. I wanna get ready to haul ass up those ladders if we ram."

70

"What's the difference?"

"Because it might tear off these bottom plates, that's all!"

"We're not going to ram."

"How the hell do you know—you got a private phone to the bridge?"

The other could find no suitable answer to this, so they made their way to the foot of the ladder leading to the communications mess, and stood there, tense and self-conscious before one another.

"I'm hungry," Robinson said, wanting to say something, and not caring very much what it was he said.

"So am I. I could eat a lobster, claws and all."

"If this baby rams anything, the lobsters'll be eating us!"

Allison reported to the Captain, "Echo red one-oh—range five hundred yards." He shouted down the voice pipe to the throwers and the rails, "Set pattern B for Beer!"

Back aft on the ack-ack platform Smith-Rawleigh gripped the rail and stared ahead, purposefully, into the darkness. Behind him, the Supply Assistant and Able Seaman Williams held tight to their loosely-swivelling pairs of machine guns, and shuffled their cold feet on the wooden firing steps. The Assistant Cook, who was an ammunition number, backed into the relative protection of the armoured shelter. He laughed tensely, and said, "I won't be able to bake any bread tonight."

"Keep silence!" muttered Smith-Rawleigh, as though they were hunting ducks.

As the ship closed with its target the echoes began hammering into the asdic cabin until they became a blur of sound. Allison reported, "Lost contact—last bearing dead ahead—range three hundred yards!"

In the engine-room the Chief and E.R.A. Talbutt stood together on the oily fibre mat before the throttle and the telegraph, and kept their eyes on the smashing arms of the wildly punching engine.

"I wonder if those bastards on the bridge know what they're doing?" asked the Chief. "They're going to smash us up down here. They'd better not ask for any more revs or this God-damn thing'll take off like an aryplane."

As he spoke, the rev counter jumped another ten revs to 180.

"Maybe I'd better secure some of this loose gear," said Talbutt, wanting something to do which would take him away from the side of the angry Chief. "When we drop our charges, they'll fly all over the place."

"All right. Hey, Sanderson, give Talbutt a hand here!" cried the Chief to the stoker who was oiling.

250 yds . . . 200 yds . . . 150 yds . . .

The gun crew inched around the gun as though seeking warmth from the biting wind which knifed through their wet clothing. McCaffrey, pretending a disinterest he did not feel, watched the others to see how they were reacting. He thought, it's like rushing down a dark hill, not being able to see ahead, yet knowing there's a brick wall waiting at the bottom.

Allison stood at the H.S.D.'s shoulder staring intently at the instruments before him. As the ship closed on the contact, he pressed the depth-charge buzzer, counted slowly to himself, pressed it again, counted some more, and pressed it a third time. It was like ringing a house bell which cannot be heard— nothing happened for what seemed, to him, minutes. Then the ship heaved with the explosions of the ten depth charges, and a window shattered behind him in the cabin.

On deck there was the popgun sound of the throwers as they heaved their weighty burdens in slow, graceful arcs, into the sea. At the stern, the L.T.O. and his assistant pulled the bars and allowed six charges to roll into the wake. Those on the bridge and the after gun platform stared astern, bracing themselves for the explosions, but in the waists the thrower crews were struggling with new charges for the throwers.

"Get off my feet, you son-of-a-bitch!" Cowboy cried as he and the other members of his crew bulldozed a new charge into place.

"If we'd go by the drill, you wouldn't be standing there!"

"To hell with the drill, this isn't the torpedo school in Slackers!"

Behind the little ship the sea turned itself inside out in massive convulsion, and the spume and froth settled in a spreading white blanket over the darker water. On the bridge it felt as though the ship has been caught momentarily in a pair of giant pincers, only to shake itself loose, and fly on again. The gun deck pitched, and sent McCaffrey sprawling against the gun shield. There was a clatter of pans and stove lids from the galley. In the wireless cabin there was a rattle of gear, and the waste-basket spilled its papers and cigarette butts over the feet of the telegraphists.

In the boiler-rooms the stokers, unaware of what was going on above, went about their work beneath the straining tension of the giant boilers. There was a clanging thud, followed quickly by a series of them, and the deck plates and sand buckets heaved and rattled. Some light-bulbs shattered from their stems, and a cloud of lamp-black obscured everything, as it fell with a slow, agonizing reluctance from above. There was a short scream from Frenchy as a feed line cracked and sent its arterial flow pulsing out in a heated spray.

Jimmy Collet groped his way along the bulkhead in the dim glow of the auxiliary lighting, beneath the clouds of soot, and found Frenchy rushing around in the blackness, groping at his back. With one quick movement he ripped the shirt over Frenchy's head and threw in the bilge trough. Then he lay the moaning boy on the footplates and covered his scalded back with wiping rags. He called for assistance from the other boiler-room, and using his jersey as a shield, fought his way under the cascading spray and shut off the broken line. Then with the help of the others in the darkened pit the fuel was re-routed to feed the gasping hunger of the fires. Only after this was done was a call made through the blower for aid to the injured Frenchy.

On the bridge the Captain gave an order which brought the ship around ready for another run across its former course. "Can you give me a new bearing, Mr. Allison?" he asked of the navigating officer in the asdic cabin.

"No, sir, we seem to have lost contact," answered Allison.

"Oh damn it! Try to pick it up again."

As he spoke, the convoy was relighted with the white glare of star shells, and over to its starboard side could be seen the pin-prick flutterings of small-arms tracer fire.

"They've seen something over there," Lieutenant Harris said. The Captain mumbled assent as he raked the sea with his binoculars.

Bodley picked his way along the deck, towards the ladder leading above to the stokehold hatch. He passed two members of the fire party crouched in the lee formed by the indentation of the Captain's entryway. "How's things, Tiffy?" yelled one of them above the wind. He recognized the voice as that belonging to Stoker P.O. Forsyth.

"Not bad, Fred. I'm going below to look at Frenchy."

"What happened to him?"

"Burnt his back."

He moved aft, feeling with his feet in the darkness for the raised man-hole covers on the deck. The crew of the starboard forward thrower were grouped around their weapon, two of them engaged in a bicep-punching contest as though they were standing before a drugstore window at home. "Who goes there?" murmured the disguised voice of Cowboy Henderson.

"Joe Blow," answered Bodley.

"Hey, guys, it's the tiffy sneaking aft to drink the alky out of his first-aid bag," whispered Cowboy. "Hey, Tiffy, can I go below? It's time for my pills!" There was a burst of laughter from the others. Bodley smiled.

Nothing more was found that night, though the ship executed a complicated sweep over the area of its last contact, and widened its patrol on the flank as far as effective torpedo range. Hot cocoa was carried to those on the bridge, and one by one the members of the gun and thrower crews were relieved, to go to the galley for a cup of warming brew. Some of the men sneaked a wink of sleep on the warm plates above the boilers. In the communications mess, the magazine party made thick sandwiches from the signalmen's supply of Spam and bully beef, and a pot of aromatic coffee percolated on the hot-plate. After midnight the convoy settled down on its interrupted course toward America. The star shells no longer lighted the sky, and the nervous bubble of machine-gun fire had ceased.

Two of the corvette escorts had been left behind to search for survivors of three ships which had been torpedoed, and the remaining ships closed ranks and waddled on their way. The *Riverford* took up its station again, making a lengthened sweep as it tried to cover the whole port flank of the convoy to make up for the diversion of the *Milverton*, which had stayed behind. The Bosun's Mate piped the "All Clear" around the decks, and the new watch-keepers, grumbling about their loss of sleep, took over the middle watch.

"How good an echo did we have on that run?" the Captain asked Mr. Allison.

"Very good . . . almost perfect, in fact."

"Was it Jerry?"

"I'm certain it was. The paper gives us a good reading too."

"It's funny we didn't bring him up. I expected him to surface and fight it out."

"I did too. We shook him up, anyway."

They were sitting in the wardroom drinking cocoa. The Captain had kicked off his sea-boots and opened his sheepskin, and now he sat on the settee rubbing his head, his face still burning from the wind and lack of sleep. Mr. Allison half lay along the locker behind the wardroom table, still wearing a long woollen scarf round his neck.

"They took another three of them tonight," the Captain said, conversationally.

"I hate to think of the *Port Moresby* getting it. I served in her five years," Allison said.

"What was she, a McCallum and Henderson ship?"

"Yes, U.K. to the Levant. Forty-five hundred tons."

"The way things are going we won't know any of them after the war. They got the *Empire Badger* too; she was a beauty."

"They didn't get our friend the little Greek," said Allison smiling.

"No. They never do get those smoky little buggers," the Captain laughed. Then he called, "Roberts!"

"Y-y-yes, sir," said the steward, appearing in the doorway.

"You may as well turn in. Leave everything until morning."

"Right, s-s-sir. Thank you."

After he had gone the Coxswain came down the companion-way and stood against the wardroom door.

"Yes, Cox'n?" asked the Captain.

"I thought I'd let you know, sir, that one of the stokers had his back burned tonight. The Chief was busy, so he asked me to tell you."

"Was it very serious?"

"I don't think so, sir. Our pattern broke an oil feed and it spattered his back with hot oil. The tiffy says he has a few second-degree burns."

"Where is he now?"

"In his 'mick, sir. He managed to walk to the stokers' mess."

"Which one was it?"

"Camille Turgeon, sir. The one they call 'Frenchy'."

"All right. Tell Bodley to keep an eye out; we don't want anything to happen to *him*." He nodded his head in a gesture of dismissal.

"There's something else, sir," said the Coxswain, twirling his cap in his hand.

"Yes?"

"The Chief has a man in the rattle."

"What for?"

"Refusal to carry out his duties, sir. He was an oiler and he refused to o¸ the shaft."

"What damned nonsense is this? The man must have had a good reason," said the Captain, sitting upright.

"He told the E.R.A. on watch that he refused to go into the Engineer's stores. He said that—that the body of Ordinary Seaman Clark had been thrown from the bench where it was lashed and was lying on the plates looking at him."

"Looking at him!" exclaimed the Captain and navigator together.

76

"Yes, sir. And it was true; I saw it myself after I came off the wheel."

The Captain turned and looked to the navigator for confirmation of what he had heard. When he faced the Coxswain again he was sitting on the edge of the couch. "What, exactly, did you see?" he asked with purposeful calm.

"Well, sir, the boy's body had been thrown—"

"You told me that before. Go on about his looking at you."

"The hammock that he was sewn into had opened up and his face was pushed through. One eye was closed and the other open, like he was winking, sir," answered the Coxswain, not pausing for breath.

The Captain rubbed his hand across his face.

"And, sir, there's lots of talk going on around the ship that it's bad luck to carry him. This stoker was burned, and we got into action again tonight, and——"

The Captain's head snapped back. "And what, Cox'n? Do you subscribe to these old wives' tales also? Do you believe that Jerry attacked us because we are carrying a corpse?"

"No, sir, if you put it like that, sir, I don't."

"Then why report such things?"

"I thought you should know, sir."

The Captain stood up. "I was not aware, until now, that this galley bilge was being mouthed around the ship. It almost seems as though you have been delegated to inform me, in the hope that I will order his burial, posthaste, in the morning——"

"No, sir, nothing like that."

The Captain ignored the interruption. "Let me say now that if such hopes have been engendered in the crew through their silly superstitions, they are wasting their time thinking of them. We are carrying Clark's body into Newfoundland where he will be buried in the Naval Cemetery. If any further talk of this sort is reported to me I will deal most severely with the offenders. Do you understand, Cox'n?"

"Yes, sir," answered the Coxswain, his lips pressed together in frustrated anger.

"And furthermore, I am relying on my chiefs and petty officers to see that this order is carried out."

"Yes, sir," automatically.

"Has the body been properly stowed now?"

"Yes, sir. We sewed up the hammock and lashed him under a bench."

"Good. That's all, Cox'n. Good night."

CHAPTER 8

On the morning following the attack on the convoy the crew were tired and grouchy, the middle-watch keepers because their only sleep had been a cat-nap after coming off watch, and the others because their sleep had been interrupted earlier in the night. To make matters worse the breakfast was an old Navy standby, "red lead and cap tallies", or stewed tomatoes and bacon, as it was called ashore.

"Hey, what's the matter, Cookie?" asked Cowboy as he came off watch, and advanced into the galley with an outstretched plate. "Not red lead!"

"Yes, red lead," answered Peebles, who was angry that anybody should have the temerity to question a breakfast while standing in the sacred precincts of his galley.

"Why don't you save that kind of stuff untill we get into port? I know that it's good for hangovers, but nobody's got a hangover out here."

"Here," said Peebles, sharply, pushing the plate into Cowboy's hand. "Take it or leave it."

The smile vanished from Cowboy's face. "Listen, you fat ape, don't hand me that kind of stuff or I'l shove your thick head into that stove! Now give me my bread ration. Everybody's eaten in our mess, and there's no bread left."

There was a look of crafty triumph on the cook's face as he pointed to an opened, tin-lined wooden box on the deck. "Help yourself," he said.

"What's the idea of sea-biscuits?" asked Cowboy.

"It so happens that my assistant cook was standing Action Stations last night and couldn't get around to baking bread for signalmen," Peebles answered.

Cowboy picked up a handful of hard-tack and stalked from the galley.

It was the same all around the ship. In the seamen's mess Newfy Powers and Able Seaman Pearson were regaling some of the younger hands with stories about the bad luck which follows a ship carrying a dead body.

"I'll be glad when we get in this trip," a seaman said. "After all this time away from Canada I don't want anything to happen now that we're only a couple of days from St. Johns."

"Suthin' *has* happened, ain't it?" asked Newfy. "We gets in trouble wit' the Jerries last night, an' one a' the stokers gets his hide burnt wit' oil. Ain't that enough for a start?"

"Newfy's right," said Pearson, who didn't believe all that the other said, but liked to scare the younger ratings.

"A' course I'm right. I been sailin' vessels out to the Banks man an' boy for forty year an' I knows what I'm talkin' about."

The younger seamen sat and listened to the older men, only half believing Newfy's yarns but feeling an apprehension nevertheless as they thought of their leave only a week or so away. The two-day trip from Newfoundland to Halifax did not count, but they were worried about the immediate few hundred miles which lay between the ship's position and the harbour gates at St. Johns.

Butch Jenkins had stood the middle watch, alternating between the after look-out's position on the ack-ack platform, the port bridge look-out and the wheel-house. Had the ship posted a look-out in the crow's-nest at night, he would have volunteered for the whole four hours of the watch, so that he could be alone with his thoughts.

He stood now, in the early morning light, leaning on the griping spar which kept the starboard sea-boat swung out on its davits, staring at the convoy, and at the wide expanse of water which lay between the *Riverford* and the nearest ships.

Some gulls were twisting and diving a hundred yards from the ship. They fell so that their breast feathers brushed the water, before soaring again in tight spirals. Butch noticed that they were smaller, whiter birds than he had seen the first few days out of Ireland, and much smaller than the large black-winged birds which had intercepted the convoy off Iceland. He wondered what sustained them when they tired of their constant flight. Did they sleep on the water, or fly to the nearest land? They were strange birds, bred through the centuries to expect titbits floating in the wake of every ship, but frustrated during the war by an order prohibiting the dumping of garbage during the day, lest it point the convoy's path to a sharp-eyed submarine. One of them glided above the ship on languidly rigid pinions, keeping pace without apparent effort, its bright little eyes taking in the scene below. With a few slow beats of its widespread wings, it circled the ship, and dived gracefully towards the sea.

After the first excitement of the Action Station bell the night before, Butch had felt a recurrence of his fears, and had stood at his station in the port waist, shivering involuntarily, imagining that every moment would be his last. The crack of the four-inch gun had frightened him almost to death, and he had fought against the urge to run, the urge to get away from where he was, even if it was over the side into the rushing sea.

He had backed his body against the bridge structure and had prayed that the ship would not find a submarine to attack. He had ignored the questions put to him by Roberts, the steward, stationed below him through the hatch, lest his voice give away the fact that he was reduced to quaking cowardice. One of the seamen had come down the ladder from the wheel-house and had informed him excitedly that they had a "ping" on the asdic and were going in to make an attack. He had flattened himself against the steel plates and watched with panic-stricken fascination as the depth charges were fired from the throwers on the port side.

Above the fear of a hurtling torpedo was added that of the corvette's own depth charges exploding prematurely. After they had fallen into the sea, he had felt a surge of relief to know that he had escaped that possibility, at least for the time being.

When the submarine failed to surface, and they had lost their contact with it, he had been glad, and when the ship returned to its station and the "All Clear" was piped, he had gone on watch, keeping to himself, letting his mind run over all the possibilities of violent death which the ship afforded. He had savoured each one, masochistically: the explosion of a torpedo; of a depth charge in its rack (if water pressure can cut the firing pin in the primer, why should there not be one with a slight defect which will do the same thing through the accident of a slight jar?); a boiler explosion; a slight concussion which would fire the shells in their racks up forward . . .

When he came off watch he did not return to his hammock in the mess, but chose, instead, to sleep on the warm plates over the boilers, where he lay until morning, his head buried under the hood of his coat.

The mess, which had been a warm, friendly spot to return to after a watch in the cold and darkness, now was a steel trap ready to close in on its occupants with the buckling of side plates and jamming of hatches when any of the possible explosions occurred. If the others wanted to take the chance of being trapped and boiled alive in hissing steam, or drowned by a slowly rising floor of cold green water, let them. For himself he would stay out on the upper deck where at least he stood the chance of being flung away by the impending blast.

There had been times during the night when he had envied Knobby lying below, away from the fear that alternately froze and boiled in his marrow. He was not afraid of death, he told himself, but only of the explosive shock of being killed; of the searing agony of breaking bones and tearing sinews; of being blinded by a flash of burning cordite; of being pinned on a sliver of sharpened steel.

The few times that he had thought of his mother and sister it had been to envy them their good fortune, safe in Montreal, a thousand miles from the things which stood ready to burst with devastating suddenness, and among which he was forced to live. He had prayed to God to protect him for the next two days until they reached Newfoundland. When he got ashore this time he was through. One trip in a death trap such as a corvette was enough. They'd never get him aboard a ship again. He'd go and tell them that he was in the Navy illegally; that he had lied about his age when he joined up. They'd have to let him go . . .

82

He took a firmer grip on the spar as he heard the Bosun's Mate piping the hands to fall in at the waist.

In the wardroom the officers were ranged around the table tackling the bacon and stewed tomatoes. The First Lieutenant occupied the chair in which the Captain sat when he came down to his meals. On his right, sitting on the locker, was Lieutenant Harris, and beside him was the navigating officer, Allison. Across the table from them sat Sub-Lieutenant Smith-Rawleigh. The Captain and the only other officer aboard, a quiet, unobstrusive Sub-Lieutenant named Sundcliffe, were standing a watch on the bridge.

"It looks as though we made it all right this trip," said Harris, pointing to the Mercator's Projection hanging on the bulkhead. A piece of blue tape was pinned in a crooked line from Ireland to a point about two inches from the north-east tip of Newfoundland, showing the convoy's course. About a quarter of an inch back from the end of the tape was a group of five white-headed pins denoting the submarines which had been the ones, presumably, to attack the convoy during the previous night.

The others looked up at the map. Down the middle of the Atlantic were thick clusters of white pins, beginning just south of Iceland and continuing in an almost unbroken line to the Azores. Other small groups were dotted here and there across the length and breadth of the ocean; thick around the Straits of Gibraltar and the Western Approaches, with a few scattered into the Arctic from the Shetlands to Norway's North Cape. There were single pins up the west coast of Africa and around Bermuda and the West Indies, with a thin line of them along the Atlantic Seaboard from Sable Island to Hatteras and down the tanker lanes along the Florida coast.

"Jerry's got almost as many subs as we have ships," said Lieutenant Bowers.

"It's always a mystery to me how we get through without meeting fifty of them."

"It was lucky that we struck heavy weather near Iceland," said Allison. "As it was, they got two ships."

"And three last night makes five for the trip," said Smith-Rawleigh. "That's not a bad average."

"I don't think we are very accurate with those pins,"

Allison went on, buttering a biscuit. "There are lots of subs, but when we get a new disposition we place another pin in the chart, and for all we know it may be one which is already marked. On a map as small as that one they seem to be clustered pretty compactly, but there would probably be spaces of a hundred miles or so between some of the groups."

"There's one lying outside Belle Isle Strait," Harris said, pointing at the map. "He's in a good position to spot everything coming that way."

"There's a small striking force hunting him right now. I saw the signals last night," the First Lieutenant said.

"I don't think we have much to fear from him," Allison continued. "He's a weather ship, probably, and so is that one off Cape Farewell. That's where we have the advantage over Jerry, he is unable to get long-range forecasts except from a couple of submarines spotted on this side."

The steward brought back two cups of coffee, placing them before Smith-Rawleigh and Harris.

"One of the stokers was burned last night, I hear."

"Oh? Not badly, I hope?" asked Harris.

"Superficially. A feed line parted or something when we dropped our pattern."

"It did shake things up. We could feel it on the bridge."

"Did you hear what happened below?" asked Smith-Rawleigh, stirring his coffee. "It seems that the body of Clark the seaman was wrenched loose from its moorings in the Engineer's stores and rolled on the floor. One of the stokers went through to oil the shaft and there was Clark's face staring at him with one eye open and one closed." He glanced around the table, ready to smile when they did.

"Pass the marmalade, will you, Win?" asked Allison of his next-door neighbour, Winfield Harris.

"Sure," said Harris quickly, reaching for the jar in the middle of the table.

"How do you account for us losing contact so soon after our first pattern, Allison?"

"I can't account for it," he answered, "I guess you can put it down to sloppy work by yours truly."

"Did you have a good contact before that?"

"Yes, perfect."

"What it our E.T.A.?" asked Smith-Rawleigh.

"We should rendezvous with the triangle escort about fourteen-hundred tomorrow, Peter. If all goes well that will get us in tomorrow night."

"Good-O!" exclaimed Smith-Rawleigh. "It's my girl's birthday on the fifteenth. I'll be able to air-mail her something from St. Johns."

Jimmy Collet woke up with the breakfast din of the Chiefs and Petty Officers' mess ringing in his ears. He sat up in his bunk and kicked the blankets down to the foot. Then, with a gargantuan yawn he stretched his arms as far above his head as the low deckhead allowed. Those sitting at the table looked up at him, startled by his animal bellow.

"King Kong is ready to be fed, Sammy," said an E.R.A. named Talbutt to the messman.

"He's too late. Breakfast is over at eight hundred hours, except for watch-keepers," the messman answered, winking.

"Hear that, Collet? Even your stokers refuse to feed you."

"The servant problem is the same all over," the Coxswain remarked.

"What's for breakfast, Sammy?" Collet asked, before his eye caught the crimson debris on the others' plates. "No, not red lead!"

"More than that," said Talbutt. "Hard-tack."

"All I can say, 'Swain, is that you get rid of that cook before we all die of ulcers," said Jimmy, swinging his feet over the bunk's edge, and dropping to the linoleum-covered deck.

"What's the matter with tomatoes?" asked the Chief E.R.A. "They're a protection against scurvy."

"To hell with that, I'd rather have the scurvy."

"Okay, if you don't want them, I'll polish them off myself. Sammy, go forrard to the galley and get a plateful, an' keep 'em warm."

Collet searched around the foot of the bunk until he found a not-too-dirty towel, and with this over his arm he mounted the ladder to the washroom.

He had turned in at four o'clock, after being in the stokehold since the previous evening at eight. They had changed the broken line from the fuel pump after the "All

Clear" had sounded, and it had been slow, exasperating work down below on the heaving plates.

The taps in the wash-bowl ran dry when he turned them on, and he remembered that it was after hours for washing. He swooshed his face with a handful of second-hand soapy water which someone had left in the bowl, and scrubbed his hands with a small brush he carried in his kit. After drying himself on the towel he hurried below again to his place at the table.

He interrupted a conversation which was being led by the Coxswain as he entered. "I never saw the Old Man so mad," the Coxswain said. "You guys know how he's usually a gentleman and all that stuff, never gets rattled or anything. Well, you should have seen him last night when I told him about Sanderson refusing to go in the stores, and about how the crew kicked about carrying a body."

"What did he say?" asked a Stoker P.O.

"Oh, he ranted and raved about how we were going to carry the kid to Newfy, and how all Chiefs and P.O.'s should watch out for talk among the men, and things like that. He practically accused me of being a delegate taking a squawk to him."

"Did you tell him that Sanderson was in the rattle?" asked the Chief.

"Sure. He asked what for, and I told him."

"Have you got him in your charge book yet?"

"No. I'll put him in later."

"I hate to run the guy in," said the Chief. "I wouldn't have liked to see a dead man's face staring up at me, winkin', during action like that. The stores is a spooky place anyhow."

"What I can't understand is why they didn't bury him before this," said Talbutt.

"It's because the Old Man's got a bee in his bonnet about it," the Coxswain answered. "If we'd only been seven or eight days out we'd have dropped him over the side, *and Bob's your uncle,* but just because we happen to be a couple of days from Newfy we got to carry him in and bury him ashore."

"What's this about Sanderson?" asked Jimmy as he took

the cup of hot coffee from Sammy's hand and stirred some Carnation into it.

The Chief told him what had happened.

"Did he go in later?"

"Sure, after Frank here and a couple of seamen had covered the kid up and relashed him under the bench."

"Sanderson's a good man. I wouldn't want him to get into trouble; he's supposed to be going for an M.T.E. course, isn't he?"

"Yes," answered the Chief.

"He's been waiting for it since we left Halifax last year. It'd be a shame for him to lose it now."

"Maybe we won't bother running him, Frank?" the Chief asked the Coxswain.

"Okay by me."

"How's the weather look, Coxswain?" Talbutt asked.

"It's going to be good, I expect. We should have good weather all the way into St. Johns."

The mention of good weather, and the fact that they were only a day or two's steaming from port, put them all in a good humour.

"How is the pea-souper this morning?" asked Jimmy of the messman.

"He was still in his 'mick when I left the mess, sleeping like a baby," answered Sommy.

"I must take a look at him later."

"Who's that? Frenchy?" asked another P.O.

"Yeah."

"I heard about him getting burned. Was it bad?"

"No, it shocked him for a couple of minutes. He's got some blisters on his back."

"You can turn in again, Jimmy, after breakfast," said the Chief. "Forsyth is down below taking your watch."

"Okay, Chief."

There was a cry from the top of the companion-way, "Chief! Is the Chief E.R.A. down there?"

"Yes, what is it?"

"He's wanted down in the engine-room right away."

The Chief lifted his bulk from the bench and reached into his small cabin for his cap before going above.

In a few minutes he returned to the mess, his fat, good-natured face haggard with anger. Those who were still sitting around watched him as he stalked into his cabin, then they glanced at each other significantly.

He came out again and said to the Coxswain, "I have another man to be put in the rattle. Disobedience of the order of a superior officer, or refusal to carry out an order, or whatever the hell they call it. It's O'Brien—First Class Stoker O'Brien. The charge is laid by E.R.A. Fourth Class Bullock."

"What happened, Chief?"

"The same thing as early this morning. Bullock asked this mick O'Brien to go to the stores and bring him some light torpoyle, and he refused. He told Bullock that none of the stokers were going to set foot in the stores until they dumped the body that's in there. Damn him to hell, I've had nothing but trouble since he came aboard! My E.R.A.'s don't have to do their own oiling, and we've got to put a stop to this tomfoolery right now. After that nonsense he got into in Gibraltar I should have had him drafted back to the R.N. They know how to handle guys like him."

At the mention of O'Briens escapade in Gibraltar the others grinned. They remembered the occasion: the Captain was showing a guest of his, a Royal Navy Commander, over the ship, and they were standing on the bridge admiring the view of the rock, when there was a commotion above them, and looking up they spied the naked, drunken form of Stoker O'Brien sitting on the cross-trees near the top of the mast, singing an unintelligible song while he brandished a half-empty rum bottle in a wildly waving hand.

"It's nothing to laugh at," said the Chief, glancing about him. "If this stuff keeps up we may as well drop our hooks and swim for it."

"I'll report him to the First Lieutenant right away," the Coxswain promised.

"That goes for Sanderson too."

"Who's charging him?"

"Who was it? You, Talbutt, wasn't it?"

"Yes."

"I'd hate to be them, going before the Old Man on this charge. He'll give them a trip to chokey for sure," said the Coxswain.

CHAPTER 9

An unmistakable change for the worse had come over the ship's company during the past twenty-four hours. Everyone felt it. There was a tension in the air, apart from the insubordination among the stokers, which should have evaporated by now, when they were so close to home. It may have been due to the superstitious tales of Newfy Powers and Able Seaman Wright, or to the awareness that they were close to the end of the trip, and were all afraid of something happening which would stop them from completing it.

Up to the time of Knobby's death, the ship had been what the Navy calls "a happy ship". In the two years since its commissioning, it had enjoyed its share of good runs and bad. Even during dirty runs, the men had not groused, or shirked their jobs. Everyone had liked their ship, though they had called it a "banana boat" and a "fruit packet". They had been proud of it, and had bragged about it to those whom they had met from other corvettes. Though they were not given to using the feminine vernacular "she", or calling it "a grand old lady", as ex-naval officers do in their memoirs, they had felt at home when aboard.

Now, this feeling of oneness with the *Riverford* had almost disappeared, and the crew's feelings, one to the other, had undergone a sudden and devastating change. If a relief was a minute late in reporting on watch, if a messmate took an extra potato from the pan, if a man was asleep on one's locker, there were angry words, or sullen acceptance of his selfishness.

During the day following Knobby's death there had been a fight between the coders and the acting P.O. telegraphist about some wrongly deciphered groups; the Leading Cook had accused the Supply Assistant of cutting him down on his meat ration, and they had battled over it being five ounces of boneless beef as against eight of the regular carcass; McCaffrey had been forced to stand over Ordinary Seaman Jenkins until he finished his stint of cleaning up the seamen's mess; the canteen server, a leading stoker, had refused to sell a seaman named Pinchott, who was a non-smoker, any more cigarettes, and he had accused him of hoarding them for re-sale ashore. They had ended up calling each other names. And Pinchott, a Baptist Bible student, had been called a "Bible thumper" and, most odious term of all to the caller, a "Jehovah's Witness".

The men went about their work dispirited and sullen. Wright, the radar rating on loan from the Royal Navy, ran a *dhobi* firm, taking in washing for the other members of the crew for a set price per bundle. He had gone into the washroom after dinner with an armful of clothes, a scrubbing brush, and a package of soap flakes and made ready to go to work. He had filled a large empty oil drum with boiling water and had stood it in a corner until he returned from removing some clothes from the lines he had strung above the forward boiler. When he came back he found the water in the taps turned off, and his beautiful big oil drum full of a stinking pile of socks and dungarees. Without waiting to find out who had placed them there, he had dumped the water down the drain, and had thrown the odorous mess through an open scuttle into the ocean. The owner of the irretrievably lost clothing, an asdic rating, had backed Wright against a bulkhead and had almost choked the life out of him until they were pried apart by two leading hands.

"I told you that this ship was hexed," said Newfy Powers. He sat on the boat deck splicing a rat-tail for the life-lines which ran down the port and starboard waists for use in rough weather. "I've seen this happen before. I 'member one time we was comin' back from Jamaica wit' a cargo a' molasses. Our vessel was the *Thomas D. MacPherson,* a schooner outa Fortune Bay. We hit a norther off a' Cape Race an' we lost the Old Man, John Hanley. Broke 'is back, 'e did. We caried 'im 'ome and do you know, it took us a week. Yes, sir, a week it took us, an' when the misfortune hit us we were within hailin' distance a' the beacon on the

Cape. It don't do no good to carry a corpse. You wait an' see if we don't 'ave more trouble than we's got now afore us is through."

Late in the afternoon the two corvettes, *Milverton* and *Port Dover*, which had been left behind to pick up survivors from the night before, came into view on the eastern horizon. When they drew up to the convoy there was an exchange of pennants between them and the *St. Helens;* and they took their stations on the flanks of the other ships, greeted with a flag hoist, "Well Done", which emanated from the Commodore's ship, and which was passed on with a flutter of bunting from all the other vessels, including the remainder of the escort. They had picked up a total of eighty survivors between them, including seven German sailors from a sunken submarine.

Aboard the *Riverford* there was speculations as to which ship had bagged the sub, but later in the day a signal came from the St. Helens which congratulated the *Kirbyville*, a corvette that had been on a starboard stern sweep, on making the kill.

Cowboy Henderson was worried. Behind his bantering front lay a keen intelligence, and an introversion which none would have suspected from his outward demeanour. Though he pretended a nonchalance and carelessness about his physical condition to others, to himself it was a source of worry, and he was anxious to get rid of his affliction before the ship reached Canada. Although he had made the Sick Berth Attendant believe that he looked upon his forthcoming marriage as of small consequence, the truth was that he was worrying himself to death wondering how to postpone it until such time as he was sure he was completely cured.

His fiancee was a young woman whom he had met on his last leave in Toronto the summer before. She was a first-generation Ukrainian-Canadian named Janis Petroff, who was employed by the Bell Telephone as a switchboard operator. His mind was filled with the memories of Janis as he climbed to the boat deck and sat down on the engine-room skylight watching the gulls shadowing the ship.

In a group near the funnel stood several ratings huddled in their coats, enjoying the late winter sun. They were quiet and appeared to be engaged in a conservation too serious for the inclusion of the usual skylarking. Against the starboard railing leaned one of the new seamen, paying no attention to the others, his gaze seemingly fixed upon the herded merchant ships nearby. Cowboy raised himself from his perch and walked across the deck, taking his place beside the other. "How's things going, kid?" he asked.

The seaman turned quickly as though startled by his approach. "Not bad," he answered, turning away again as soon as he had spoken.

"We'll be in Newfy tomorrow. Have you ever been there before? Not a bad hole when it doesn't rain. Maybe not as good as 'Derry or Glasgow, but not bad." He stopped his monologue and looked to see what the other was staring at. All he could see were the forward files of convoyed ships.

He said, "That first one there is the *Mount Nyassa*. We took her over to the other side last summer, loaded with mustard gas."

"They should have sunk it," the boy answered, not facing him.

Cowboy did not reply immediately. He thought, this kid's either a pacifist or religious nut. Well, why not? Everybody was entitled to their opinion! When he spoke his voice was conciliatory, "My old man was gassed in the last war. Sometimes he nearly coughs his lungs out."

There was no answer. He thought angrily, to hell with the snotty little punk, why should I bother with him? But he remained where he was, unwilling to concede defeat. After a long, emabrrassing silence he asked, "Where you from, kid?"

The suddenness of the answer was unexpected. "Montreal—Verdun."

"Montreal, eh? I don't know the place very well. Do you know Mother Martin's down near the Windsor Station?"

"I know where it is."

"I've been there between trains," Cowboy continued, mollified somewhat by the breaking of the other's silence. "A stranger never really gets to know a town, especially a sailor on leave."

"It's a good town," said the young seaman emphatically. "Sure."

"They'll never get me out of it once I get back there."

Cowboy was going to say that he might get sick of it after a while, but there was something so serious in the boy's tone that he desisted. Instead he said, "You don't like it out here, eh, kid?"

"I hate it!"

"Who doesn't? There's only one good thing about it— it comes to an end finally. Tomorrow night we'll be tying up to the jetty in Newfyjohn and you'll be going ashore; then you'll forget all about the monotony out here. Don't forget that we're going for a refit this trip. That'll mean two months in a dockyard with twenty-eight days leave for everybody."

"I don't mind the monotony."

The answer to something culled from the text of what he had said disconcerted Cowboy, who groped back through his mind before he found which statement was being answered. "It's the monotony that gets me," he said.

"Why should we kill each other?" asked the boy, looking at him now. Cowboy saw the sheen that covered his eyes; the same dull glaze he had noticed in the eyes of wounded men who had been pulled aboard after a sinking.

"It's either them or us," he said slowly, knowing now that the boy was ill.

"Some people don't care. None of this bloody crew care. They laugh and joke about killing Germans as though it doesn't matter. The Germans want to live as well as we do!"

"They don't want to live any *more* than I do," said Cowboy. "Don't let things like that worry you, kid. Take it easy."

"Oh, it's all right for you to talk, you don't care about nothing. You never saw your best friend die, did you?"

"Kid, lots of my friends have died. I didn't see them, but I miss them just as much as you miss your winger that killed himself yesterday."

"They didn't die while you were holding them, though."

"No, they didn't."

"Why don't you leave me alone!"

Cowboy reached out his hand, ready to shake the boy, but instead he said softly, "Don't let your feelings turn you against everybody that wants to help you. There's times when we all feel low, like you do now, but the feeling

93

passes. One time I was on the bum, before the war, down in West Virginia. I was sleeping in a sand-house in the Baltimore and Ohio yards in Parkersburg. There was an old bindlestiff in there too, dying of alcohol poisoning. It was raining very hard and I was soaked to the skin, and cold and miserable as hell. I stayed awake all night, feeding this poor old guy drinks of water from a stand-pipe down the yards. He died early in the morning and I went and got some railroad men and told them what had happened. One of them, a big hill-billy, started hollering 'Copper!' They pinched me for trespass, and I did thirty days in the County can on a vag charge. I was nineteen years old at the time and a long way from home, and hungry as hell to boot. I figured that the whole world was against me because this big clod-hopper had me pinched, when all I'd done was try to help a poor old man. For thirty days I sat in my cell and thought of the best way to kill this guy when I got out. The day they released me I headed down towards the yards hoping to meet him. On the way I saw a crowd of kids huddled around a sewer. They had the grating lifted up, and they were poking around inside with a pole. When they saw me they asked me to help them fish for their ball that had fallen through the grate. I thought, 'Maybe that hill-billy's kid is one of them,' and I was going to tell them to go to hell, but I didn't. I went over and fished the ball out for them, and they thanked me politely. It made me feel that I was some use, and that people did appreciate a good turn now and again. Instead of going down to the yards I took the highway towards Cincinnati."

He paused and stared across the water. "It's not much of a story, but I wanted to let you know that we all feel like you do at times, and it only takes a little thing to change our feelings completely. Tomorrow you'll find that you feel better, and nothing that you're thinking now will matter any more. So take it easy, kid, will you?"

Butch made no sign that he had heard.

"I'll see you later," said Cowboy as he slapped the boy on the shoulder and walked away.

Darkness closed in around the convoy that night under a sky that was brilliant with the flickering reflections of a thousand suns upon their galaxies. The sea ran with a slow ground-swell from the coasts of Labrador and Newfoundland to the west. The moon, red-faced from its climb, pushed its way above the horizon, and turning white, sent its albedos to cover the gently undulating sea. The plodding, gently nodding, merchant ships stood white against the outer blackness of the night, looking like a turreted town upon a tipsy screen.

The Captain made one last tour around the bridge before going below to his cabin. He was vaguely uneasy over the change which his experienced eye and ear had detected in the crew, and he puzzled over it as he removed his outer clothing and filled his pipe from the jar which was secured on his desk.

On such a beautiful night, the last one of the trip, there should have been a noise from the messes and the boat deck. Missing was the usual laughter and shouted, obscene banter from below. At other times the ship had rung with loud-voiced greetings, and the comradely sound that only a harmonica can give to a group of lonely men. From the wardroom should have come the sly, schoolboy laughter of the sub-lieutenants and the gruffer, jocular tones of the older officers. There should have sounded the jet noise of water upon the bottom of a pail, and the insistent swishing of scrubbers on soiled clothing as the ratings readied their best uniforms for the morrow's evening ashore. But as he listened, he could hear none of these things, and the ship pushed forward in a silence that was weighty, brooding and funereal.

He asked himself whether the corpse below decks was to blame, but he was unable to supply an answer to his question. Perhaps it was the reaction which is set up by the achievement of a thing longed and planned for . . . he remembered the countless times when as a boy he had looked forward to a coming event with tremendous enthusiasm, only to have it disintegrate into something very ordinary upon its happening, and with its disintegration break his happiness into torpid acceptance of the commonplace. Perhaps it was so with the men; they had looked forward so much to the end of the trip, and with it the going to Canada for a refit, that now with the end in sight the reaction had set in. There had come the realization that the end could never justify its image; that reality was woven of shoddier materials than the dream.

And yet would that be true of all? Could such an hypothesis be applied to the collective thinking of more than seventy men? It was not fair of him to think so. Something deeper and more far-reaching than that was working through the ship, and eating like a dry-rot into their behaviour. It must be the result of carrying the boy's body . . . it could be nothing else. But why was this, in itself, cause for the restraint upon their feelings? He dismissed as absurd the thought that it was caused by the idle prophecies of the older men.

Why should the fact of the body being carried have affected the whole crew as it had? The boy was a newcomer to the ship and, as far as he knew, had not formed many friendships among his messmates. Most of the men were veterans of a year or two of sea warfare and had become hardened to the *fact* of death, which they had seen staring at them from the sites of a dozen sinkings. Was it an atavistic fear, a throw-back to ancient tribal *mores*? The more he thought of it the more certain he became that it was not the boy's death that had affected them, but the fact that the corpse was being carried aboard the ship, instead of being buried at sea.

Well, let them brood and titillate their anger over it; he had made his decision and he must stand by it, whether it had been wise or not. In retrospect, perhaps it had not been a wise thing to do; to impinge upon their happiness the reminder that one, at least, would be unable to share it. He lay back in the squat, heavy chair before the desk, weighing, and trying to balance, the cause and effect of his act.

Of the superstitious anxiety caused by the eerie yarns of the men he cared not a whit; they would evaporate with the entry of the ship into harbour. What did worry him was the loss of the crew's respect, and a lessening of the discipline. It was dangerous, and such a precedent was hard to defeat. If he should order the boy's burial now they would know that he had acknowledged his fault and was seeking to remedy it. He could not afford to change his decision even at the expense of adding further fuel to their anger. He pushed himself up from the chair and walked the few short steps across the length of the cabin. When he returned, he stood for a moment staring at the photograph of his wife and son, letting his greater tragedy erase the lesser from his mind.

His wife's smiling face had not changed, and it was hard to believe that she had thrown over their mariage for the love of another man. Thank God that within a few days he would be in Canada and would be able to talk to her without recourse to the cold scratch of pen upon an impersonal paper sheet. He remembered that he would be able to telephone her from St. Johns. The recollection of this fact brought their meeting much closer . . . brought it as close as tomorrow night.

Now that the inevitable conversation was imminent he found himself going cold at the thought of what to say. If she refused to listen to his plea, then the decision rested with him. He would be forced to choose one of two alternatives: refusal to grant her a divorce, and thus hold her in tenuous restraint; or let her go, and thus break up his home. The first one was an impossibility, and the second was fraught with the danger of blighting the life of his son. She had either to come back to him, hard as that would be for them both, or he would sue her for divorce and take the boy away from her. He thought, thank God that is *one* decision I can postpone until later, at least.

He sat down again at his desk and shuffled the small pile of paper work which had accumulated during the day. There were the usual decoded signals, fuel reports, logs to be signed, a flimsy of his congratulations to the *Kirbyville*, a small pile of forms to be filled out dealing with the accidental death at sea of Ordinary Seaman Wayne Clark. He read them all, signing those requiring his signature, filing his confidential signals, clipping together those which were to be passed on to the gunnery officer, signals officer, Chier E.R.A. and Coxswain. By dint of frequent recourse to *King's Regulations and Admiralty Instructions* and the signals from the escort's Senior Officer, he filled out the preliminary paper work which covered with beaurocratic thoroughness the death of Seaman Clark.

When he had finished, and everything was clewed up to his satisfaction, he sat black in the chair and tamped some fresh tobacco into his pipe. When he glanced at his watch he noticed with surprise that almost two hours had passed and he felt the satisfaction that accompanies the completion of a job well done—the self-indulgent feeling of being able to say, "There it is, all neatly catalogued and filed away." He thought, I'd make a very good shore going Johnnie. By five o'clock my desk would be clear and then out through the dockyard I'd go, stopping all careless ratings who failed to salute me, up to the Admiralty House for a double Scotch before dinner, showing off my Order of the Bloody Executive.

He lighted his pipe before placing the dead boy's small bag upon his desk. When he opened it the photograph of Alma-Doris-Peggy smiled up at him, and he placed her carefully to the side of the desk. Under the small pile of collars was a bundle of air-mail letters held together with a rubber band. He laid these down and picked up a tin cigarette box from the bag.

When he opened it a few small snapshots fell out on his knee, and he recovered them carefully, placing the box and its contents before him. The first two snaps pictured a girl (obviously English), in one of them sitting on a low wall, and in the other standing beside a bicycle before the front garden of a small suburban villa.

He knew how to pick them anyhow, the Captain thought, admiring the photographs.

He removed several negatives and another snapshot of the same girl standing with a sailor. The young man looked familiar, but it took a minute or two before he realized that it was the other new member of his crew, a young fellow named Jenkins, the one who had been holding the boy when he died.

Placing the snaps and negatives in a pile he rummaged further. There were two or three Naval Station cards, an out-of-date leave chit, a Canadian Legion membership card, two Halifax car tickets, and a pass entitling the bearer to a free swim at the Wordensely, Lancashire, Public Baths. Digging deeper he came up with several folded sheets of typescript, and he opened them to find that it was a pornographic story headed *Diane And Her Great Dane*. He shook his head, tearing the pages into small bits and letting them fall into the waste-basket at his side.

Underneath a New Testament he found three snaps of a

blowsy woman of about forty standing in a field of tall grass. In the first one she was holding her skirts high around her naked waist, and in the other two she had discarded all her clothing and stood facing the camera, on her face the most obscene and lustful expression he had ever seen on a woman. He found himself biting his lips in anger, and he cursed as he ripped the photographs to bits so that the pieces scattered to the deck.

He riffled through the other things the bag contained, making certain that there were no more mute reminders of the dead boy's secret past. He tried to temporize with his feelings, remembering his own youthful prurience, but his anger was unreasoning and could not be calmed.

Picking up the snapshots of the young girl again and the large photograph of Alma-Doris-Peggy, he compared them. It would be a hard choice between the two. Then he thought, what do these two know about this boy . . . about his dirty little thoughts and acts . . . about the lewd photographs which rest beside their own in his bag? What do any of us know about each other? Then, bitterly, what do I know about my own wife? He placed everything back in the bag with the exception of the bundle of letters he had removed at first. He picked these up, hesitatingly, afraid of the filthy things they might contain, and turned them over in his hand before slipping the elastic band.

They were all addressed to the boy care of G.P.O. London. The writing was a peculiar, angular script, undoubtedly feminine. The postmark was obliterated or indistinct on most of them, but they all bore a Canadian stamp. He found one on which he could read Medicine Hat, Alberta, on the cancellation. He opened the torn end of the envelope and removed several pages of thick, hard paper. He flattened them out with his hand and began to read.

My Dear Wayne:—   *Dec. 29, 1942*
    Your last letter reached here this morning. Daddy come home for lunch at twelve and I read it to him. We are very happy to know that you are safe and well. I am sorry that you could not visit your Auntie Flora in Leith. Be sure to call on her soon if you can. Her address, in case you have lost the one I give you, is

93 McDonald Court, Pendrith Rd. She is looking forward very much to seeing you, and in her last letter she says that your cousin Bob will be home from Egypt in the new year.

Marilyn and Dorothy just come in from school and they wanted me to read your letter for them. Marilyn's teacher in getting the names of all the young men in the services, and I think that the Home & School Club is going to send you all some cigarettes and candy. Did you get our Xmas parcel yet? We mailed it on Dec. 4th. so that you would get it by Xmas. I guess the mail is late with you moving around so much.

I was talking to Edna Penney and her mother last night. I met them in front of the Safeway Store. Edna asked about you, and she said that she'd mailed you a photograph two or three weeks ago but she hadn't heard whether you got it yet. I guess you know that she stood first at Mrs. Litchter's conservatory exams . . .

The Captain reached across the desk and pulled the photograph of the girl toward him. So that is your name, Edna Penney? My first impression of you was wrong, wasn't it? "What will you do now that your sailor is dead?" he asked the photograph. It returned his stare with the fixed, proud smile it always wore.

Picking up the letter he read on.

Your daddy has a better job now at the plant. He took Mr. Summerville's job when he joined up and he's had two raises already. Clarence Hefferman is in the Air Force at Rivers, Manitoba. He was home here for the holidays.

The Captain skipped the next two pages, and read the final paragraphs on the last page of the letter.

A family called Turner had their house burned down from a blazing Xmas tree and they lost everything they had. The Salvation Army made a collection for them of furniture and bed clothes. I gave them your old Meccano Set because I knew you'd like to see their youngest boy have it, and you can't buy them since the

100

war started. It was only gathering dust on the stairway shelf, anyway.

But I see that I've filled five pages already so I'll close now. Remember that we pray for you every night, and I know that you also pray to the Lord Jesus to watch over you. You need have no fear if you are in His care. Read 1 John 3, verse 16 and I know that it will give you strength to fight temptation.

With love from Mama and Daddy and the girls.
God Bless You.
Mama xxxx

For some minutes he stared at the closing paragraph which lay before him in his hand. He then cleared his desk, and taking a sheet of paper from a drawer he unclipped the pen from his breast pocket and began:

Dear Mr. and Mrs. Clark,

It is with the deepest regret that I take my pen in hand and begin writing this letter. Nothing I can say will ever be able to lessen your grief at this time, but I want you to know that the heartfelt sympathy of myself and the whole ships' company of H.M.C.S. Riverford is yours in your bereavement. You may be sure that your son Wayne went to his Maker as a true young Christian of whom you might well be proud. We are sending along his personal effects post-haste. He is to be buried in the Naval Cemetery at St. Johns, Newfoundland . . .

CHAPTER 10

Frenchy Turgeon was very unhappy. His back was stiff, and caked with the liberal application of gentian violet with which the "Teefy" had covered his blisters. And now they had awakened him to stand a watch. As he sat up in his hammock, wiping the sleep from his eyes with his sleeve, he noticed that the ship had a very peculiar roll, and that it did not seem to be making way. He swung himself down to the mess-deck table and pulled on his shoes. Tying an old piece of towel around his neck for a sweat-rag, he took his gauntlets from beneath a rolled-up blanket in his hammock. He shook his watch-keeping mate, then climbed up the companion-way leading to the seamen's mess, and went out through the blackout curtains to the weather deck.

It was dark, and strangely still outside, and water dripped from the overhang of the fo'castle. He stood in the waist and looked over the side. The ship was scarcely moving through an oily sea, while a thick fog stood around it like a wall, and transient vapours detached themselves from the wall of fog and curled around the funnel and the mast. From close at hand came the mournful hoot of a ship's whistle, and immediately there was the sound of a voice from the bridge, and the ship veered slowly to port.

He hurried to the galley door and pulled it open.

"Shut the door, for Christ-sake!" came the strident voice of the cook from the darkness. "I've got the oven door open and a pan of dough in my hands!"

Frenchy pulled the door shut behind him, and its automatic switches clicked, sending the galley lights on again.

"Hello, Frenchy," the assistant cook greeted him as he placed the bread pans in the oven. "How's your back?"

"Not too bad," Frenchy replied, finding himself a seat on an upturned canned-goods case.

"Did you notice if it was still foggy out?"

"Yes."

"It's still foggy?"

"Yes."

"It's been like that since two o'clock. We're only doing thirty revs. If this keeps up we'll never even see the other escort today."

"We will not go to New-found-land today?" asked Frenchy.

"God, no, not if this fog doesn't lift! There's some coffee over there in that pot, and the milk—now where the hell is it?—there it is, on top of the flour bin."

Frenchy rinsed out a cup over the sink, which was filled with the cook's dirty shirts and underwear, and poured it full of thick black coffee. After he had turned it grey with milk, and had stirred some sugar into it, he sat down again on the box.

"You standing the next watch?" the cook asked him, as he kneaded a large blob of dough on a bread-board.

"Yes."

"Is that all you can say this morning? Maybe I should learn to parly-voo the ding-dong, eh, Frenchy? Then we could talk about those little French babes of yours in Mo'real, eh?"

Frenchy smiled but did not answer. It was maddening to him to be the butt of their jokes; to be called "pea-souper" and "froggy" even though he knew it was in jest. His lack of English kept his conversations with the others down to a monosyllabic level, so that they looked upon him as being little better than a moron. His inability to counter this—to show them that he was literate and intelligent in his own language—drove him to despair.

His appearance did nothing to counteract their impression of him. He was short and broad, with a weightlifter's muscles knotting his back and shoulders. From his navel a twisted growth of black hair triangled across the width of his chest and spiralled down the backs of his arms. His face was the black-bearded face of a Puck, scarred lips opening on a mouthful of false teeth, a legacy of parochial indifference to dental hygiene.

103

His solitude among the English-speaking members of the crew, his muteness caused by his lack of English, had left him lonely and frustrated. He had tried to excel in his work and thus receive an accolade from Stoker P.O. Collet which would acknowledge that he was one of them, and that they recognized him for something more than an *opéra-bouffe* fool. But nothing that he had been able to do in the five months he had been aboard had changed their attitude to him, and Collet had never once said, "You're okay, Frenchy, you're all right, kid!"

With the exception of a few conversations with other French-Canadian sailors whom he had met, the only real talk he had enjoyed during the past few months was one with a Free French sailor off a corvette in Londonderry. The Free Frenchman had been a revelation to him. This young man, a former apothecary from the *Midi* named Paul, had taken Frenchy in tow one night, after meeting him in a fun-fair, and had bought him several drinks in a bar. When he had become slightly tipsy he had confided to Frenchy that he was a socialist and a free-thinker, and he had discussed with him the lack of culture in French Canada due to the strangulation of the Church.

"What literature have you?" he had asked. "None! You have none because the crows will not allow you to have any except *La Vie Des Saints* and other innocuous Papal tripe. Last year when we were undergoing repairs in Halifax I took my leave in Quebec, and believe me, *mon vieux,* I was appalled at conditions there. As a joke I walked into a bookshop and browsed through the shelves searching for something to alleviate my boredom. All I could find was cheap, paper-backed editions of 'romantic', but unworldly, fiction. I searched in vain for a good book. No Baudelaire, no Racine, no Anatole France; and as for the good French moderns, it was as though they had never lived. You *Canadiens* are living in the Middle Ages."

"We have preserved our French culture against the in-roads of English and American filth and anti-clericalism," Frenchy had replied.

"*Our* French culture! It is not my culture you are protecting. And as for the English and Americans, you are boasting now of your stupidity. Do you few million *Canadiens* think that your insularity hurts the English and Americans? Do

you think that a New York American or a Halifax Englishman cares a pinch of *merde* that you refuse to be assimilated?
Your views, my friends, are too provincial for the twentieth
century."

"You talk like a veritable *Communiste*," Frenchy had
answered. "It is the things you are saying now which have
brought France to her knees. France has become a house
divided because of the things you advocate for us in Canada."

"Not because, but in spite of. But we were talking about
Canada, were we not?" asked Paul. "What are the *Canadiens*
doing about the war, eh? In Quebec I heard them laughing
at me behind my back. Young men on the streets jeered
at me because I wear this uniform. They avoid conscription
by going into the woods or the seminaries. They attempt to
hide their ignorance and cowardice by saying that they do not
want to fight England's war—"

"It is true," Frenchy interjected.

"It is a lie! *Regardez moi,* am I fighting for England?
Is a Greek or a Slav or a Norwegian? No, no, my friend,
we are fighting to save ourselves from slavery. If we lose,
do you think that the *Boche* will make *Canadiens* the bosses
in your paper mills and textile factories? Do you think that
you will become a favoured people? Do not make that
mistake: the *Canadien*, whether he fought against Germany
or not, will help to fill the concentration camps, and the
Fuehrer of your country will not be one of your piss-pot
fascists, but an Englishman."

Frenchy was surprised by the other's knowledge of things
which had been troubling him. He said, "If the Germans
ever invaded Canada, we would fight them to the last man."

The other shrugged. "Oh, your friends would urge you
to fight then perhaps, because you could do your fighting
at home. *They* do not want you to come to Europe to fight,
because then you might meet people like me."

"They show wisdom," said Frenchy, laughing, his anger
melted by Paul's good-natured sincerity.

They had talked on into the night, after the pub closed
walking the empty, blacked-out streets. When they parted,
with the dawn coming up behind the barrage balloons
across the river, they had promised to meet again. Three
weeks later he had heard that the Free French corvette

Marguerite had been sunk with all hands off the African coast.

He was thinking of his meeting with Paul, and of the things the young Frenchman had said, as he sat in the galley drinking the muddy coffee and watching the cook fashion the loaves in the pans. He wished that he was able to talk to some of the Englishmen, and get their reaction to the things which were troubling him, but instead he was forced to sit in silence listening to their staccato jabbering (their talk was too fast for him ever to be able to learn it, he thought) and laugh at their jocular aspersions to his race and its customs.

"Hey, Frenchy, I hear that some of your leading stokers are in the rattle for refusing to go into the Engineer's stores," said the cook, breaking into his solitude.

"What you say?"

The cook repeated his remark with the slow, tantalizing condescension of a man talking to a child.

"Yes. Dey are in trouble wit' da Chief."

"Scared of a stiff, eh?"

"A steef?"

"Yeah, that dead seaman they got stowed down there."

"Oh! Yes."

"It wouldn't bother me none. They coulda left him in here for all I care."

"In 'ere?" asked Frenchy. He was thinking, what an ignorant lout to entrust with the cooking of food. Some of these people were obviously of the *canaille*. It was ridiculous to look upon them as the boss class. But of course the bosses were of the class represented by the officers. The Captain was a man who would command respect, and the navigator. The First Lieutenant might. The other Lieutenant, Harris, was a *juif*, but an educated one. He was a very nice man.

"They shoulda thrown the body over the side," the cook wen on. "I hear that it's starting to stink."

"No!" Frenchy said. He did not see how anybody could speak like that about the dead boy.

"I know that all we've had is bad luck since we been carryin' him. First we get an attack, an' then we lose contact with the sub, after we got it cold. Then everything goes

106

wrong with everybody. You get burned, and now this fog is going to keep us out here for God knows how long."

"It was not 'is fault I got burned," Frenchy said, standing up and dragging on his gloves. He turned at the door and said, "T'anks," before he opened it and plunged the galley into darkness as he stepped outside into the weather.

He climbed the short ladder between the starboard depth-charge throwers and crossed the boat deck to the stokehold hatch beside the funnel. Pressed against the raised funnel housing was a shivering figure wrapped in a duffle coat. He stooped and lifted the hood which was closed about the figure's head. Inside he could see the cold, soot-streaked face of the young seaman who had been the friend of the dead boy. He was sleeping fitfully, his lips working above his chattering teeth. The duffle coat and the trouser legs which protruded from beneath it were soaking wet from the fog and the water which dripped from the funnel guys.

Peter Smith-Rawleigh stood before the small wash-stand in his cabin and mixed a bubbling tumblerful of liver salts. He waited until the precise moment of effervescence before upending it and letting it fill his gullet and nasal passages with its gaseous salubrity. He then removed his pyjama jacket and began laving the soap and water along his plump brown arms.

"Y-y-y-your breakfast is ready, sir," came the voice of Roberts the steward from outside the door.

"Right. Have we met the triangle escort yet?" he asked.

"No, sir."

"Why aren't we under way, then?"

"W-w-w-we're in a thick fog."

"Oh damn it! How long have we been piddling about like this?"

" I c-c-couldn't say, sir; s-since before I got up at se-se-six, sir." The noise of his retreating boots along the passage-way immediately followed his last statement.

What a rum go! He had looked forward so much to arriving in St. Johns that night. They would probably flounder around for hours in this fog while the other escort waited at the rendezvous or searched for them with their radar. He concentrated on his toilet: washing, shaving, and brushing his teeth carefully, pausing now and again to admire their flawless brilliance in the mirror.

When he had dressed, he walked into the wardroom and took his seat. The news of the fog had not improved his spirits, and when he saw that the room was occupied by Lieutenant Harris he said nothing, but stared angrily at the bulkhead.

"Hello, Peter," greeted the other, who was sitting across from him, a book of tide tables propped against the sugar bowl.

"Hello," said Smith-Rawleigh. "I hear we're hove to in a fog?"

"Not exactly. We're doing about thirty revs."

"What rotten luck! I'd planned on being in St. Johns tonight."

"Yes," Harris answered, turning back to his book.

Smith-Rawleigh glanced at him. Studying tide tables, he said to himself. Even in the Navy their Jewishness made them scheme and study to get ahead. Not that Harris was the worst type of Jew, but still it was a bit thick having to acknowledge him as a superior.

He rang the small bell on the table. When the steward failed to put in an appearance he rang it again, with an insistant emphasis.

"Roberts has taken a cup of tea to the bridge, and the other chap is getting some grub from the galley," Harris said, his eyes glued to the book.

"What in hell's wrong with the stewards!" Smith-Rawleigh cried, peevishly. "They know that I have less than fifteen minutes before I go up top."

There was no answer from Harris, who concentrated on his book.

After a time the steward came down the companion-way and entered the wardroom door, carrying a covered plate in his hand. He set it down before the Sub-Lieutenant and removed the cover.

"What do you call this mess?" Smith-Rawleigh asked, staring over his shoulder at him, a finger indicating the plate.

"Kidneys, sir."

"What kind of kidneys are they?"

"They could be any kind, sir. We got them from NAAFI, I believe."

Harris chuckled.

"I didn't ask for any smart answers," Smith-Rawleigh said. "What kind are they, or is that too difficult a question to answer?"

The steward's face drained of colour, and his hand clenched around the empty plate he had removed from atop the kidneys. "I don't know, sir," he answered.

"That's better," said the officer, toying in the *saute* with his fork. "Get me some toast . . . brown toast."

"*Brown* toast, sir?"

Lieutenant Harris looked up from his book and smiled at the steward, then shook his head slowly from side to side in a gesture of caution. The Sub-Lieutenant did not fail to catch the movement. When the steward had gone, Harris said, "What is the matter with you this morning?"

"Are you sticking up for the men? You heard him give me an impertinent answer."

"He didn't mean it to be impertinent; he was only making a joke. I thought it was good too—'They could be any kind, sir, we got them from NAAFI.'"

"I don't think that it is a *Lieutenant's* prerogative to condone impertinence," said Smith-Rawleigh sharply, staring pointedly at the double stripe on Harris' sleeve.

Harris blanched, but before he could answer, the steward returned and set a plate of toast on the table.

"That's the trouble on this damned ship," Smith-Rawleigh said, tossing discretion to the winds as soon as they were alone again, "there's not enough discipline. Some people don't know enough to preserve the line which divides officers and ratings. There are too many tradesmen being promoted from the lower deck." This was an obvious jibe at Harris who had joined the Navy as a telegraphist.

Harris rose to his feet, and with his fists clenched on the table top, said, "I'll see you later about this. A wardroom is not the plate to bring in personalities."

"It's as good a place as any! I'm tired of being ordered about by every other God-damn officer aboard. I'm getting off this bloody packet as soon as we reach Halifax, and I'll have a few things to tell them ashore!" He ignored Harris' unspoken plea to quiet down. "I'll tell them too that I won't take any more crap from a dirty Jew!"

Lieutenant Harris was transfixed, his eyes staring over the other's shoulder, his mouth agape. Smith-Rawleigh spun on his heels as though pulled with wires, and stood stockstill for a moment before his head fell on his chest.

The Captain removed his cap, unbuttoned the oilskin coat he was wearing, and handed it to the steward. Attired in oilskin trousers and his familiar roll-necked sweater, he took his chair at the head of the table and sat down. He wiped the moisture from his face with a handkerchief before he said calmly, "Smith, go and relieve Lieutenant Bowers up top. Tell Mr. Allison to discontinue the fog signal unless it closes in again. When you come off watch I'd like to see you in my cabin."

After Smith-Rawleigh had stumbled through the door, the Captain said, "Sit down, Harris." And glancing at the propped-up book, "How are you coming with the tables? Damned hard things to memorize, aren't they?"

CHAPTER 11

After breakfast the off-duty hands were piped, and they formed into two ragged lines in the starboard waist. The Coxswain and McCaffrey detailed them to the morning's work: two hands to straighten out some cable in the port anchor-cable locker, a man to give the stewards a hand scrubbing out some of the officers' cabins, a man to clean the washroom, some hands for various painting jobs.

The First Lieutenant stood off to the side, putting in a token appearance at the unceremonious ceremony. As though to justify his presence he said, "Cox'n, do you need the communications ratings?"

"No, sir," the Coxswain answered. He turned to the work party and shouted, "Fall out all the tel's, signalmen and coders. Report back to your work below."

"You have a small party this morning, Cox'n. Is anybody missing?"

The Coxswain turned to McCaffrey. "Are they all here, Buffer?"

"One absentee."

"Who's that?"

"Jenkins."

"What's wrong with him; is he ill?" asked Mr. Bowers.

"In a way, sir."

"How do you mean?"

"He hasn't been right since Clark was killed. He's nervous; won't stay in the mess."

"That's no excuse for him not falling in."

"No, sir, but he probably didn't hear the pipe."

"Where is he?"

"He's flaked out on the boat deck. He's been there for two days."

The First Lieutenant's face assumed an official mien. "Get him down and put him to work. What kind of a ship is this getting to be? We have three stokers in the rattle now for refusing to work. We can't allow any more of this nonsense."

"Right, sir."

McCaffrey climbed the ladder to the boat deck and shook the prostrate form of Butch Jenkins. "Come on, kid, get up," he said. The figure stirred beneath the duffle coat but refused to rise or answer McCaffrey's summons. The Leading Seaman reached down and pulled Butch to his feet. He pushed back the hood of the boy's coat and looked into a pair of wildly staring eyes. "Jesus, kid! What's wrong with you?" he asked.

Butch turned his head away, refusing to answer.

McCaffrey shook him gently by the shoulders. "Listen to me for Christ's sake," he ordered, "I'm trying to help you! Don't make it tough for us. Tell me what the trouble is."

Butch allowed his eyes to meet the other's stare. "Can't you guys leave me alone? I'm all right."

"You're not all right as far as the Jimmy is concerned. He sent me up here to get you. You've got to pull yourself together. Now tell me what the trouble is."

The boy averted his eyes as he said, "I don't know what's happened to me. I'm scared of things. I'm scared of everything."

"That's all right; we're all scared sometimes," McCaffrey said slowly. He could feel the shivers running along the boy's arms as he held him.

Butch began crying, trying to wipe his grubby face with his sleeve. "I don't know what to do. Sometimes I feel like killing myself. I can't eat or sleep."

"You'll be okay. We should be in Newfy today or tomorrow."

"I hope we get in today," the boy said eagerly.

"We might if this fog ever lifts. Now come on down below and I'll see that you get fixed up in your hammock. You won't have to stand your watch." He tried to lead the boy by the sleeve.

"No! No, Mac, I can't go in the mess deck!"

"Sure you can; you'll be all right. There's nothing to be afraid of. Are you still thinking of Knobby?"

"No, I don't give a care for Knobby. I hate him! Jesus, I hate him, Mac!" His face tightened under the tear streaks until McCaffrey sensed, rather than saw, the intense hatred he had brought forth by his mention of Knobby's name.

"Come on, anyway. You can't stay up here in the cold. You'll freeze."

"No, I won't go!" the boy cried, striking at McCaffrey's arm. "I'm going to stay here!"

"Like hell you are!" McCaffrey said, maddened by what he interpreted as the other's obdurance. He let go of the boy's coat and walked across to the port railing. "Hey, you two," he shouted, motioning to a couple of seamen who were painting the degaussing cable, "come up here a minute. Drop your brushes and come here."

Two seamen, Wright and Pinchott, came up the ladder.

"We've got to get this kid into the mess," McCaffrey said. "It's the Jimmy's orders. He's too dumb to know that we're only trying to help him. Give me a hand to get him below."

"I won't go!" cried the boy, backing against the rail.

"You'll go all right," McCaffey said, trying to remove his hand from its grip on the rail. The two seamen stood apart from them, reluctant to interfere. "Come on, Wright, grab his other arm," McCaffrey ordered. The older man tried to pull the boy's hand from the rail.

Pinchott stood apart from the struggle, saying, "Why don't you go below, Jenkins? They're only trying to help you."

"Come on, Pinchott, give us a hand too, don't just stand there giving advice. The first thing we know the Old Man or somebody on the bridge'll spot us and then there'll be hell to pay."

"Come on, son, let us take ye below, ye'll no be harrmed if ye go quiet like," said Wright as he succeeded in breaking the boy's desperate grip on the rail. Butch struggled at first, but finally gave in, and crying and blubbering, was led down the ladder and forward to the black-out screen at the break of the fo'castle.

Smith-Rawleigh gave Allison a surly greeting as he arrived on the bridge. He resented the fact that he was not trusted to stand his own watch, but must always play second fiddle to the navigating officer or the Captain. Allison gave him the course, and went into the asdic cabin where he busied himself with the charts.

He stood against the dodger watching the slight bow wave fall away in conflicting angles to port and starboard of the ship. The fog lay in a solid mass which retreated thirty yards ahead of the fore-peak of the slowly moving corvette. As the ship swung off course he shouted the deviation through the wheel-house voice pipe, and listened for the quartermaster's answering reply.

He was fed up, he told himself. Now that matters had been brought to a head he would ask for a draft to Fairmiles where he should have been sent in the first place. A Fairmile was a much smaller ship than a corvette, and there were usually only two officers carried. On a Fairmile he would be able to command the respect that was lacking on the *Riverford*. When he had received his commission on the West Coast it had been planned between himself and an uncle, a Commodore, that he would be given one of the small sub-chasers. There was faster promotion and the opportunity to obtain a command of his own in a year or so; at the rate he was going now the war would be over before he was even a First Lieutenant.

There was a noise from below, and he looked over the bridge shield at the men lining up in the waist to be told off for their morning's work. The First Lieutenant and the Coxswain stood apart from the men, talking with the "Buffer", Leading Seaman McCaffrey.

"We'll need two men in the cable locker," McCaffrey said, his voice loud against the sounding board of the fog.

"You and vou," the Coxswain said to the outside files. "Break off and get that cable unfouled. You'd better wait down below until McCaffrey comes."

There was the sound of further orders being given and McCaffrey's voice came drifting up to the bridge. Smith-Raleigh hated McCaffrey with the undying hatred of one who knows he is held in contempt by the other. He thought, if I ever get anything on him I'll make sure that I get him dipped back to an A.B. at least.

He walked back to the middle of the bridge and watched the slowly knifing prow cut through the water. Allison came out, and they stood in uneasy proximity, each intent on his own thoughts.

When the dragging, crying figure of Butch Jenkins reached the blackout screen he refused to go any farther, and all the coaxing of McCaffrey and the others could not persuade him. He took hold of the heavy canvas screen and began kicking out at the escort, screaming at the top of his voice. They let go of him, startled by his terror. As soon as he was free he turned and ran back along the starboard side to the stern, leaving behind him a gathering crowd of curious onlookers who had been drawn by his cries.

Smith-Rawleigh leaned over the bridge and shouted. "What's wrong down there?"

The faces of those below were turned to him momentarily, but nobody answered.

"McCaffrey!"

"Yes, sir," answered the leading hand, looking up at the bridge.

"What happened?"

"We were taking Ordinary Seaman Jenkins into the mess, but he struggled and broke away."

"What right had you to lay hands on him? Don't you know that a leading hand has no right to use force on a seaman?"

"We were obeying the order of the First Lieutenant," shouted McCaffrey. There was a mumbling among the others who were standing nearby. One of them gave Smith-Rawleigh a Bronx cheer.

"I'm going to put you on the First Lieutenant's report!" screamed the Sub-Lieutenant, his voice cracking into a falsetto with anger and frustration.

"Go soak your head!" cried a voice from the crowd below.

"McCaffrey, who was that!"

There was silence at first, then Able Seaman Wright looked up and said, "McCaffrey's nae doon here, sirr."

"I was just talking—he's down there all right! Get him here at once——" He turned to the spot where Allison had been standing, but saw that the other officer had moved

115

back into the asdic cabin where he could be seen through the window busily engaged on the chart table. On the starboard side of the bridge the duty signalman and the lookout were watching him, their blank faces unable to conceal their obvious enjoyment of the scene. He realized that his anger had forced him into an indefensible position, and he turned back to the voice pipe, his body shaking with shame and anger. There was a quick movement behind him, and Allison glanced quickly at the compass before shouting through the voice pipe, "Quarter-master, one-nine-five!" The ship swung slowly on to its course. "Steady!" The echo came back from the quarter-master on the wheel. "Better keep a better eye out in weather like this," said Allison curtly. Smith-Rawleigh stared ahead into the fog.

Hector McCaffrey rubbed his hand across the growth of beard which covered his chin, before deciding that he would not shave. He combed his hair and jammed his blue issue cap on his head, squaring it above his eyes in strict regulation manner. Then he set out towards the First Lieutenant's cabin.

He was resolved to have it out this morning. For the past two days he had been aware of the change in the attitude of the crew, and he had recognized the danger if it was allowed to continue. For six years now he had taken a pride in the Navy, and he was unwilling to see it reduced to an unruly mob due to the blunders and lack of discipline of several "plough jockeys" and "bank tellers" to whom it was only a wartime berth.

All his life he had taken trouble by the horns, going out to meet it, and from so doing gaining the advantage of aggression. When he was fourteen years of age, living in a small New Brunswick bush town, his mother had died and left four children to the lackadaisical ministrations of a father whose life had been thwarted. The old man had allowed the penury and insecurity of a pulp-cutter's life to overwhelm him through the years, so that his only escape from the wild-eyed knowledge of his position were terrible and frequent bouts with the bottle.

After his wife's death McCaffrey's father had gone away to the pulp drive along the Miramichi, and had not returned to his children. Hector McCaffrey, the oldest of the four,

116

had sold nearly all of the family's possessions to buy food, and when this source of income had been exhausted he had taken them to the railroad line and had lifted his younger brother and sisters into the open door of a freight car and set out for Moncton.

On arrival in that city he had led his small brood to a police station and told the desk sergeant the story of his mother's death and his father's desertion. While the four children were sitting there awaiting the arrival of a representative of a charitable institution, Hector had slipped a piece of paper into the hands of the younger ones containing their names, age and birth dates. Then, without letting them know that he was going, he had walked from the police station and had made his way to the edge of town where he hailed a passing truck. Two days later he arrived in Halifax where he found a job at five dollars a week on a fish wharf. For the first week he slept in malodorous sheds along the water-front, and lived off handouts which he begged at back doors of houses in the west end of town. With his first pay envelope he rented a room in a scratch house on Water Street, and began buying his meals.

For the next three years he worked at a number of jobs around the city, ending with his employment as a gas-station attendant for a Syrian who owned a motor camp on the outskirts of town. While he was employed there he joined the Naval Volunteer Reserve, and attended parades once a week during the winter, and took cruises during the summer months.

The Navy had a fascination for him which nothing could douse, and as soon as he was able, he made application for enlistment in the regular force. There followed months of impatient waiting while he greased and gassed cars at the Syrian's camp. When he received his summons for a medical examination his heart beat so much that the M.O. made him sit for ten minutes in the office before he examined him with the stethoscope.

His peacetime rise in the Navy had been slow, as all promotions are slow in a force which was small and static, but he had progressed, first from ordinary seaman to able seaman, and later to leading seaman. As soon as they got back to Halifax he was going in for his Petty Officer's Course, and was studying with this end in view at the present time. It was this fact, along with his distaste for confusion, that forced him now to go to the First Lieutenant.

He ran down the companion-way to the wardroom flats and looked through the wardroom door. "Hello, Mac," said Roberts from his pantry.

"Hello, Robby, is the First Lieutenant around?"

Roberts pointed with his finger. "He's got his head down, I expect. He's in his cabin, anyhow."

"Will you take a look?"

The steward pushed past him and went down the narrow corridor which opened on the officers' quarters. When he came back he said, "He's s-s-sitting there r-reading. G-go down and knock at the door."

McCaffrey knocked at the partly-open sliding door of the First Lieutenant's cabin. "Come in," invited Lieutenant Bowers. McCaffrey pushed the door open, removed his cap, and entered.

"Oh, it's you, McCaffrey," said Mr. Bowers, grinning. "What's up?"

"Several things, sir. I'd like to have a talk with you if you have the time."

Bowers saw that something was troubling the other and he closed the book he was reading and indicated a small folding seat against the bulkhead. "Sit down."

McCaffrey laid his cap on the small desk and took the seat that was offered.

"Cigarette?"

"Thanks, sir." They lighted their cigarettes, and Bowers looked the other up and down, wondering what could have brought him there. He asked, "Is it about Jenkins?"

"Partly, sir. We couldn't get him to go into the mess deck. He broke away from us and ran aft to the stern. I don't know whether he's there now or not. He might have thrown himself into the drink."

"What's the matter with him?"

"He's terrified to go below decks, sir. I don't know what caused it, whether it was the fact of the other kid dying in there, or what. He says he's scared of everything now. It might have been the bit of action we had the other night, but I don't think so. Maybe he's just been brooding about things, and he's gone off his rocker."

Bowers listened to the other. He tapped his fingers on the closed cover of Fitzgerald's translation of *The Rubaiyat* which he had been reading. "Do you think, then, that he is a mental case?"

"Well, not exactly; I'd say that he is shell-shocked or something. He might be all right in a few days."

"Is he standing his watch?"

No, sir. I'm two men short now. The H.S.D. and the radar mechanic have been standing watches since yesterday morning."

Bowers sat thinking. Along the ship's side could be heard the moaning brush of the Atlantic as it sizzled along the slowly moving plates, and the hum of the wire cable which held the asdic dome came through the dead-lighted scuttle. "We'll have to get the kid attended to," Bowers said.

"Sir."

"Yes, Mac?"

"This ship is going haywire. Everybody's on edge, it seems. I've never seen things like they are, before. I'm afraid that if something isn't done soon there's going to be a lot of trouble aboard before we get into St. Johns."

Bowers straightened up. "What do you mean?"

"Well, sir, take the stokers. I hear that some of them are in the rattle because they won't go into the Chief's stores?"

"That's right."

"And then there's this kid Jenkins. I get around quite a bit and I hear lots of the men complaining about carrying the body of Clark into St. Johns. I don't think it's right, sir, either. I think he should have had a sailor's burial at sea. Some say that carrying him brings bad luck. I don't believe that, but lots of them do. First we lose contact with Jerry the other night, then we hit this fog — "

"Those things could happen at any time."

"Sure they could, sir. I'm not worrying about them, but it's the talk that's going on around the messes. Everybody's ready to pick on everybody else. There's been more fights and squabbles the last couple of days than I've ever seen before. Some of the men are planning how to get off the ship as soon as we hit port. There's buzzes flying that we're going to continue on to Boston with the convoy — "

119

"I can tell you that that particular buzz is entirely wrong."

"I'm glad to hear it, sir. The latest rumour is that the body in the stores is beginning to stink."

"Who the hell says?"

"I don't know, sir; it's all around the ship."

"Yon won't tell me, eh, McCaffrey?"

"I don't know who started it; it's just a galley buzz. No names, no pack-drill."

"I had no idea that things were getting as serious as all this," Bowers said, squeezing out his butt in an ash-tray.

"There's something else, sir."

"Let's have it."

"I think that Sub-Lieutenant Smith-Rawleigh is going to put me in the rattle for man-handling Jenkins. He spotted us from the bridge when we were trying to get the kid into the mess."

"I'll attend to that," said Bowers. He stood up and paced across the cabin. "What do you suggest we do about all this, Mac?"

"I think that we should get to the bottom of it, sir."

"That's just what we'll do. You stay here for a minute or two while I go up and see the Old Man." He grabbed his cap, and lowered his long frame through the door.

When McCaffrey entered the Captain's cabin he found it occupied by the Coxswain, the Chief E.R.A. and the First Lieutenant. The captain stood against his bunk lighting his pipe. "Oh, McCaffrey," he said, after he had drawn a light into the tight-packed tobacco, "the First Lieutenant tells me that you are worried about the behaviour of some of the men."

"I am, sir. I'm worried about the behaviour of most of them."

"Quite so. Do you mind telling us again, please?"

McCaffrey told them, briefly, what he had heard and what he had observed. When he finished, the Captain turned to the others. "You know, what McCaffrey says is true, I've noticed it myself. Not as much as he has because I haven't as much contact with the lower decks, but I've noticed it."

The Coxswain nodded, and looked to the Chief E.R.A. for support. The Chief was staring at the Captain, saying nothing, his fat cheeks working over the bones of his face.

"About the condition of the boy's body, can you give us any information on it, Chief?"

"No, sir. I ain't heard nothing about it before."

"Good. Now, Cox'n, you and McCaffrey can go. I may call on you both later." As they started out, the Captain said, "Thanks, McCaffrey."

"Right, sir."

When they had gone the Captain talked for a few minutes with the Chief E.R.A. "What are the names of the stokers who refuse to go into the stores?"

The First Lieutenant read the names from the charge book: "First Class Stokers Sanderson and O'Brien, and Leading Stoker Dunderfield, sir."

"A leading hand, too? What do you make of it, Chief?"

"I can't explain it, sir. They seem to have the wind up since Sanderson saw the kid winkin' at him."

The Captain took another match to his pipe. "We'll hold off the charges until later, Bowers." The First Lieutenant nodded. "Now, Chief, I want you to put these three men into the stokehold and replace them with others. Have you three other men whom you can put into the engine-room?"

"I think so, sir."

"All right, switch them around." He reached into the closet and pulled out his coat. "Let's go down and see how things are," he said. The other two followed him out of the door and down to the Engineer's stores.

The body of the boy was securely lashed under the bench. The Captain felt of it, opening the canvas hammock and inviting the others to come closer. "Do you smell anything?" he asked them.

"No, sir," they both answered.

"It seems fairly cool down here. Have you any idea of the temperature, Chief?"

"No, sir. I would say that it's about forty degrees."

"Mmm, yes. Do you agree with me that there is no sign of decomposition yet?"

"Yes, sir."

"Which of the stokers is oiling on this watch, Chief?"

The Chief E.R.A. walked to the door of the engine-room and called out above the din of the engines. The officers

121

could see him waving his arm at somebody. A stoker attired in a blue denim smock and small wool *toque* was with him when he returned to the stores.

"Come over here, Sanderson," ordered the Captain. When the rating stood before him, he asked, "Did you refuse to enter this place when you were ordered by the E.R.A. of the watch?"

Sanderson scraped his oily boot on the deck-plates. Without looking at the Captain he answered, "Yes, sir."

"I understand that you were frightened during the action of the other night by the fact that this boy's body broke loose from its lashings."

"Yes, sir."

"You know the penalty for refusing the order of a superior?"

"Yes, sir."

"You are expecting to take an M.T.E. course?"

"Yes, sir."

"And you let your fear jeopardize your chances of promotion? Did you inform the other oilers that they would be 'saps' if they came into these stores while the body was here?"

"Not in so many words, sir," answered Sanderson. "I said that we should all stick together——"

"Did you know that you were inciting to mutiny?"

"I—1 guess so, sir."

"We'll hold over the charges until we reach port. I am sorry, but I will not be able to recommend you for your course. You will do your future watches in the stokehold. The Chief here will give you your instructions." He turned and made his way to the door, followed by the First Lieutenant. "Are you afraid now, Sanderson?"

"No, sir," the stoker answered in a whisper.

"See that he carries on the normal oiling routine for the remainder of the watch, Chief, and if there is any more nonsense from him or any of the others I want them to be reported straight to me, and we'll put them under close arrest—down here."

When the officers reached the wardroom the Captain sat down and ordered a pot of tea from the steward. "What do you make of it, Bowers?"

"I can't figure it out, sir. I certainly don't believe that it is a deliberate collective act of disobedience on the part of the stokers."

"I don't either. It's strange that everyone aboard should have a feeling of almost psychic tension. I'm glad that it didn't happen when we were only a few days out; it might have meant trouble during action. Some of the more high-strung young men may have gone the way of this lad, Jenkins."

"Yes, sir."

"I have been giving it some thought. Are you familiar with the study of psychology? No? Well, neither am I for that matter. I have a very superficial knowledge of the subject gleaned from reading several volumes on it when I was hospitalized for three months in Accra before the war. It was very dull reading, let me tell you." He laughed dryly at the memory of it.

The Captain's face grew serious again. "I am inclined to believe that all the trouble among the ship's company is a form of mass psychological tension. Here we are, over seventy of us, on our way home after almost a year away from Canada. We all have our private reasons for wanting to get home quickly and without mishap. Everybody is keyed up and it takes very little to anger us or get on our nerves. This boy meets with this unfortunate accident and we all, consciously or not, see him as a symbol of our own frailty. We look at him, and see ourselves slipping on a ladder, or washing over the side, or being scalded or blown up. Do you follow me?"

Bowers nodded. He thought, the Old Man's head is screwed on the right way, anyhow.

"I admit now that I made an error of judgement in not having the boy buried at sea. I assure you that my motives were good ones: I thought that it would be nice for his parents after the war if they could come and see his grave in Newfoundland, or even have a photograph of it. Were I to do it again I would have him buried."

Bowers nodded. He had been wondering what had gone on in the Captain's mind when he had decided to carry the body to port.

"By carrying the body with us I have antagonized the feelings of some of the men who believe that a sailor deserves to be buried at sea; to tell the truth, I do myself. I have also pandered to the superstitions of those who believe—or pretend to believe—that it is bad luck to carry a corpse. And then, as I said before, I have kept him with us where he reminds everyone that 'there but for the grace of God go I'."

The steward entered with the tea-things. When he had gone Bowers asked, "What will we do about Jenkins, sir?"

"Leave him alone for a while. Tell the look-outs to keep an eye on him. I think it is better to let him work it out himself. Don't let him know that anyone is concerned about him."

"Yes, sir."

"When you were a boy did you ever do something of which you were very much ashamed, and then go and hide, and pretend an anger against others, as though they were to blame?"

"I suppose so."

"That's all that he is doing. He'll be all right." The Captain searched through his pockets for his tobacco pouch. "What with all the trouble among the stokers, I have forgotten the fuel report. I certainly hope that the Chief has enough bunker to take us in. The way this fog is hanging on I'm afraid that we won't be able to rendezvous today."

"McCaffrey told me that there was a rumour going the rounds that we would carry on to Boston."

The Captain laughed. "Where in hell did that one start?"

"In the galley I expect, sir."

CHAPTER 12

Before dinner Smith-Rawleigh was closeted in the Captain's cabin for almost a half hour. One of the stewards mentioned to a seaman the incident in which Smith-Rawleigh had called Harris a dirty Jew, and before long it was the topic of discussion in all the messes of the ship.

In the Chiefs and Petty Officers' mess Frank Cartwright, the Coxswain, said, "'I don't like Jews any more than the next man, but if it came to a toss-up between Harris and that other son-of-a-bitch I'd be for Harris every time."

"I wonder what the Old Man said to him?" asked Jimmy Collet. "The cooks say that he was in the Old Man's cabin for over half an hour. I'll bet he gave him hell."

"They should dip him to an O.D.," one of them said. "Going around with that trick talley: Smith-Rawleigh. How the hell do you get a name like that? Do you tack your old lady's name in front of your own?"

"It's so your name won't be plain Smith like a million other guys."

"And that accent! 'I siy, you cawn't do that there 'ere, y'know'."

"That's the phony West Coast for you," said E.R.A. Bullock. "It's full of those scissor-bills. They think they belong to the aristocracy, and their grandaddies used to beg lumps on the skid row."

"Bullock always has to get his oar in about the West Coast," said Talbutt, who was a professional Westerner.

"It's not that; I just detest those guys. I don't mind an Englishman like the Captain or the radar mechanic talking like that, but for some Canadians to try and imitate the lingo, it puts me off about five left."

Stoker P.O. Forsyth entered the mess and held out his cup to the Coxswain who poured a tot of rum into it from a white enamelled jug on the table. "This thing's got ashes in it," said Forsyth. "Who the hell would be low enough to put ashes in a jug of bubbly?"

"Here, I'll buy it off you, Freddy," said Jimmy Collet, tendering a dime across the table.

"Listen to him ! He's got over a quart saved now!"

"Yeah, but that's my shore-going supply."

"We won't be going ashore for a few days yet, boys," said Forsyth after he downed his drink. "Moody, the coder, just now told me that we're going straight to Boston for our refit."

"You can tell Moody to pound sand up his back," said Collet. "McCaffrey asked the Jimmy about that, and it's just a galley buzz."

"Moody ought to know, he's a coder. He deciphers the bloody signals, doesn't he?"

"He couldn't decipher a God-damned cross-word puzzle," said Collet.

They talked about their favourite refit yards, some hoping that it would be Boston, and others wanting to go to Montreal or Quebec. "I'd even settle for Halifax," said Forsyth.

"I think that Harris should press charges against Smitty," said the Chief, bringing the conversation back to the subject of the moment.

"What happened now?" asked Forsyth. The Chief told him. "He called him a dirty Jew, eh? And the Captain heard him?"

"Sure."

" Harris is all right," said Forsyth. "He's what I call a white Jew."

"Have you ever seen a black one?" asked Collet.

Forsyth ignored him. "What I say is that any Jew who joins up and fights is a white Jew. The last time I was home on leave I saw hundreds of them hanging back, keeping out of the Army. When most of them do join up they become home guards in the Air Force. Don't forget that Harris joined up as a Tel'."

"As far as I'm concerned a Jew's a Jew no matter if he joined up in the Commandos on September the third, nineteen-thirty-nine," said Talbutt. "I agree with Hitler, they should be wiped off the face of the earth."

"Oh, for Christ's sake, Talbutt, don't talk like a God-damned Kid!" cried the Chief.

The Coxswain jumped up. "Here, we've got three tots left in the jug; who wants to roll for it for a dime?"

"Clear the table, Sammy," said Forsyth to the messman.

When the table was cleared and wiped they threw a dime apiece into a tobacco tin held by the Coxswain. Then, each in turn, rolled a pair of dice down the table. The Chief crapped with a three, followed by Collet with a nine, and Talbutt with a five. The Coxswain also rolled a five. Bullock and Forsyth rolled an eight and a four. "You win, Jimmy," said the Coxswain, handing the jug to Collet. Jimmy poured the raw, brown liquor into a glass, draining the jug, with its sediment of charcoal from the inside of the keg.

"Bottoms up!" shouted Forsyth in the custom of the mess.

Jimmy pulled a wry face as he sniffed at the rum.

"You've got five seconds to make up your mind," said Cartwright, "One – two – three – " Bracing his feet on the deck Jimmy drained the glass of its six ounces of pure West Indian rum. Then before he drew a breath he reached to the table and put out the fire in his gullet with a long swig of cold tea. "Long live my bastard children!" he cried through the tears which were springing to his eyes.

In the seamen's mess there was the usual scramble for the duff. "What do them cooks call this stuff 'ere?" asked Newfy Powers, fishing out a second helping from the pan. The piece on his fork was one sent down from the galley for Ordinary Seaman Jenkins who was not there to eat it.

"You don't know what it's called, but you've eaten enough of it," answered Pinchott, keeping his eye on the piece that belonged to him.

"What's it called, Williams?" asked Newfy, ignoring Pin-chott's remarks.

"Cottage pie or cottage pudding or something," said Williams.

"It has a nice gravy to it."

"Gravy!" exclaimed Pinchott. "Gravy on dessert!"

"It's good, anyhow." Newfy went on, devouring a forkful.

"Is it better than boiled 'taters and cod's heads?" asked Williams.

"There's nothin' on land or sea can beat 'em," Newfy answered. "What do yez call dis stuff on it?"

"Sauce," answered Pinchott.

Able Seaman Manders came through the bulkhead door and took a plate from the cupboard. "Did you guys hear about Smitty and Harris?"

"What happened?"

"Smitty called Harris a dirty Jew in front of the Old Man."

Williams whistled. "What happened to him?"

"The Old Man had him in his cabin. I guess they'll court-martial him."

"Good for the bastard!" cried Williams. "When're they going to do it; as soon as we get in?"

"I don't know. I just heard about it from Benny Peebles the cook. It happened this morning before Smitty came on watch. He didn't look too good up on the bridge. When he hollered down to McCaffrey about Jenkins, he caught me and Cowboy Henderson staring at him. He gave us a look that'd melt the knackers off a statue."

" Do you remember when we ran off course?" asked Pearson. "He gave me starboard five, and then forgot. We pretty near ran around in a circle before Allison caught it."

"They shouldn't allow a dough-head like him to stand a watch. He'll have us all killed before we get home," said Williams.

"Did you hear about McCaffrey going to the Old Man? One of the stewards told me that he reported Smitty for threatening to run him in after the Jimmy told him to get Jenkins below."

"Where is Jenkins? Up on the engine-room fiddly?"

"Yeah."

"Somebody should get him outa there, he's gonna starve to death or freeze. We don't want another stiff on our hands. How does the fog look, Manders?"

"Still the same."

"I've seen 'em last four er five days in these latitoods," said Newfy.

"Listen to old Laughing Boy," Manders remarked, filling his plate with bully beef and dehydrated cabbage.

Down below in the wardroom there was a quietude even more pronounced than that in evidence before. Smith-Rawleigh took his seat and ate the bully beef without remarking about it to anyone. Lieutenant Harris and Mr. Allison pretended to carry on a normal conversation, but it was forced. Sub-Lieutenant Sundcliffe ate his dinner at the lower end of the table, now and again glancing at Smith-Rawleigh to see how he was faring since his session with the Captain.

"Where are you going to spend your leave, Junior?" Allison asked Sundcliffe.

The young man, a boy really, cleared his throat before he answered. "I'd like to go up to the Laurentians for some ski-ing, but I'm afraid I'll be too late by the time we go on leave."

"I've always meant to go up there," said Allison. "They say it's beautiful."

"It sure is. Have you ever been there, Win?" Sundcliffe asked Harris.

"No, I haven't. I guess I'm not one for winter sports."

"We have a nice club at a place called Ste. Marie de Corbierre. If you take your leave the same time as me I'd like you to stop off for a few days in Ottawa and go up there. The ski-ing may be over, but it's lovely any time of year," he said.

"I'll keep it in mind, Junior, thanks," answered Harris. He thought, it's nice of him to ask me, but I'll bet a dollar to a doughnut that the club is restricted to Gentiles.

"I guess you'll be going to Winnipeg, Win?" asked Allison.

"Yes."

"That's another town I should see."

"It's not bad there."

"Are all your relatives there?"

"My parents are. I have a brother and sister in Los Angeles," he answered. Then from some perverse source deep within himself he said, "My father runs a Kosher delicatessen. He has the best business in Winnipeg in baby beef, liverwurst and dill pickles."

Sundcliffe looked up quickly. He had known that Harris was a Jew, but it had seemed better, somehow, before it was thrown up in their faces like that. "Liverwurst is my

129

favourite sandwich," he said to break the silence. "I'm crazy about liverwurst on rye."

Smith-Rawleigh kept his eyes on his plate, but a triumphant smile was developing around his mouth. Harris noticed it, and he went on recklessly as though hurling himself into an abyss in a frenzy of self-abnegation. "You should take a trip to Winnipeg. If you like liverwurst I'll get you all you can eat. I'll get it for you—wholesale!" he said.

"Ring for the steward, will you, Allison?" asked Sundcliffe. "I could use another cup of coffee."

"Sure, so could I."

Harris sat staring at the table-cloth, his knife drawing doodles in its virgin whiteness. "I'm going to ask for draft ashore when we hit Newfy," he said slowly. His remark was met with a silence that was painful. "Pete here was right this morning when he said that he wasn't going to take anything more from a Jew. I don't blame him, and I admire him for his honesty. I'm sorry that the Old Man caught him saying it though because he will be punished now for something that every man aboard the ship feels. Why should any of you take—orders from Jew! I wouldn't if I were you — "

"Oh hell! Cut it, Win, please," said Allison.

"I wish that I were the same as you fellows are," he went on, his face ashen now, the words pushing one after the other, as though he feared to stop talking—afraid to meet the onrushing silence. "I'm sorry that I'm a Jew . . I'm ashamed of being a Jew. Do you know what I'd like to be for a while? I'll tell you, I'd like to be a God-damn white, Gentile, Anglo-Saxon. You fellows don't know how much you are the envy of every Yid and Wop and Nigger in this world. You don't know how nice it is to be always one of a majority . . . to be able to turn away insult with a righteous shrug . . . to be able to go anywhere, and feel the confidence that you wear like armour-plate. I'd give five years of my life to be one of you for a month, to walk down the street in Haifa or Lisbon or Port Au Prince, and know I was the envy of mankind. I'd like to go anywhere on the face of this earth, and know that was king. Do you know what being an Englishman is? It's knowing that you're *right*, arrogantly *right*! That's why a Jew is — is so — Jewish, because he's eaten up with envy of you — "

"Excuse me, sir, did you want another cup of coffee?" asked the steward.

"No. No, thanks," Harris said, getting up, and hurrying through the door.

"Well!" exclaimed Allison, when he had gone. He looked down at the table-cloth in front of Harris' place. Cut into the linen, as though with a razor blade, was a swastika that Harris had made with his knife.

CHAPTER 13

After lunch, and aroused by the three extra tots of rum he had drunk, Jimmy Collet was filled with the drunkard's desire to share his well-being with his fellow-men. The mess was too quiet, its only noise being the mumbled "Fifteen-two, fifteen four . . . " of Talbutt and the Coxswain playing cribbage on the end of the table. Jimmy's few attempts at conversation had ended with the Coxswain's terse remark that he should either go to sleep, or go on deck and let the wind get at him. "That's just what I'm gonna do too," he said, and he staggered up the companion-way to the weather deck where he stood against a depth-charge thrower and made up imaginary conversations to be held with his girl friend Daisy when he reached Hamilton.

The after look-out leaned over the side of the ack-ack platform and shouted down, "Hey, Collet, you got a match?"

"Oh, hello, Billy! Sure, just a minute; I'll bring you one up." He circled around the quarter-deck and climbed the ladder to the gun platform. Billy Turner, the lookout, reached down through the hole in the deck of the gun platform and gave him his hand.

"What you been drinkin', Collet?" he asked.

"Sssh!" cautioned Jimmy, holding his finger to his lips. "I won the roll today for the spare tots. I won three of 'em."

"Spare tots? What spare tots?"

"Well, it's like this, see. The Cox'n brings all the spare tots down to the mess, an' then we each throw a dime in a can for the chance to roll for 'em. The winner gets the rum and the money we put into the can goes for the beer the first night ashore."

"So that's what happens to all the tots that that old

132

phony chisels off the hands up forrard. I always wondered!"

Jimmy sat down on the wooden step which circled the machine guns. "You know, we're not going to get into Newfyjohn tonight," he said.

"You're telling me, mate," answered Turner.

"Look at that fog. We haven't seen another ship all day. If you ask me, it's getting thicker all the time."

Turner looked out over the side. "It's just about the same."

"Which direction's the convoy, Billy?"

"On the starboard beam."

"Have you seen it?"

"I saw a fog buoy about an hour ago. I pretty near reported it to the bridge for a periscope. I'm getting as jittery as the rest of them aboard this packet."

"Cheer up, we'll be in soon. Are you takin' the first or second leave?"

"I'm taking the first I can get on; I'm not going to take any chances of missing this one. You heard what happened to me last summer? I was all set to go on leave from the *Port Dover,* when I'm drafted here and miss my leave. I've got a kid sixteen months old I've never seen."

"Where do you live, Billy?"

"Calgary."

"I'm from Hamilton; Hamilton, Ontario. You know where that is, Billy? The ambitious city. Toronto is a suburb of Hamilton."

"Yeah."

"I used to have a girl friend in a restaurant there, but I guess she's married now or joined the Wrens or something. Her name was Daisy. Isn't that a hell of a name for a dame? Daisy! It sounds like something you'd call an Airedale bitch, or a horse. She was all right, though; she was one swell kid."

"Sure," said Turner, taking a puff of his hidden cigarette. He thought, anything I hate is a drunk who bores you taking about his wife or girl friend.

Jimmy stood up and staggered to the side of the platform. "Who's that guy's been sleepin' on the upper deck for the last coupla days? he asked.

"A kid called Jenkins; one of the kids we picked up this trip."

"What's the matter, is he sea-sick or what?"

"I don't know. He won't go below decks; says he's scared."

"I think I'll go talk to him; maybe I can get him to go below," said Jimmy, climbing down through the hole in the platform.

When he reached the side of the bundled-up figure in the duffle coat, he reached down and opened the hood. A pair of wide, frightened eyes looked up at him, and at the petty officer's badge on his cap. "Is your name Jenkins?" asked Jimmy.

"Yes."

"Get up; you've been here long enough. I've pretty nearly tripped on you every time I've gone on watch for the last couple of days."

The boy scrambled to his feet.

"What's wrong, kid, you scared to go below?"

"No."

"Well, what are you stayin' out here for, freezin' to death?"

"I want to."

"What've you been eatin'?"

"Nothing."

"That's no good. I was once on a bat for nine days, and didn't eat a thing. It almost killed me, and I had the jitters for a month after."

Something like a smile whisped across the boy's face.

"I'll tell you what I'll do. If you promise me to drink it, I'll bring you a cup of good beef-tea. What do you say?"

"Okay," the boy said in a low voice.

"Right! Now you stay here until I come back." He made a circuitous path to the top of the boat deck ladder, and went below to the mess. From his locker he took a package of Oxo Cubes, which he had received in a package from home, and made his way to the upper deck again. He shouted down the engine-room ladder to the oiler on duty, and when the oiler came up to see what all the shouting was about, Jimmy gave him the Oxo and a cup and told him to make a brew out of it on the steam line and bring it back to him in a hurry.

When the stoker returned with the steaming cup of beef

tea Jimmy carried it with a drunkard's tenderness to the boat deck.

"Here, kid, drink this," he said, shoving the hot cup into the shivering boy's hands. Jenkins placed it to his lips and downed it in several fast, hungry gulps. "See, it'll warm you up," said Jimmy.

They sat together in the lee of the funnel for several minutes, and Jimmy told the boy highly coloured stories of being out West before the war, and about the many jobs he had held, and lost. As the hot drink began to warm him, and fill the void left by his two-day fast, Butch felt his confidence returning, and he smiled several times at the things Jimmy said.

"You know, those punks up forrard would have let you starve to death up here. You should have joined as a dustman, kid—as a stoker. All the good eggs are stokers. Now I don't wanna scare you or nothing like that," he went on in a conciliatory tone, "but you've got to get cleaned up, and get your head down in a hammock. We'll be in Newfy tomorrow, and you wanna be on your toes or they'll draft you off, and you'll never get home on leave for another six months. Now all I'm gonna ask you is, will you let me fix you up? I can fix you so you'll have the best sleep you ever had, an' no trouble. Will you do as I tell you?"

Butch nodded his head.

"Okay. Now, what we've got to do first is to go and get you cleaned up. We'll use the P.O.'s washroom, where it's not too far from the open deck, so's you won't be scared. You'll take a good wash, and you'll feel like a million bucks. After that I'll give you a coupla big, stiff shots of pusser's rum an' then you'll be able to sleep like a baby all night. Okay?"

"Sure."

"Right. Follow me."

Jimmy gave the boy a towel and some soap and left him in the washroom. When Butch emerged his face was shining, and with his hair freshly combed he appeared a different person. "Now, kid, take a good drink of this," Jimmy said, handing him a bottle which he whipped from under his coat. "Even if you don't like the stuff, drink it down."

Butch placed the bottle to his lips and took a long swallow. When it went down he spluttered a bit, but held on to it. "Now take another one, a bigger one this time," ordered Jimmy. The boy drank a good shot of the fiery liquid, but this time it threatened to come up again. Jimmy was ready for this emergency, and he shoved a cup of water into the boy's hand in time. "Now just sit down there until you feel like singing, and then we'll go along to your mess, and you turn in," Jimmy said, taking a long drink himself.

When Jimmy returned to the washroom the boy was drunk, and was almost asleep. "Come on, kid, it's bedtime for you," he said, and taking Butch by the arm he led him down the deck and into the seamen's mess.

McCaffrey was lying on a locker when the drunken pair entered the door. "What happened, Jimmy?" he asked, getting up and walking towards them, where they stood, swaying together, inside the door.

"I just fixed up one of your seamen, Mac," Jimmy answered. "Where's this kid's 'mick? He wants to turn in."

McCaffrey scratched his head in bewilderment. "If I hadn't seen it, I wouldn't believe it!" he exclaimed.

Pinchott leaned over the side of his hammock and took a look at the tipsy tableau. "That kid's drunk, Mac," he said. "It's a fine thing when a P.O. goes and gets a kid his age drunk.

Jimmy peered around the mess, trying to find the speaker, whom he had recognized by his voice. "Listen, you Holy Roller, for all you care that kid could have froze to death outside," he shouted. "I got him in here, an' that's what counts, eh, Mac?"

"Sure," McCaffrey answered, trying to hide a smile.

"Did I do right, Mac?"

"Sure, you did a good job, Jimmy."

"Sure I did. You tell that sanctimonious Baptist, wherever he is, that when they need help, nobody should go to a Bible-thumper, will you? The on'y cure they got for anything is – is hymns."

"Okay, Jimmy, we'll take care of Jenkins now," McCaffrey said. "You'd better go and turn in yourself, if you're going on watch tonight."

"That's just what I'm gonna do," answered Collet. "You're not mad at me, are you, Mac?"

"No, you did a good job, Jimmy," said McCaffrey, humouring him.

"You're damn right I did," he said, and with that he staggered with dignity from the mess.

McCaffrey took the boy's shoes off, pushed him into his hammock, and covered him up. Before he finished tucking the blankets around his feet, he saw that Butch was asleep, his breathing regular, no longer afraid.

CHAPTER 14

The morning of March twelfth began with a lessening of the fog, and by nine o'clock the sun's position was marked on the ceiling of grey mist by a yellow blob which grew brighter as the daylight advanced. The grey, thickened sea slapped languidly against the ship's plates with off-hand playfulness. There was a new smell in the air: of far-off forests and snow-covered earth; and the wings of coast-wise birds dipped and soared through the clinging fog, their voices raucous with insatiable greed. On occasion the ship ran into clear patches of sunlight with a suddenness like the opening of a door to a lightened room, and at these times the wraith-like silhouettes of one or two of the merchant ships could be seen, before they disappeared again into the anonymity of the mist. The sight of them after twenty-four hours of solitude was miraculous and unreal as is the first rays of sunshine peeping from beneath a thunderhead.

As the clearings became more numerous the speed of the ship was increased, and it pushed its way through the fog banks recklessly, breaking out again with porpoise playfulness into the open sea. To those above decks the quick changes of temperature between the fog and the clear air was exhilarating, and occasionally there was the view to be had of a convoyed ship above a low-hanging surface mist, pushing its way through deck-high cottonwool.

The Captain, who had been on the bridge all night, returned again after breakfast, and together with Allison shot the sun and worked out the ship's position on the chart table in the asdic cabin. The First Lieutenant detailed four hands to go below and bring up the body of the dead seaman, and place it in the shade of the after gun platform.

The men went below and unlashed the corpse from beneath the work bench in the stores.

"'e's as stiff as a side a' mutton," said Newfy Powers as he struggled with the tightened knots around the legs.

"You didn't expect he'd be liquid, did you?" asked Pearson.

"I've seen 'em liquid afore this."

"Keep silence, you two! This isn't a picnic," McCaffrey said.

"The whole bloody thing's a picnic, if you asks me," said Newfy.

"Nobody's asking. Hurry it up, for God's sake and let's get out of this hole."

With two men at each end of the bundle they removed the body from its resting place and carried it through the engine-room. E.R.A. Bullock pulled his hand from the pulsating engine, where he had been feeling for hot rods, and together with Frenchy Turgeon stood watching the macabre struggles of the four seamen with their stiffened cargo.

"What you do wit' 'im now?" asked Frenchy, whose sense of propriety towards the dead had been outraged enough on this trip.

The others did not answer at first, but when he repeated his question, Pearson said, "We're taking him up for some air, he can't stand the smell of the stokers."

They struggled up the slippery ladder and out to the deck. Newfy bent a line around the corpse, and they hauled it aloft and stowed it in a cleared place beneath the gun platform.

"Let's hope they let him stay here now until we get in," said Pearson, looking down at the twisted canvas bundle at his feet.

"The poor devil's had a time of it," Newfy said. "There's no peace for the livin' nor the dead aboard a plague ship like this 'as gotten to be. An' our ill luck's not finished with yet, you mark my words! Last night I dreamed of a derelict vessel. That's always a goodly sign a' misfortune."

"Stow that stuff," McCaffrey broke in. "You can start laying your lines. Newfy, I want you to get that new spring line from the locker, and Pearson, you and Wright give him a hand. Starboard side."

"Do you think we'll tie up today?"

"We'd better."

"Somehow I can't believe it," said Pearson. "We'll founder, or run into a minefield or something."

"Bowers says we'll be meeting the triangle escort in an hour."

"Yeah, but how long will it take us to run in after we meet them?"

"Not long; four or five hours, I guess."

"I hope so, I want to be able to make the Wets when they open at six."

The fog disintegrated under the evaporating suction of the sunshine until the sea lay wide and clear. Scattered haphazardly on its surface were member ships of the convoy, two here, a half dozen there, several more lying mast down on the eastern horizon. There was a hurried interchange of flashing signals, and the scattered ships reformed their lines, the stragglers hurrying under a plume of black smoke to regain their positions, herded by the ubiquitous little corvettes. A smudge of smoke dead ahead soon evolved into a picket fence of masts and sampson posts, and then became a small herd of maverick merchantmen shepherded by the *St. Helens*.

When the convoy found its course again, and the ships had reformed their ranks, they were counted and it was found that only four were missing, two swift Norwegian tankers which had broken away by themselves, the dirty little Greek, and the R.N. trawler which had stayed fifty miles astern to look after it. The convoy pressed on speed again and headed south-west towards its destination.

Butch Jenkins awakened after the fog had gone and poured himself a cup of lukewarm tea from the pot standing on the mess deck table. His head was light and fuzzy from his long sleep, and the rum, but he felt better than he had done in days. His first reaction upon awakening was to wonder how he had been induced to sleep in the mess, but as the memory of the night before came back to him he felt only a burning sense of shame at his conduct of the past two days. To prove to himself that he was afraid no longer, and to make up for his former refusal to work, he helped the messman wash up the dishes and clean the mess deck. When it was finished he wandered outside to watch the convoy being gathered together.

McCaffrey approached him. "How do you feel now, kid? Okay?"

"Better," he mumbled, before turning away.

"Go and find some place to scull . . . get out of sight," McCaffrey instructed him.

Butch made his way aft and stood in the stern watching the green water turn white as it frothed and bubbled in the wake.

The look-out in the crow's-nest spotted the relieving escort first. He shouted their position to the bridge, and the news was passed on by signal lamp to the other ships. Before long they came into view: a Royal Navy V-and-W destroyer and four Canadian corvettes and minesweepers, which would escort the convoy from there to Cape Cod.

As they came closer the men of the *Riverford* watched them manoeuvring for position, feeling a little superior to the crews of these craft whose run was almost coastwise in comparison to their own.

"How do you get these jammy numbers?" asked Jimmy Collet, who stood on the quarter-deck and watched the minesweeper which was to relieve them, come up astern.

"You give the drafting officer a bottle of bubbly," answered Talbutt.

"It must be great—Halifax to Boston, then up to Newfy. They're only at sea a few days at a time. Boy, could I use some leave in Boston!" said Jimmy, enviously.

A Bangor class minesweeper ran alongside, and its Captain spoke a greeting through the loud-hailer. "Hello, *Riverford*, nice trip?" he asked.

"Fair," answered the Captain. "We had some rough weather earlier."

"Lose any ships?"

"Some."

"I understand you may refit? I'll see you in Halifax."

"I'll look forward to it."

"Well, carry on. Don't drink everything in the Crow's-nest," shouted the other Captain, referring to the sea-going officer's club in St. Johns.

"So-long, *Humber Bay*," answering the Captain, as the

Riverford heeled to starboard, and set out to catch the others of the escort.

The five ships, with the *St. Helens* in the van, formed a broad arrow formation as they raced in a north-westerly direction towards the Newfoundland coast. As they settled down, they took a bone in their teeth, and with long slaps against the ground swell hurried to make the harbour before nightfall. To those standing on their decks there was now a feeling of comradeship between them; a feeling that they had gone through things together; that their association was something exclusive and friendly. On the funnel of each was a large green-painted maple leaf bearing the figure 1 in black. It was their escort number, talisman, escutcheon, the crest of their team.

Cowboy Henderson walked aft and stood beside the watching figure of Butch Jenkins. "How do you feel now, kid?" he asked. "Lost the jitters yet?"

"I feel all right," answered Butch.

"That's the stuff. They should open this thing up. I'll bet if they did, we'd leave that there old four-stack tin-can twenty miles astern."

"Could we beat it in a race?" asked Butch, forgetting the fact that he did not want to speak to anyone.

"Sure," answered Cowboy, with more pride than probity. "Why don't we put on more speed then?"

Cowboy looked at him to see if he was joking before he answered. "The *St. Helens* is the senior ship. If she could only make four knots, we'd have to slow down to four knots too. Senior ships are very sensitive things."

"The others look nice going along like this, don't they?"

"Everything looks nice when you're heading for home."

About four o'clock in the afternoon two small smudges came into view on the horizon. The news that land was sighted passed around the ship. At first it seemed to be a series of small islands, which later were joined together and became high bluffs, between which the high, rolling country could be seen stark and white beneath its mantle of snow. As the ships drew closer, those who watched from their decks could see the small scattered communities nestling in the shelter of the cliffs. Later, the shore-line broke up into a series of bays, and above them, in the valleys that cut inland from the sea, there were dark patches which marked the small, stunted vegetation, sheltered from the tearing force of the wild Atlantic gales.

The ships steered for a point of land capped by the white-painted finger of a lighthouse. As they passed around it, there opened up before them a wide, protected bay whose waters were still and smooth compared with those outside. Several fishing vessels lay beneath the heights of land, and a small grey naval patrol craft came across and sniffed at their heels as they passed. They headed in line astern towards an inch-wide crack in the solid face of the cliffs.

"Where's the town?" asked Butch, gazing at the long low shore-line of the point where a few scattered houses could be seen.

"It's behind that cliff, kid. You see that narrow opening there? Well, we go through it, and we're home," Cowboy answered.

"It doesn't look wide enough."

"It is, though."

"Is that a castle on top of the cliff?"

"A wireless tower, kid. That's where Marconi received his first signal from across the ocean."

"Who're you kidding!"

"You asked me, didn't you?"

When the ships were a mile or so from the harbour mouth they swung out of position in answer to a signal flashed from shore and hove to, their engines barely turning over, while those on board stared through the frame of the cliffs at the sight of the hill-side city beyond.

"You'd never know it was there," said Butch, gazing at the terraced heights of the roof-tops, and the flickering Aldis lamp signalling from the roof of a large hotel directly across from the harbour entrance. There was something of magic in the sight of the small city which lay protected by its cliffs, a few hundred yards back from the terrible anger of the wide, green Atlantic.

When it came her turn to enter, the *Riverford* felt her way between the cliffs, while the fore, aft and waist parties stood to attention on her decks.

The rocky shore-line ran past them at arm's length, first the gun batteries, and then the jerry-built homes of the fishermen, leaning crazily atop their stilts at the water's edge. The harbour was crammed with ships: destroyers, corvettes, minesweepers and tugs stood four and five abreast against the jetties; and tied to trots in the middle of the harbour were crippled merchantmen, and a large captured German tanker.

The smell and the taste of the town were strange to their salted palates, so that they were able to separate the ingredients: dust, manure, sewage, month-old snow. The drab water front streets were broken and sagging after the beautiful symmetry of the sea, and the colours were dark and sombre with blackened paint and paintless wood. The crowded harbour gave promise of a seething town behind the hedge of masts and spars, a promise of warmth, and drink, and gaiety.

As they slowly felt their way along the harbour, swinging to miss the bumboats and water taxis, the men aboard the *Riverford* enjoyed a surge of pleasurable anticipation in thinking of the coming hours, as some feel it entering a circus tent, or a gay, lighted café.

"It's not a bad town," said Cowboy. "It used to be a hell of a good town in nineteen-forty, but we spoiled it. We spoil every seaport town sooner or later. We forget that we can go on a spree nearly every night we are ashore, and we never seem to realize that the natives never go on one at all. We expect them to act like we do, and we're as mad as hell at them when they don't. I once worked as a bus-boy in a night club, and I used to wonder what the people saw to have such fun about. I know now that they only came into town from the suburbs once a month, while I was there all the time. It's the same with us. Tonight we'll raise hell because it'll be our first night ashore in two weeks."

"It feels good in here, surrounded by land. I never knew how safe the land could feel before," said Butch.

"Yep. You know, I'm just thinking; I mentioned that it used to be better in nineteen-forty. This war is lasting too long. I'm beginning to compare the good old days already."

"It can stop any time," said Butch. Forgotten now was the picture of himself winning the Victoria Cross.

"It'll stop when we're too old or rum-dum to work."

144

"The harbour looks nice, with the snow all around it," Butch said. "Knobby would have liked to have seen this; he always liked visiting new places."

"Did you know him long?" asked Cowboy.

"Nearly six months, I guess."

"You'll miss him now."

"Yeah. The other day I said I hated him, but I don't. I guess I was crazy when I said that."

"That's nothing; nobody remembers those things. Don't worry about it."

"They've got him under the gun platform now."

"Yeah, that's so they can get him ashore easy when we tie up."

"I wonder if they'd say anything if I went and looked at him? I just want to see if he's okay."

"Go on if you want to," Cowboy said. He watched the figure of Butch climb the ladder to where his friend's body lay, wrapped in its canvas shroud.

CHAPTER 15

The Captain bathed, and dressed himself in his shore-going uniform. In the mirror, wearing a collar and tie, he looked taller and thinner. His hair was turning grey around the temples, and he badly needed a hair-cut. He took a pair of nail scissors, and trimmed the hair around his ears.

The palms of his hands were damp and he thought, I'm worrying too much about my phone call. He was reminded of a time when he had called Joyce from South Shields. They had been courting then, and the incident returned to him sharp and poignant, so that he re-lived it: the battered telephone kiosk, smelling vaguely of fish and chips; the difficulty he had in finding the correct change; his breathlessness, and her knowing, happy laughter; his saying, "I'll come, even through fire," and her intimate little reply. The memory flickered momentarily like the warmth from a new-lit log upon a hearth, before it expired.

He thought, this time it will not be the same, for the only emotion it is possible to recapture is sorrow. They would pass the time of day, and he would tell Joyce to expect him home in a fortnight or so. They would bandy some small talk back and forth, very correct, civilized and intelligent, and that would be all.

Then he thought, of course, whether we have a telephone conversation or not depends upon what she has to say in her letter. There must be a letter or two from her in the mail which has been redirected here to meet the ship.

There was a knock at the door. When he opened it he found the Yoeman of Signals standing outside. "Yes, Barton?" he asked.

146

"I sent the signal about the ambulance, sir. They just flashed that it will be down to pick up the body in half an hour."

"Very well. Has the mail been brought aboard yet?

"Yes, sir. They are sorting it now."

"Have it distributed as soon as you can, will you?"

"Yes, sir."

"Thank you."

He closed the door, and opened the drawer of his desk. Inside was a small pile of papers which he was taking ashore. On top of them was a memo which said, "Funeral Arrangements (?)". He took this out, and began writing headings in a short column down the page. He wrote, "Flowers", then "Padre (Prot.), Hearse (Gun Carriage?), Naval Party, Band, Route to Cemetery, Undertaker, etc."

Tied neatly into a parcel on the corner of his desk was the dead boy's personal gear. Clark's uniforms and equipment were packed, and stored in the steward's pantry in readiness to be shipped ashore. He took the letter he had written to the dead boy's parents and placed it in his pocket, to post in the wardroom mail box. After ascertaining that everything was ready at hand, he placed the papers in the drawer again, and went below to the wardroom to await the distribution of the mail.

When the signalmen returned to the ship with the mail, the table in the communications mess was cleared of supper things, and the letters were sorted for distribution to the messes.

"Here's one for Clark," said Cowboy, holding up a thick white envelope.

"Put it over here, I'll take it to the wardroom later," said the Leading Tel.

"I wonder if his people know he's kicked the bucket yet?"

"Sure, the Navy sends a signal."

"What would they say? 'Killed on Active Service'?"

"Sure."

"I'd sooner be killed in action; it sounds better," said Moody.

"I want to live to be ninety, and then be hanged for rape," Cowboy asserted.

The piles of letters and parcels grew in size as they were

147

taken from the bags. "Without reading the name on it, I know who this one's for," said Moody. He held up a once-brown parcel, slightly squashed, upon the wrapping of which there spread a large greenish stain. "It's Wally Crabbe's old lady sending him quince jam again. Look at the mess; she must bottle it in Kleenex or something! Quince jam!" He made a face as though he were about to vomit. "They might have won the last war on plum-and-apple, but we'll never win it on Mrs. Crabbe's quince." he said.

"Look at all the mail for the tiffy. He's got about twenty letters already."

"Hey, Bodley, what else have you got except wavy hair?" one of the sorters called across the mess.

Cowboy said, "He writes to all the lovelorn columns, 'Young sailor, lonely, not hard to look at, twenty-two years old, five feet ten inches tall, weighs one-fifty pounds, desires correspondence with lonely member of the opposite sex, object true friendship'."

"Never mind, you guys, it'll pay off some day. There's one who writes to me, owns a mink ranch."

"Keep away from her," said Cowboy. "A setting like that would give her ideas."

"Here's one with a monogram on it for *Lieutenant* Smith-Rawleigh. When did he get promoted?"

"He promotes himself when he's on leave."

"Yeah, like the ordinary seaman I seen on the train, sewing a hook and a good conduct badge on his sleeve before we got to Montreal."

"There's one here from the International Fertilizer Co. for Fred Forsyth."

"That explains all the B.S. in the Petty Officer's mess. They send it to them in envelopes."

"Here's another one for Clark; it's different from the first one. Must be from a dame. Baby, you wasted at least one air-mail stamp in your life."

"I see they got the kid standing a watch under the gun platform."

"He's going ashore as soon as the ambulance gets here. Barton just received a signal from shore."

"That reminds me, they haven't piped the leave yet," said Cowboy.

148

"What are you worrying about? You're confined aboard—C.D.A., the Contagious Disease Act. Ain't he, Bodley?"

"Oh yeah, not this chicken!" shouted Cowboy.

There was a piercing blast from the top of the ladder, followed by the sing-song ritual of the quartermaster, "Shore leave for all non-duty men. Rig of the day Number Twos and jerseys. Leave expires at oh-seven-three-oh, Chiefs and P.O.'s at eight hundred hours. First liberty boat at eighteen-thirty hours!"

The conversation slackened as the Captain entered the wardroom. Bowers and Allison were sitting with their drinks at the table, while Smith-Rawleigh leaned against the book-case, a glass in his hand. Draped on the settee was a Pay-master Lieutenant named Orsonby, a friend of Lieutenant Bowers. "Greetings, sir," said Orsonby as he spied the Captain. "It's been a long time no see."

"Hello, Orsonby, how've you been?" It was amazing how people such as Orsonby heard that a ship was coming in; there was hardly time to tie up before they were down cadging drinks.

"I'm bored, sir, just bored. If they don't get me out of here soon I'll be screech happy. I'm now nearing the end of my second year fighting the battle of Newfoundland."

"I hope you'll have our pay down tomorrow. We've had only one casual payment since leaving Gibraltar the last time."

"You can depend on it, sir," Orsonby asserted with tipsy sincerity.

Roberts looked through the doorway.

"Give the Paymaster another drink, Roberts, and I'll have a whiskey and water."

"Y-y-yes, sir."

The Captain took a seat on the lockers. "Bowers, would you mind standing by when they take the body ashore? You might inform the Coxswain to muster four men. The ambulance should be here within the half hour."

The First Lieutenant prepared to go.

"Finish your drink first; I expect the ambulance will be later than promised. By the way, who is the officer-of-the-day?"

"Sub-Lieutenant Smith-Rawleigh, sir."

149

"Smith, have the quartermaster pipe the usual leave for all hands."

"Blacklistmen too sir?"

"Everyone," answered the Captain. Then he said, "Just a moment, please," and turned to Lieutenant Bowers "We have no men under stoppage of leave, have we?"

"No, sir. McCabe was the last, and his Number Eleven punishment stopped four days ago."

"Good. Will you take your requestmen and defaulters tomorrow, Bowers?"

"Very well, sir."

"That will give all defaulters and men awaiting punishment the chance to have their good time tonight," the Captain said. He turned to Smith-Rawleigh. "Tell the Coxswain that the First Lieutenant's requestmen and defaulters will muster in the morning."

"Yes, sir," answered Smith-Rawleigh indolently.

After he had gone, the Paymaster asked, "Did I hear you say 'body', sir, a moment ago?"

"Yes, we had a lad fall down a ladder and kill himself."

"That's too bad. Just before a refit too. Had he been aboard long?"

"No, we only picked him up before this trip."

"Just a kid, eh?" asked Orsonby.

"Yes, his first run on a corvette."

"It just shows you, doesn't it?" asked Orsonby, sombrely leaving the others wondering just what it showed, except that the cause of death is always its meeting with one's own frail self.

There was the sound of clattering boots on the stairs and the steward entered with a bundle of mail, which he set before the First Lieutenant. Bowers began sorting it into piles for those officers who weren't present, and handing their mail to the Captain and Allison. "Here's an official looking one for me," he said. "Probably dunning me for an insurance premium, or asking why I didn't file my last year's income tax."

"One of our chaps received his army call-up in a letter last week," said Orsonby.

Bowers and Allison laughed. When they glanced at the Captain, he was shuffling his mail in his hands as though searching for a letter which had escaped him.

"Are you missing one, sir?" Bowers asked.

"Eh? Oh no; the mail is rather skimpy though, isn't it?"

"Probably more to come tomorrow."

"Yes, I suppose so." He stood up, and forced a smile their way. "I'll trot along; I have quite a bit to do ashore tonight. Good night, Orsonby."

"Good night, sir," the others said as he left the ward-room.

Jimmy Collet unfolded a clean shirt from his bag, and put it on, and followed this by the donning of his "drinking" uniform. He lifted the three-parts empty bottle of rum from his locker, and held it against the light, trying to make up his mind to save it for the morning. He said to himself, "If I drink it now, tomorrow I'll be sick and sorry; but if I keep it for the morning I'll only drink it when I come back to the ship tonight. By drinking it now I'll get the full benefit from it, which I won't do by drinking it later, when I'm already drunk." Logic defeated caution in his monologous argument, and he took a long drink "for the road".

He made his preparations carefully, placing a clean hand-kerchief in his right-hand-trouser pocket, a small hondful of silver in his left, and a wallet, denuded of everything but his naval registration card and a five-dollar bill, in the buttoned-down pocket over his left hip. He took his cap from its bag, and shined the peak with his sleeve, before cocking it over one eye. Then he took another drink because the first one did not seem to have had any effect. He suddenly realized that there were no other preparations to make, so he poured the remainder of the rum into a cup, and drank it down. This done, he executed a little dance step before reporting his departure to the Chief.

"Don't forget that leave is up at eight hundred hours in the morning," said the Chief, impaling him with a stare.

"No, Chief. You know me, I'm always back when the pubs close."

"See that you are; we're oiling ship in the morning. And watch coming inboard over that gang-plank."

"I'll use both my hands and feet."

"I know *that*."

"If I'm not at the P.O.'s Wets I'll be at the Queens Hotel," said Jimmy, "and if I'm not there I'll be beating the drum for the Sally Ann."

"Yes, and in the morning you'll be beating your head on a stanchion to shake out that Jockey Club brew."

"That's tomorrow," said Jimmy, falling up the first step of the ladder.

Frenchy Turgeon read his mail in the relative privacy of a corner in the stokers' mess. He divided it into courses, his hunger for news from home being first titillated by the unwrapping and laying aside of a small parcel of periodicals: a January issue of *Le Samedi*, several dog-eared and food-stained copies of the Quebec daily, *Le Soleil*, and two monthly issues of the ecclesiastical *Annales de la Bonne Sainte Anne*, forwarded by his mother. With these piled close at hand, he opened the unfamiliar envelope of a letter from Roger Ouillete, one of his fellow-workers at the foundry. Inside were two ruled pages filled to overflowing with Roger's sketchy reports on doings at the stove company. Many of the items referred to happenings unknown to Frenchy, so that he turned the pages over once or twice to see if any were missing or misplaced. He smiled at Roger's attempts to be wordly through the inclusion of several English slang expressions. When he finished it he sat back and enjoyed the warm, friendly feelings it had brought.

There were two letters from his mother, their phraseology terse, as though she had been afraid that her feelings might flow through the pen. Both began with an injunction to attend mass as often as he could, and pray nightly to Ste. Anne. Thus having taken care of the spiritual Frenchy, the remainder of the letters were filled with more temporal things: endless paragraphs full of neighbourly and family affairs, an attempted condensation of all the happenings of the town into four pages of writing.

As he read the letters, he could see her composing them on the kitchen table, hesitating, pen to mouth, before writing the short, sharp sentences as though possessed. Behind her, leaning back against the brown-painted wall-board, his father was sitting, twirling the dials of the radio, interjecting his approving comments above the dialogue of the radio plays. The picture that the letters brought to mind, more than the

152

contents themselves, carried Frenchy home, so that for a few minutes he was with the family in the kitchen, surrounded by the laughter of his young brothers and sisters, and the cleanliness of newscrubbed paintwork and spread-out papers on the floor. His hunger was only partially appeased by the letters from his mother, so he lay them aside and began the dessert, a letter from Gabrielle.

There were five pages of Gabrielle's beautiful, girlish script. She mentioned how much she missed him, and asked him to forgive her penmanship, because she was writing the letter while lying in bed. (He sensed the feminine attack upon his susceptibilities by this transparent, off-hand, mention of herself in bed.) She gave him the names of three or four of his friends who had received their Army call, showing him her disapproval of such things, and expecting him to sympathize. She wrote that things were very slow in town, and that some of the girls were going to Quebec to find jobs in the arsenal. At the end of the letter was a brief sentence telling him that his rival, Paul Gregoire, had been transferred to the Lake St. John district. He re-read the sentence, searching for a clue to her feelings when she had written it. Was she sorry, or glad? Was it a hint to him that he now stood alone in her affections? Lover-like, he was unable to read into the few words the protestations of affection he wanted it to contain. She signed it, *Your Little Gabrielle,* and he tried to give even this phrase a connotation in line with his feelings.

He took the letters and magazines from the table and stowed them in his locker for later perusal, before going about his belated job of washing up the supper dishes.

By the time he finished this chore the ship was quiet. Those who remained aboard were either reading their mail, or were scrubbing clothes in the washroom. The chop of the harbour ran between the *Riverford* and its jetty mate the *Port Dover* with an impatient splash-clop-splash against the side plates. The scuttles were open, and a cold, fresh breeze blew through the mess, erasing the closed-in stink of the past two weeks, and bringing out the clean ship-smell of paint, cordage and tar.

Another stoker lay in his hammock, luxuriating in unaccustomed nakedness beneath the blankets. He was reading a letter, now and again chuckling over some small, secret

153

item it contained. Frenchy climbed to the top of the lockers with a pan full of dish-water, and threw the contents through the port-hole. As he did, there was an ominous rattle, and several knives and forks followed the water into the harbour. "Oh Frenchy!" shouted the reclining stoker, leaning from his hammock.. "Oh, you goofy Pea-Souper!—there goes half our bloody cutlery! If the seamen don't steal it, the mess cooks throw it away!"

"I did not do—it is my fault," confessed Frenchy, in the hope that confession would alleviate the look of simulated horror on the other's face. "It is my fault it 'appened. I did not see—I did not wait to see — "

The other stoker broke into a laugh. "It's nothing, Frenchy. Never mind explaining it. This harbour bottom must be covered with R.C.N. cutlery by now."

"It is covered?"

"Yeah, every mess peggy throws the cutlery overboard in port. It's like the pongos do after they drink a toast—they throw their glasses into the fireplace."

"What is dat—pongo?" Frenchy asked.

"A soldier," the other explained. "After a victory, army officers drink a toast to K.G. 6, and then they shatter their glasses against the fireplace. In the Navy we do it different like: we throw all the bloody cutlery into the drink!"

He began to laugh, and Frenchy joined with him, not fully understanding what they were laughing at, but laughing because he wanted to, because the mood was infectious.

When they calmed down, the other said, "I just got a letter from my wife. She says my kid is looking forward to me bringing him home a lanyard and a whistle. I've got a couple of lanyards, but who the hell ever heard of a sailor carrying a whistle?"

"A whistle?"

"Yeah, like kids have in the pocket of their sailor suits—you know, a toot-toot affair. You blow on it."

"The same like the quartermaster got?"

"No, not like that——" He scratched his head. "How do you illustrate a whistle?"

Frenchy did not want to appear completely obtuse. He made another stab at it: "Like dat on a life-jacket?" he asked.

"Frenchy, you're a genius! Sure, on a life-jacket. Now, why didn't I think of that? I'll take my kid a lanyard, and fasten my life-belt whistle to it. Frenchy, *merci beaucoup*, you're a genius!"

They began laughing again.

The duty stoker came down the ladder. "What are you guys stayin' aboard for? Are you broke?"

"No," spoke up the stoker in the hammock. "I want to read my mail."

"You should have took it ashore. I read all my mail in the wet canteen; then if the news is good I can celebrate, an' if it's bad, I can drowned my sorrows in beer."

"How's everything back aft, Red?"

"So-so. The subby is feelin' no pain. He looks as if he's been into the liquor with a syphon. They took the kid's body ashore a while back. I seen the Jimmy supervisin' a party carryin' him on to the *Port Dover*."

"Maybe the ship'll brighten up now that he's gone. It's been as cheerful as the day before pay-day ever since he kicked off."

"Yeah." He sat down on a locker, wiping the grime from his face with his sweat-rag. "Sanderson an' the others'll be weighed off tomorrow. I wouldn't be surprised to see the Old Man give them detention. He's pretty hard on that stuff."

"No, they'll get fourteen days Number Eleven, and Dunderfield will lose his hook and good conduct badge," the other said, judicially.

"It's a hell of a night out—the blackout here is worse than in the U.K. I wouldn't want to be that kid bein' buried in this hole," said Red.

"When are they going to bury him?"

"Tomorrow, I guess. That means clear lower decks, an' everybody has to go."

"Not stokers. We've got to oil ship tomorrow."

"We'll do both, mate."

"How about a pot of tea, Frenchy?"

"Yeah, Frenchy, put a handful of tea into the pot an' I'll take it down to the engine-room an' brew it. I've got to flash up No. 2 boiler first, but it won't take me long."

Frenchy placed a fistful of tea in the pot, and prepared to re-wash the cups.

Lieutenant-Commander Frigsby stood for long minutes inside the telephone booth in the lobby of the Newfoundland Hotel. Though the receiver came the low, but distinct, hum of far-away voices, audible through his phone due to some technical or cosmic pick-up: "—Here is your party, sir"—"The Lord Nelson Hotel, Halifax? Toronto calling Mr. S. D. Westland"—"We are not allowed to connect you with that number, Madam"—"From Fort Dix, New Jersey? Yes, sir, we'll try the Post Exchange at Fort Pepperell."

Outside the booth the hotel lobby was filling up with its evening quota of Army and Navy brass-hats and their women, who after entering, stood in small knots around the room. Now and then the door would open from the blacked-out vestibule, spilling into the brightness a fresh bevy of pleasure-seekers.

The far-off hum of the telephone operators' clipped speeches could still be heard as the Captain turned his head and watched the narrow panorama of the hotel through the glassed-in door. He recognized some of the Canadian officers, and also some of the women. They were paired in polygenous disarray, this wife with that other officer. The sight of them, innocent though their juxtaposition might have been, was distasteful to him.

The operator said to him, "There is no answer to your call to Montreal."

"Are you sure?" he asked, startled by the intrusion of her voice, which sounded as though she were peering over his shoulder.

There was another feminine voice, with a French-Canadian accent, then the Newfoundlander's again, "Sorry, sir, I can try again, and let you know."

"No—no, thanks. I'll call again, myself, later," he answered, hanging up the receiver reluctantly. He glanced at his watch, computing the difference in time between St. Johns and Montreal. It was now ten o'clock his time, or eight o'clock in Montreal. "Where could Joyce be at eight o'clock?" he asked himself. It was easy to excuse her absence from the house; there were a hundred reasons why she would not be there just then; but coupled with the fact that she had neglected to write to him, it made her absence ominous. The matter-of-fact terseness of the conversation he had planned was forgotten; if he could have spoken to her at that moment his voice would have been filled with anxiety and concern. He decided to have a drink and a sandwich before he tried again.

CHAPTER 16

At ten-thirty o'clock that night two-thirds of the crew of the corvette *Riverford* were seeking escape and entertainment depended on their age, marital status, and individual taste. By far the greater number of them were engaged in spending a traditional sailor's evening—drinking in the wet canteens. But others, the non-conformists, were scattered across the breadth of the city in pursuit of pleasures more mundane, urbane or esoteric.

Geographically, the ones farthest afield were Sub-Lieutenant Sundcliffe in a taxi on the gravel highway coming in from Bowring Park (with Loretta McPherson, ledger-keeper in a Water Street Bank), and Able Seaman Scotty Wright walking back in the general direction of the ship from a sight-seeing trip through the snow to the top of Signal Hill.

Leading Seaman Hector McCaffrey was esconced in the kitchen of a second-floor flat in the western suburbs of town, drinking his sixth glass of "kickapoo" in the company of the flat's tenant, Petty Officer John Pinnett, a naval diver, who occupied the place with his wife and five-month-old son.

"This stuff is powerful, Johnnie," McCaffrey said for the fourth time, looking into the top of the earthenware pot at the pinkish liquid with its flotsam of lemon rinds, sliced beets and vagrant rice kernels.

"It's cheap and it's good. Marie is the best little brewmaster that ever came out of Truro, ain't ya, Pet?" asked Johnnie. He smacked his smiling wife on the thigh.

Ransome Bodley was dancing in the U.S.O. canteen with a girl named Betty, from Cornerbrook, while across the floor three *Riverford* stokers talked to a pair of Wrens, and a Canadian girl employed as a telegraphist at Gander Airport. Two young seamen from the ship, Drewery and Natale, sat on stools at the soda bar and ate their second David Harum sundaes.

Lieutenant Harris was leaving, after paying a social visit with a good friend of his, Morris Silvers, a St. Johns clothier. "See us again before you go, Win, won't you?" Morris asked.

"I'll drop around. I'm going to ask for a draft off tomorrow, despite what you've said against it, and so you might see a lot of me," he answered.

"Any time, any time. The house is never locked to you, Win."

"Good-bye, Winfield," Mrs. Silvers said warmly. "Don't forget to let your mother know I was asking about her, if you do go home soon."

On La Marchand Rd. two *Riverford* seamen were trying to entice a pair of girls into a field behind a row of stores. "What's the matter, are you scared of us or somep'n? Don't be ascared of my chum here, he just *looks* like Jack the Ripper."

"It's not that; we haven't only met wit' yez this evenin'," said the fattest girl of the two.

"Listen, Baby, *Go where I'm to, or I'll come where you're at,*" said the second seaman, in an imitation of Newfoundland *patois.*

"Your friend-boy t'inks he's a fly one," said the thin girl.

"Baby, I'm the lovin' champeen of Brandon, Manitoba," the seaman answered.

"We's got to go 'ome," the fat girl said. "We's decent girls."

"Sure you're decent, we never thought nothin' different, did we, Alex? That's why we picked you—talked to you on the corner. Now listen, it's half-past ten, and we've got to go back to the ship soon, 'cause we're going to a funeral tomorrow———"

159

"Whose funeral? Yer own?" asked one of the girls, giggling.

"Never mind," a seaman said, not liking such trollops to joke about it. "Tomorrow night we'll meet you early, in the same place, and take you to the movies," he lied. "Now let's go in here, and sit down for a minute, and talk things over."

"I knows what you'll talk over. There's no place to sit in there, I'm thinking," said the fat girl.

"You can sit on my knee, Baby," the first seaman said, steering her by the elbow.

They made their way along a rough path between two buildings, the girls, heads coyly bowed into their collars, giggling with excitement and expectation.

On one of the hilly streets sloping towards the harbour, the Yoeman of Signals and Moody, the coder, were returning to the ship from the movies. "I like musical shows best," Barton said.

"So do I, if they're good."

"Oh sure, if they're good."

"I used to like Fred Astaire's pictures," said Moody.

"Yeah. You don't see him much now."

They passed the door of a fish-and-chip café, and from inside came the loud, strident voice of Benny Peebles, the cook. Moody turned back, and opened the shuttered door. Inside, Peebles was engaged in an argument with an American soldier. "It's only a talking fight," said Moody.

"I hope the Yank fills him in," the Yoeman remarked, as they continued their walk.

Scattered around in the taverns of the Queens, Ritz and Crosby Hotels were several *Riverford* men, drinking beer. Their state of intoxication was relevant to their finances, and the length of time they had been there. The majority were in pairs, but one table in the Crosby held the supply assistant, two seamen, and a telegraphist, in the company of two members of the *Milverton's* crew, who were playing "chug-a-lug" with pints of beer. They were all fairly drunk and they sang a continuous ditty, to the accompaniment of which, in turn, each had to drink a pint of beer without stopping. Their cracked and maudlin voices filled the room:

160

Here's to Pearson, he's true blue,
  He's a good one through and through;
He's a good one, so they say,
  But he'll never get to heaven if he looks the other way;
  So drink chug-a-lug, chug-a-lug, chug-a-lug,
So drink chug-a-lug . . .

Lieutenant Bowers sat at a table in the Crow'snest with Paymaster Lieutenant Orsonby and a Lieutenant Pilbright off a Royal Navy salvage tug. Pilbright was saying, "You can't deny the possibility of an after-life any more than you can deny the fact of a pre-natal one. Before birth— even before conception—there is life in the spermatazoa."

"I'll give you that, George, but after death the body cells atrophy and die. If there is an after-life it cannot be physical, and the soul must have substance."

"Not at all."

"I agree with Harold," said Orsonby, opening his eyes and fixing the Englishman with a stare, before he closed his eyes again.

"This heaven, or nirvana, or whatever you like to call it, must be populated with wraiths," said Bowers.

"Perhaps it is—that's my point exactly."

Bowers glanced at the glasses on the table. "What will you have, George? Another of the same?" he asked, holding up a finger to the waiter.

"Yes, please."

"Orsonby, what about you?"

Orsonby roused himself. "Give me a rum and Coke." He pushed his sagging frame higher in the chair. "You meta—metaphysicians want to hear a good joke?" he asked. "All your talk of spermatazoa and things reminds me of one I heard the other night."

Butch Jenkins walked the dark, lonely streets of the city by himself, wondering where to go. In the blackout there was no indication which of the boarded-up doors opened to a café, and, to him, they all appeared the same. After walking up and down hills for more than an hour he was fortunate enough to find himself before the door of a small lunch counter when the door opened to emit some customers, and he went inside and ordered a cup of coffee and a piece of pie. After he had eaten, he would have liked to linger inside a while, savouring the warmth and light, but he could see the proprietor glancing at him with a look that held something less than friendship, so he emerged again into the darkened streets. He climbed a hill to a better part of town, and found himself before the massive doors of a cathedral. He made his way up the steps, and entered the building.

The inside was dim and quiet, and he was alone but for three kerchiefed heads bowed in a forward pew, and an old man making the Stations of the Cross. He smelled the old familiar church smell of musty cushions and candle wax. Genuflecting, he stepped forward and found a seat in one of the rear pews. He sat for a time in quiet thought, letting the peaceful quietude wrap itself about him, before he began praying for the departed soul of his friend, Wayne Clark.

The Assistant Cook sat at a writing desk in the Salvation Army Hostel penning a reply to a letter from his brother-in-law in Sarnia, Ontario. It was the fourth letter he had answered that evening, and with the exception of the first and last paragraphs, they all contained the same material. From memory he wrote:

> One of our seamen was killed this trip. He was a fellow about my age. He fell down the ladder from the wheel-house. We are going to bury him tomorrow. He was a nice kid. I baked bread for eight nights this trip. The English bread doesn't keep as long as the bread from this side. This is the first time we've seen snow this winter. We were running to a place where there is no snow before this, although I can't tell you where it is, of course. I expect to be home on leave next month . . .

Seaman Manders strolled over to the writing desk. Hanging on his arm was a young woman wearing the skirt and blouse of a CWAC. "Hya, Cookie," he said in greeting. "Got your letters written yet?"

"This is the last one."

"I hear that Smitty is drunk as hell. You want to watch yourself going aboard; you know what he's like. The steward was in here a while ago. Smitty tried to keep him aboard, but Roberts broke ship."

"I'll watch myself," the cook said.

Allison sat in a cabin aboard the freighter *Goldhaven,* chatting with a friend of his, the Second Officer. The *Goldhaven* was tied to a buoy in the middle of the harbour, awaiting a tow to a dry-dock to have a torpedo hole mended in her bow. "How do you like the Navy compared with the Merchant Marine?" Allison's friend asked.

"It's not so good. I wish I'd have stayed where I was."

"How are the blokes aboard your ship?"

"The Old Man's all right. He was First Officer on the Imperial Oil tankers before he joined the Navy. The other officers are V.R.'s, but they're nice fellows, most of them. The First Lieutenant comes from Toronto; he's a pretty good man on navigation; used to be a yatchtsman on the Lakes. The other looey is a Jew from Winnipeg named Harris, a hell of a good head; he's going in for a long N course after refit. There are two subbys, an Ottawa kid just out of college, and the other comes from the West Coast."

"I wouldn't want to cross the pond on those corvettes. They seem to bounce around like corks."

"Yeah, they're pretty rough in a sea, but I never heard of one foundering yet."

"Neither have I, come to think of it."

"They're a hell of a lot safer than these big babies against tin fish. We only draw about nine foot forrad, and fourteen foot aft."

"But when they get it, they get it," said the *Goldhaven's* Second Officer.

Allison looked up at the bulkhead. "How's the time, Barney? Is that clock right?"

"I think so."

"I'd better get going. Can you supply me with transportation home?"

"Have another wet first, and I'll take you back in the whaler."

Three members of the crew of the *Riverford* were already in bed ashore. E.R.A. Fourth Class Bullock was sleeping

163

blissfully in a double-decker bunk at the Canadian Legion Hostel in town. His face bore a care-free expression, for he had checked his wallet at the desk downstairs; his shoes were hidden beneath his pillow; he had bought, and mailed to his wife and daughters, a parcel containing souvenir leather goods; and his name was on the wake-up list for six o'clock in the morning.

Leading Stewart Roberts was also asleep, but in the Salvation Army Hostel on Water Street. He had feared returning to the ship before morning, after wilfully disobeying the direct order of Smith-Rawleigh to stay aboard and pour drinks. Before leaving the ship he had stolen a half bottle of London Dry Gin from the wine cupboard, and had entered it on chits bearing the signature of the Sub-Lieutenant. It had been his experience that no officer cared to question his drink chits while suffering from a morning hangover; and as for them taking him before the First Lieutenant or the Captain, none ever would, because that entailed a post-mortem of the evening before. To counteract any charges which Smith-Rawleigh might press, he had formulated a counter charge of his own, which had sounded good after the half bottle of gin had been drunk; he would claim that an officer when intoxicated was no longer in authority, and so had no right to issue orders of any sort.

First Class Stoker Sanderson was in bed in a shack high above the south side of the harbour, in the squatters' section known to three or four allied Navies as "Dogpatch". His companion was a young woman who frequented the jetties during the day, begging drinks from the ships, a character known as "Corvette Annie". Annie was asleep, but Sanderson sat up in bed drinking luke-warm beer from a bottle, and remembering that this would be his last night of freedom for some time to come.

At eleven o'clock Lieutenant-Commander Frigsby tried again to get his wife on the telephone, but the operator informed him that she was unable to get an answer. He hung up the receiver and walked slowly from the hotel.

The streets were dark above the old, grey snow, and only an occasional chink of light showed from beneath a blind, or was aimed by the slit-lights of an army truck or taxi.

Up above the city a few stars glittered dully, like ice chips scattered on a rug.

"Cab, sir?" a voice asked at his elbow.

"Yes, thank you. Job's wharf, please, on the South Side," he answered, groping his way into the taxi.

"I knows where 'tis, sir," said the driver, pulling out from the curb.

It was a terrible feeling, not being able to contact Joyce. Of course, anything could be the cause, despite the absence of mail. Perhaps she had taken Ronald to the movies, or to visit friends. Perhaps her letters had gone to England by mistake. He would get a letter from her in the morning, and then he would laugh at his present feelings. A thousand things could have happened—silly little ordinary things which happened to everyone at one time or another. He soothed himself with these thoughts as the taxi felt its way through the town.

When his eyes grew accustomed to the lack of light, he could see people walking along the sidewalks, some of them with the aid of flashlights. There was a commotion in the street ahead of the taxi, and it slowed down, revealing in its headlights the sight of Stoker Petty Officer Collet, stripped to the waist, staggering about in the snow, his arms held in a fighting pose, challenging anyone in the world to come and fight.

The Captain leaned back against the cushions so that he would not be seen, while the driver remarked, "E's pretty drunk, that one."

"He's all right," the Captain said. "He's one of the few really happy men I've seen tonight."

"I'll allow that, sir," answered the driver, steering the cab around the lonely gladiator.

When he arrived aboard, the quartermaster was absent from his station at the gang-plank. Without being seen, the Captain traversed the few feet of deck to the officers' entry, and made his way to his cabin. As he passed the wardroom companion-way he could hear Smith-Rawleigh's laughter, and the tinkle of glass from below. Then the voice of Allison shouted a goodbye to somebody from the starboard side.

Cowboy Henderson and Able Seaman Pinchott crossed the stone bridge leading to the south side of the city. A more ill-matched pair would have been hard to find, and they were only together because it had been Pinchott's misfortune to stop and help a fallen figure from a snowbank. To the consternation of both of them, the figure had proved to be that of Cowboy, and the Good Samaritan had been pressed into involuntary service as a reluctant guide back to the ship.

Every few steps Cowboy would stumble in the mud and snow, and Pinchott would grab at him and haul him back to an even keel.

"Pinchott, you're not a bad guy, you know, even if you are a Christian," Cowboy said.

"That's no way to talk," Pinchott answered, hauling his charge around a pot-hole.

"Why isn't it? The trouble is, you think I'm drunk, but I'm not. After I get a few drinks my legs give way, that's all; but up here (he tapped the top of his cap) I'm perfectly lucid."

"Why do you drink at all, Cowboy? You could be a sensible fellow if you tried."

"Could be—what do you mean, could be?" Cowboy asked, stopping, and pulling Pinchott by the arm until he faced him.

"I mean just that."

"Listen, Pinchy, I'm always sensible, that's why I drink."

"It's not sensible to drink."

"It's sensible for me. I don't criticize what you eat, so don't you criticize what I drink—fair enough, Pinchy?"

"I can't help it, it seems so—well, wasteful."

"Pinchy, what I like about you is your damned innocence. Of course it's wasteful; all fun is wasteful. It's like eating cotton candy: you get a mouthful, and then it's gone."

"But there's so many other things you could do—sensible things which wouldn't disappear at once," Pinchott said, warming up to his best proselytizing pitch.

"What kind of sensible things, for God's sake?" Cowboy asked, his face thrust forward belligerently.

"Well, reading, and things like that, which would enlarge your knowledge."

Cowboy stopped in his tracks. "Why, you—you smug son-of-a-bitch! I've read more than you will ever read! That always hands me a laugh, when some goody-goody with a brain about the size of an olive tells me I should search for knowledge instead of having pleasure. There's a few things you should know, my friend.

"Now let's take you as one of the better examples of a soul-saver. You're not very bright, but you're brighter than most of your kind. Right? Right! You have the audacity to stand there and tell *me* that I should read. What the hell have you ever read, Pinchy, except the New Testament and Genesis? You don't even know when the Bible was written, or who wrote it, do you?"

"I know who inspired it."

"See! It's always been a mystery to me how any of you bloody joy-killers could have the supreme egotism to claim you're God's chosen people. You insult God just by thinking it."

"I know that it's the drink talking," Pinchott said.

"Sure it's the drink talking, but you want to know why people drink? Eh? Whether you want to or not, I'll tell you—it's because they have to live with other people like you."

Pinchott said, "Let's get going, I'm getting cold." They began their tortuous way again.

"I wish you'd let me help you, Cowboy," Pinchott began.

"Don't try to save me, Pinchy. I don't want to be saved . . don't believe in it . . . and don't, that's all!"

"My church doesn't believe in saving people, the way you mean it. However, we do believe in showing a man the error of his ways." He was beginning to wish that he had not done the Christian thing in pulling Cowboy from the snowdrift.

"I know my errors. I drink too much, and now I've got myself set up by that little Irish bag——"

"But if you know you're living the wrong kind of life, why don't you change?"

"Because while I'm in this frigging outfit I *want* to drink. Okay? If I didn't drink, I'd be like you, Pinchy, going to all the free movies, mailing postcards home, or learning to make women's purses in the "Y" hobby-lobby club. Purses!" He laughed drunkenly, slapping his escort on the back.

"What's wrong with that? If you'd have done those things you wouldn't be in the shape you're in now."

167

"Shape! What shape? You talk as though I should g
around ringing a bell."

"You're not exactly healthy, you know."

"I'm not exactly rotting with leprosy either."

"Why don't you get yourself fixed up, Cowboy?" Pinchot
asked, switching his argument from morals to health.

"Maybe you've got something, Pinchy. The tiffy can'
seem to help me, and I can't seem to drown the bugs i
beer. Now you're really cooking on both burners."

"Go to the tiffy and ask him to get you into hospital."

"I'll do that, you old Psalm-singing so and so. I'll d
that first thing in the morning."

"You won't regret it," asserted Pinchott, wincing, bu
amazed at his success.

"Okay, don't make a song about it. You've sold me
bill of goods, be satisfied."

"Watch out, Cowboy!" Pinchott shouted as the othe
lurched towards the side of the road.

"Thanks, Pinchy, you saved my life. Let's sing togethe
What'll it be, *Onward Christian Soldiers* or *The Nort
Atlantic Squadron*?"

Whatever Pinchott's answer, it was aborted by Cowboy'
off-key baritone:

> *Away, away with sword and drum,*
> *Here we come, full of rum,*
> *Looking for someone to . . .*

CHAPTER 17

One by one the other officers went ashore, until Smith-Rawleigh was left alone in the wardroom. At first he began drinking through loneliness and ennui, but later on he imbibed automatically, with the wild, fanciful tippling of the solitary drinker. His mind was a carousel upon which his spirits rode, attempting to pluck the brass ring of reason from the revolving panorama of imagined slights and misunderstandings of his fellows. With intoxicated cunning he acted circumspectly enough as the half-hour liberty parties went ashore, giving them only a cursory inspection. He read to them, with slightly exaggerated *bonhomie,* a notice issued by the Senior Naval Medical Officer of the port, dealing with the prevalence of veneral disease in St. Johns. This dry, factual warning he embellished with an impromptu aside to "Keep everything in its accustomed place," which was received by some of the men with a burst of unfamiliar laughter.

When the last liberty boat had left, he occupied his time listening to the inter-mess public address system, which gave out with "She Had To Go And Lose It At The Astor" and "She Said No—I Said Please," as the communications ratings played their current favourites over and over again. He sat at the table sipping his drinks, and tapping his foot to accompany the music.

Roberts cleaned up the pantry, and appeared at the wardroom door. "M-m-may I have your p-p-p-permission to go ashore, sir?" he asked.

"I'd rather you stayed aboard, Roberts. I'm expecting guests to drop in later," Smith-Rawleigh answered, constructing the fabrication out of whole cloth. He had some old scores to settle with the stewards.

169

Roberts remainded in the doorway, unwilling to accep what he knew was a lie. The officer asked, with calculate urbanity, "Is there anything else, Roberts?"

Without answering, the steward returned to the pantry

As the evening lengthened, Smith-Rawleigh reviewed th insults, real or imaginary, to which he had been subjecte aboard the ship. His hatred, while embracing all th members of the *Riverford's* company, narrowed itself dow to one or two, and was strengthened by its concentratio One of those he hated was Harris, whom he blamed fc his present position, and another was Leading Seama McCaffrey, whose contempt and mute impertinence toward him was known to all on board.

When the quartermaster piped, "Clean Up For Rounds' he did not stir from the table, but sat pasting beer labe on the table top, finding pleasure in his refusal to b roused from his drunken sulk. The quartermaster calle on him to ask whether he was ready to make his rounds c the ship, but he waved him away, airily.

He emptied his glass, and shouted, "Steward!" The was no immediate answer. He shouted it again, bitting off like a curse, but Roberts did not appear. He jumpe up from his chair, and fell against the door frame. "Stewar where the hell ar you !" he cried.

The quartermaster appeared at the top of the compani way. "Is anything wrong, sir?" he asked.

"Where's the steward?"

"I haven't seen him. Do you want me to get him, sir'

"Is he ashore?"

"Not that I know."

Smith-Rawleigh turned from the doorway, and with savage twist tore the knob from the loud-speaker. *"She sa no—I said please, pretty bab—"* the music was cut o sharply in the middle of a word, leaving a silence as lo as the crack of a gun. With a kick, he fired the brok dial into a corner. Steadying himself against the table, l said, "I've got him now—the little stuttering bastar Complete disregard of a direct order, and breaking ship He smiled to himself, the corners of his mouth turne down.

The pantry had been cleaned up by Roberts, and the was no sign of any liquor. Smith-Rawleigh brushed sever glasses into the sink with the back of his hand, where they shattered with tinkling harmony. He retraced his steps, and tried his keys on the door of the confidential keyboard. After a few attempts to unscramble the contents of the miscible key ring, he broke the glass and pulled from its hook the wine cupboard key. He made his way to the cupboard and took out a bottle of Scotch. Then he sat down again at the table and poured himself a drink.

After drinking some of the Scotch, his head began to whirl, so he climbed to the washroom and threw up into the bath-tub. He felt much better after this, and he walked out into the open air. The ship was completely dark, but for the light cluster which shone above the gangway to the *Port Dover*. The quartermaster busied himself with something on his desk, retreating into his duffle coat.

Smith-Rawleigh spied the holstered revolver hanging from the seaman's belt. 'Let's take a look at your gun," he said, standing above the seaman.

"I can't, sir," answered the man, defensively.

"Why not?"

"It's against orders to give up your arms."

"You're a bright boy," the officer sneered. "You're a bright little sea-lawyer."

The seaman watched him covertly, wondering what to expect next.

"Where's the steward?"

"I don't know."

"You don't know what?" snapped the Sub-Lieutenant.

"I don't know, *sir*," the man answered, getting a good grip with his heels on the deck. His face hardened, and his hands slowly clenched, under the other's scrutiny.

With a slow turn of his body which was almost a spit, Smith-Rawleigh felt his way forward again towards the officers' doorway. He heard footsteps along the deck of the *Port Dover*, and saw the figure of Ordinary Seaman Jenkins coming aboard. He waited until the boy had retrieved his card from the quartermaster, and was heading for the seamen's mess, before he said, "Jenkins, come here!"

With a start of surprise, the boy approached him.

"Are you just coming aboard?"

"Yes, sir."

"Do you know anything about mixing drinks?"

"No, sir."

"Well, this is a hell of a good time to learn. Come wit me."

Butch removed his coat and cap in the steward's pantry and mixed a Scotch and soda. He carried it to the ward room, and set it down before Smith-Rawleigh. As he turne to go, the Sub-Lieutenant said, "Stick around here for while, I'm going to need you. Find something out there make into sandwiches."

The boy was not quite sure whether he should act as steward or not, but he knew that he should obey first, an question the order afterwards. He sliced some brea opened a box of cream cheese, and made some sandwiche

"Are you still afraid of your pal's ghost?" asked Smit Rawleigh.

"No, sir."

"What made you get the wind up, then? Were you ju afraid of everything?"

"I—I dunno, sir."

"You don't like to admit it, eh?"

Butch placed the sandwiches on the table.

"You had a pretty soft draft. One trip, and now you' going home. I guess you'll be a real war hero when yo get home, won't you?"

The boy did not answer, but stood inside the door, th shame moistening his eyelashes.

"You'll tell the girls about the Battle of the Atlant won't you? I know how every stinking little coward ac when the danger's over. You should have been with running into Bone and Oran, then you'd have somethin to talk about. I wonder what you'd have done when v were attacked for five nights in a row off the Azores. You have jumped over the side, wouldn't you?"

Butch turned, and went into the pantry.

The voice of the Sub-Lieutenant followed him wi drunken cadency, as though its owner were talking himself . . . "There isn't one of you who has any guts . real guts . . . that always spells the difference . . . lik and reliefees . . . when it's tough, breeding counts . . say what they like but it's true . . . " His high laught

172

filled the enclosed space, and there was the sound of a breaking glass.

"Get me another drink," he ordered, imperiously.

Allison came down the companion-way. He stared at the seaman mixing drinks in the pantry, and glanced into the wardroom at Smith-Rawleigh.

"Hullo, Allison, come and join me in a drink."

"Where's Roberts?"

"He broke ship. I've got another steward," answered Smith-Rawleigh, brushing aside such irrelevant questioning. "Come on and have a nightcap."

"Sorry, Peter, I've got to turn in, I'm afraid," Allison said, and with another questioning look at Jenkins he carried on to his cabin.

Jimmy Collet was deposited on the jetty by the Naval Shore Patrol, and told to get aboard out of sight, or they would have to run him in.

"I'm going straight aboard, boys," he shouted. "Thanks for the ride." He insisted upon shaking hands with each of them in turn, and invited them down to the ship at "Up Spirits" the day following, for a drink.

He tottered over the ships without mishap, navigating the steps and planks from one to the other with a drunken man's care-free caution. When he reached the *Riverford* he patted the quartermaster on the shoulder, and entertained him with a long harangue about offering to fight every cop in town. He was tieless, and his shirt had been pushed beneath the waistband of his trousers carelessly, so that it was bunched in hanging folds. His cap was awry on his head, and his coat flapped in unbuttoned freedom. When he finished his tale he made his way forward in the direction of the fo'castle.

His appearance momentarily interrupted an angry discussion in the seamen's mess. "He's got no right to make the kid go down there and get his drinks," a seaman said. "If McCaffrey was aboard, he'd soon stop that."

"That big fat punk ought to be thrown over the side anyway," said another. "Corbett says that when he came out on deck an' asked for his gun, he felt like letting him have it through the guts."

173

"Wait till the Old Man hears he was pie-eyed on duty. He'll go around the loop."

"I'll go to the Old Man right away when he comes aboard," said the Leading Torpedo Operator, who was acting P.O. of the watch.

"What's the matter—what's all the beef?" asked Collet, shouldering his way into the small crowd.

The L.T.O told him about Smith-Rawleigh's actions, and that young Jenkins was being employed as a steward in the wardroom.

"He can't get away with that," said Jimmy.

"He won't get away with it, don't worry. I'm going to the Skipper as soon as he comes aboard."

"What the hell do you wanna wait till then for? Let's go down and get the kid now."

"No, it's no use, Jimmy."

Frenchy climbed the ladder from the stokers' mess, and took Collet's arm. "You 'ave a good time, Jimmy?" he asked, trying to calm the other.

"Hello, Frenchy. Yeah, I had a good time, but I'm gonna have a better one fillin' in a dirty fat rat on this ship!"

"Don't you bodder wit' 'im, Jimmy. You wait till after you sleep."

"I'm gonna get that kid outa there. Let go my arm!" He shook himself free, and pushed his way through the door and the blackout curtains beyond. The group of seamen and stokers followed him at a distance.

When he reached the officers' entry-way, he climbed inside and shouted below, "Jenkins!"

Butch looked up at him from the pantry doorway.

"Come on up here right away! What the hell're you doing down there?"

The boy reached behind him for his coat and cap, then hurried up the steps to where Collet was standing. "Go to your mess, and get into your hammock," Jimmy ordered. Butch stepped outside into the crowd clustered around the door.

Smith-Rawleigh emerged from the wardroom, and stood at the foot of the steps, looking up with an insolent stare at the dishevelled form of Stoker P.O. Collet. "What are you after?"

"You like picking on kids, don't you?" Jimmy shouted.

"Go back aft where you belong. I'll attend to you in the morning."

"You can't attend to me any time, you fat phoney. Take off that monkey suit and come up and fight man to man."

"Get back to your mess, you—you scum!" shouted the officer, his voice rising.

"You're yellow, you bastard!"

With a short cry, Smith-Rawleigh threw himself up the steps. As he did so, Collet backed out to the open deck, and threw off his coat. The officer emerged into the light from the gang-plank cluster, and Collet took two steps forward, and punched him in the face, causing him to trip on the coping in the doorway. He recovered quickly, and grabbed the stoker P.O. by the lapel with one hand, while he smashed his fist into Collet's eye with the other. They closed, and fell to the deck, rolling around in the cleared space formed by the feet of the onlookers.

"Smash his head, Jimmy!"

"Give him the knee!"

Smith-Rawleigh broke away, and stood up on a pair of teetering legs. He waited for his adversary to rise, breathing hard, his nose dripping blood down his shirt front. Collet got up slowly, measuring his opponent now, respecting the other's prowess. They closed again, their fists striking each other with hard, whacking sounds above the tense cries of the spectators. Again they clinched, and rolled on the deck, the sound of muffled curses accompanying their gasping breaths.

The crowd was on Collet's side to a man, but their partisan vociferousness was stilled somewhat by the courage and good sportsmanship, rare in a drunken brawl, shown by Smith-Rawleigh.

The figure of Allison came through the doorway, clad in shirt and trousers. He bent over the writhing forms on the deck, and pried them apart. They released each other reluctantly, and stood up, glaring with hate and caution in each other's direction.

"Collet, go back aft immediately!" shouted Allison. The stoker P.O. moved toward his mess, helped along by Frenchy, and Fred Forsyth, who had just returned aboard. Smith-Rawleigh retrieved his fountain pen from the deck where it had fallen, and went inside, looking neither to right or left.

When Allison had accompanied Smith-Rawleigh below, the unexpected voice of the Captain summoned the navigating officer to come up top.

"I didn't know you were aboard, sir," he said, as he climbed the steps.

"I only arrived a short time ago," answered the Captain, calmly.

"They were both pretty drunk, sir."

"Wes, I know; I heard the whole thing. Will you take over the watch, Allison?"

"Very well, sir."

"See that Collet stays in his mess, and send Smith to his cabin immediately."

CHAPTER 18

The morning came over the hills, and spread its light along the roof-tops, spilling down from street to street until it brigthtened the awakening harbour. The *Riverford* stirred to the strident notes of the Bosun's pipe, while from afar came the cold, mellow tones of the bugles in the army posts, and the unfamiliar barking of dogs. Overnight, the ships had adorned themselves with a glittering garment of hoar frost which crackled on the rails and stays.

In the galley the cooks broke eggs into large baking-dishes, and shoved them into the oven to fry. The supply rating, sullen from lack of sleep, and his head throbbing from the previous evening's "chug-a-lug", carried to each of the messes the day's issue of butter, tomato juice and tinned milk.

The Chief E.R.A., awake for an hour now, roused the engine-room artificers and his stoker P.O.s. "Come on, you," he said to each in turn, shaking them by the shoulder. "We oil ship this morning, and we've got a bottom end to take out as well. Rise and shine, everybody!" To Jimmy Collet he said, "Get up, killer, and get shaved. You've got a date with the Old Man later."

Jimmy pushed himself up on one shoulder, painfully. He felt the contusions on his face with a hesitant palm. "Oh, good Jesus!" he exclaimed, and fell back under his blanket.

The shore sleepers came aboard, and retrieved their cards from the quatermaster. Roberts hurried across the deck, and went below to his pantry, in the hope that an early appearance would help to erase his actions of the evening before. His resolution to lay a counter charge against Smith-

Raleigh had evaporated along with the effects of the half bottle of gin, and on his way down to the ship he had decided to throw himself on the mercy of the First Lieutenant, and accept any punishment given.

Stoker Sanderson slithered down the steep slope from Dogpatch to the jetties below, unmindful of the snow and mud which he picked up on the way. He felt dirty, with the gritty discomfort of an awakening in a crowded day coach. He could feel the stiffness of the dirt on the backs of his hands, and beneath his feet. His eyes smarted with it, and he could taste it on his tongue. As he hurried towards the ship he tried to blot from memory his actions of the night before. "You deserve everything you get," he warned himself. "Anybody who would sleep with that slut deserves everything!"

Breakfast went on to the accompaniment of a buzz of talk and speculation on the events of the evening before. "I told yez that the misfortune would be wit' us yet," said Newfy. "Just 'cause we put 'im ashore don't mean our luck'll change. We's got to bury 'im yet."

"Oh, stow that crap!" shouted McCaffrey, laying a gyrating cover of bacon grease above the weird and wonderful contents of his stomach. On occasion he could taste the mixture of fermented beets, lemons and rice, and each time there arose before his eyes a picture of the bubbling vat of John Pinnet's "kickapoo".

"All I've got to say is that the sooner we get to Canada, the better off we'll all be," said Pearson.

"Amen!"

"I guess they'll weigh off Collet this morning for sure."

"He can't miss."

"Smitty's finished. The Old Man'll throw the book at him."

"Good riddance," said McCaffrey. "I'd take twenty-eight days at McNab's Island myself to see that son-of-a-bitch get his."

"You're just lucky he missed seein' you last night. I'll bet it was you he was really after."

"I wish I *had* seen him; I was feeling no pain when I came aboard."

In the stokers' mess, Frenchy Turgeon told for the fourth

time his version of the fight between Smith-Rawleigh and Jimmy Collet. "Jimmy was too drunk to fight. When' 'e 'it, 'is arm went t'rough de air like dis," he said, illustrating a wild punch.

"If he'd have been sober, he'd a' killed Smitty," said Wally Crabbe.

"Don't you t'ink dat. De Sub-Lieutenant is good fighter too. 'E was good man last night."

"Don't tell me you stick up for him?"

"No, I don't like, but 'e fight ver' 'ard, dat's all."

In the wardroom Sundcliffe and Allison had breakfast first, talking about everything but the things which were uppermost in their minds. They pretented to ignore the broken loud-speaker, and the glass door of the confidential keyboard. The intertwined circles of the beer labels on the table-top were hidden by Allison's plate.

"They're building a new highway outside town," Sund-cliffe said.

"Oh, are they, where?"

"Out towards Bowring Park—beyond the Naval Hospital."

"This place is looking up."

Roberts poured them a fresh cup of coffee, puzzled by their complete disinterest in him. Since coming aboard, he had been wondering who had broken the loud-speaker and the keyboard door. There had also been broken glasses in the pantry, but he had brushed them up quickly, and placed them out of sight.

The Captain came down the steps, and took his chair at the table. "Good morning, Roberts," he said, cheerfully. This manifestation of normality confused the steward still further. Apparently none of them were yet aware that he had broken ship.

"This is going to be a busy day, isn't it, sir?" Sundcliffe asked.

"I'm afraid it is," the Captain answered.

"Are they going to hold the funeral today?"

"Yes, this afternoon. I'd like all the officers except the O.O.D. to attend. We're only taking twenty ratings with us. The shore johnnies are well prepared for such things. They have a band, and a drill squad or something they use for an escort. Incidentally, Sundcliffe, I'd like you to contact

179

the Coxswain and make sure that the funeral party is picked, and that they are all outfitted with gaiters. We only carry ten pairs aboard, so you might have to borrow some from the *Port Dover*. We want ten seamen, five stokers, and five communications ratings. They have to be in the rig of the day, overcoats and gaiters, by two o'clock. There'll be a truck at the jetty to pick them up at that time."

"Right, sir."

"Oh yes, and if we finish oiling in time, there'll be a make-and-mend this afternoon. Any other members of the ship's company who wish to go, may attend the funeral."

"How are we oiling, sir?" asked Allison. "Do we pull over to the tanker?"

"I'm not quite sure. There'll be a signal on that later. I believe there's a naval oil barge stationed here now. If there is, she'll come alongside, I expect."

Lieutenant Bowers made an appearance, followed by Harris. "Good morning, everybody," he said. He sat down gingerly, with the appearance of a man whose gonads were hanging on piano wires. "No more drinking for me— until after breakfast," he said, feeling his head.

"I wonder how Orsonby feels?" asked the Captain.

"Terrible, I hope."

The Captain laughed.

Bowers asked, "How many bodies are there on the crime sheet this morning, sir?"

"Too many, and now there's Collet's name to be added. Perhaps you'd better take them immediately breakfast is finished, so that I can see them all as early as possible. I've a million things to attend to today."

The First Lieutenant held court in the Captain's flats, the passage-way fronting on the Captain's cabin. He saw the defaulters first: Collet, Leading Stoker Dunderfield, and Stokers Sanderson and O'Brien. After hearing the charges, he remanded them on the Captain's report, and told them that they would appear before the Skipper in an hour. The small passage-way was crowded: Lieutenant Bowers, the Coxswain and Chief E.R.A. standing at one end, and the men, as their names were called by McCaffrey, coming through the door from the starboard entry-way, to stand at attention while the charges were read.

"That takes care of the felonies," said Lieutenant Bowers as the figure of O'Brien disappeared over the coping. "Now we'll take the misdemeanours."

The Coxswain called out, "Ordinary Seaman Andersley!"

A young seaman was ushered in by McCaffrey. He stood at attention, his face threatening to burst into laughter with nervousness, before the First Lieutenant.

The Coxswain read the charge from the book, with semi-literate concentration. " . . . did on March twelfth, nineteen-hundred and forty-three, leave H.M.C.S. *Riverford* without permission, and did absent himself for two hours, namely eighteen hundred hours until twenty hundred hours . . . "

The First Lieutenant gave him seven days' Number Eleven punishment (extra work and pack drill), one day's stoppage of leave, and one day's stoppage of pay.

Two other ratings followed. One of them had refused to lash up his hammock when ordered to do so by the Leading Telegraphist; the other had used vile language in an argument with the Chinese proprietor of the Dainty Tulip Grill.

The rating charged with the hammock incident was given three days' stoppage of leave; after ascertaining that the Chinese did not wish to press charges, the case against the other was dismissed.

The requestmen gathered in a small crowd outside the door, getting in the way of the stokers who were unbolting the fuel tank man-holes as the oil barge tied up alongside.

There was a request by Newfy Powers to be sent on leave from St. Johns rather than have to return to Newfoundland from Canada; a signalman requested permission to apply for a draft to H.M.C.S. *Niobe,* the shore base in Scotland, so that he could marry a young lady named Margaret McAlpine of Gourock; one requested a draft to the West Coast; the Supply Assistant wished to take a course in naval laundering; an E.R.A. applied for a course in diesel engineering at the Ford Plant at River Rouge; there were requests to be granted good conduct badges; and one stalwart asked to be drafted to hospital for a circumcision.

One by one they were ushered in. "Request granted . . . refused . . . placed as Captain's requestman . . . held over . . . will be investigated . . . "

"Whew!" exclaimed Lieutenant Bowers when the last one had been heard. He went below for a quick drink. The Sick Berth Attendant came down to the wardroom, and reported that Cowboy Henderson was being taken ashore to hospital.

"How long will it take, Bodley?"

"A few days I expect, sir."

"All right. Are all the arrangements made?"

"Yes, sir."

"What does Henderson think about it?"

"He asked to be sent, himself, sir."

"We won't get a replacement for him. Tell them up at the hospital to have him back before we sail."

"Yes, sir."

During the morning everyone bustled around doing the hundred and one jobs which accumulate before a ship reaches port. The fuel tanks gulped their bellies full of the black, syrupy oil from the barge. A working party passed supplies of food and provisions over the fo'castles of the ships which lay between the *Riverford* and the jetty; the men struggling awkwardly with the quarters of beef, and boxes of fresh, white bread. The signalmen went on errands to the dockyard, and returned with new current code books and stationery. The canteen servers brought aboard cases of cigarettes, chocolate bars and Coca-Cola.

As the sun climbed in the sky, the frost disappeared from the steel hand-rails and guy wires, and the ship became wet; steam rising from its flanks and engine-room skylights. Along with the vaporous heat from the engine-room came the sound of hammering and angry curses as the E.R.A.'s removed the bottom end from the engine.

In the messes, the hammocks were lashed and stowed in their racks, giving a new spaciousness to the living-quarters, while the decks were scrubbed clean of the debris which had accumulated under the lockers during the trip.

One of the leading stokers tried in vain to get new dinnerware from the Supply Assistant.

"I'm too busy right now. Jesus Christ, I got supplies coming aboard! If you needed knives and forks, why didn't you ask before this?"

"We didn't need them before. That Pea-Souper Turgeon

threw them over the side with the dish-water last night. We had to eat our eggs on slices of bread this morning."

"Swipe some from the seamen's mess," was the cryptic advice.

The Captain returned from a trip ashore, his face drawn and haggard. As the quartermaster piped him aboard, the hands stared at him speculatively. With an off-hand touch to the peak of his cap in the direction of the quarter-deck, he went below to the wardroom.

Smith-Rawleigh was sitting at the table, a bottle of beer before him. He glanced at the Captain apprehensively as he entered the room. The C.O. ignored him, and said to Allison, who was censoring mail at the desk in the corner, "Will you pack that up for now, Allison, please. You might see that the barge gets away from the starboard side."

The Captain waited until he had gone, before turning to Smith-Rawleigh. "Smith, you will pack your gear immediately. The stewards will give you a hand. You are drafted to barracks pending the decision of N.O.I.C., St. Johns. A complete report on your conduct will be sent ashore today. I might say that it was my intention, before your disgraceful conduct last night, to leave the matter of your flare-up with Harris until we reached Halifax. However, you took matters out of my hands, and left me no alternative but this. I will not review for you your actions, or tell you what my opinions are. You are not a child; you must realize your position. I might say that your good points, as well as your bad, have been reported by me." He walked to the door, before turning around. "Please be ashore within the hour."

He went to his cabin, and sent the quartermaster for the First Lieutenant. When Bowers arrived, he told him that Smith-Rawleigh had been drafted ashore, and that his replacement could be expected later in the day. "I suppose there was quite a docket of requestmen and defaulters this morning? Did you leave many for me?"

"A few sir. Most of the requests are to be held over until we reach Halifax; courses, drafts and things like that. I had one man request hospitalization to be circumcised."

"Does he want to go to hospital here?" asked the Captain, a wan smile flitting across his face.

"Yes, sir."

"Mmph! I suppose it's just as well. His leave will be less painful if left until later."

"Signalman Henderson has gone to hospital, sir."

"Oh, that's too bad; he's not cleaned up yet, then?"

"No sir. The tiffy thinks it will be a matter of a few days at the most, then he can rejoin the ship. I didn't request a relief for him."

"That's fine, Bowers." He sat down on his bunk, and motioned to the First Lieutenant to take a seat on the chair.

Bowers unbuttoned his sheepskin, and sat down. "Sir, Able Seaman Powers requested to be sent on leave from here, rather than make the trip back from Canada. I've sent a signal ashore on it."

"Good. That's reasonable enough."

The Captain's face was drawn and tight, the lines from his cheek bones to the sides of his mouth deeper, and more forbidding. Bowers throught that his demeanour was caused by the incidents of the last few days, and he was puzzled by it, for he had never associated Lieutenant-Commander Frigsby with one who would allow such things to weigh on his mind. He wondered if the Captain had been censured for his actions in bringing the body of the boy to port. "Are all the arrangements made for the funeral, sir?" he asked, in the hope that the question would elicit some information.

"Yes. You know that we are taking twenty men, don't you? The officers will all attend, except the Officer-of-the-Day—that's Harris, isn't it?"

"Yes, sir."

"I took it upon myself to order a wreath from a florist's shop, to be paid for from the wardroom funds. The ship's company have also bought one with the canteen money."

Bowers nodded.

"How did the fueling go?"

"Fine, sir."

"I noticed supplies coming aboard. Has the S.A. enough help to stow it?"

"Yes, sir, I gave him six hands."

"Fine. There are so many damn loose ends to tie up the first day in port, especially after being away from this side so long. Will you sign the victualling accounts for me, and look over the rum issue sheets? There's sure to be someone down to muster the spirits before long."

"Yes, sir."

There was a light knock on the door.

"Come in."

Lieutenant Harris stepped into the cabin. "Oh, I'm sorry, sir, I thought you were alone," he said, seeing the First Lieutenant.

"Come in, Harris. Lieutenant Bowers will go if it is something personal you wish to talk about."

"It's not exactly personal, sir. It's more or less routine— I would like to request a draft ashore."

The Captain nodded blankly, his eyes making a quick inspection of the other's face.

"I've been thinking of it since the affair the other day. As you know, the news of Smith-Rawleigh's attack on me got around the ship, and whether I imagine it or not, I sense that the men now look upon me as a dirty Jew. I've always assumed that everyone knew I was Jewish—I have never tried to hide the fact." He looked from one to the other, and they nodded. "But now it is different, somehow. I've been in the Navy since March, 1940, and as you may know, I am a survivor off one torpedoed ship. I think I've stuck my neck out long enough trying to prove that we Jews are not all looking for cushy berths. It seems to be a waste of time, when you are called the same names anyhow——" He stopped, and stared at the bulkhead behind the First Lieutenant.

"Harris, please sit down here," the Captain invited, indicating the bunk. "I'll only be a moment," he said to Bowers, and left the cabin. They could hear him speaking to the steward.

When he returned, he was carrying a bottle and three glasses, which he placed on his desk, before going back to close the door. He poured a drink for each of them, handing one to Harris and Bowers. "First today, gentlemen!"

He placed his drink on the desk, and began to speak. "As you know, there is wide leeway given to the master of a ship. At sea his decisions are final as far as the crew are concerned. This is true of a naval vessel as well as a merchantman, governed of course by certain laws and regulations which are provided for the Captain's interpretation. The biggest factor to be considered in the interpretation of these regulations is common sense. Every day I am forced to make decisions which affect the lives of seventy-odd men one way or another. Sometimes I am right, at other times I am wrong. I try to be right as often as I can.

"In dealing with your request for a draft, I am obliged to think of it as something which may affect your future, both as an officer, and as a man. What you said a moment ago may be true: you may be looked up as a 'dirty Jew' whether you fight Jerry, or sit behind a desk ashore stamping leave chits. I am not prepared to go into the question of anti-Semitism now, or any other time, and my personal views regarding the Jewish race may clash with yours. All I know is that you have been an excellent officer while serving aboard the *Riverford,* and for that reason alone, I would not like to draft you ashore. Secondly, I don't give a damn whether a man is Chinese, Jewish or English as long as he is pulling his weight, and getting along with the other members of the ship's company. Your being a Jew does not enhance you in my eyes, nor does it stand in your way to receiving the same courtesy and consideration that I try to give to every man serving under me."

He refilled the glasses, and invited them to drink up. When they had finished, he began speaking again. "Regarding your request, I would like you to reconsider it, if you will, in the light of what might happen in the future. You will never be able to defeat your problem by giving in to it, even though you may derive a certain flagellate satisfaction out of donning a hair shirt. I realize that your record in the Navy is one to be proud of, and that it is a damnable thing when your efforts are met with scorn and abuse by—er—people who should know better. But think how much worse it would be if what they said was true, if you *were* a Jewish slacker. Now, you have the right to brush off their ignorant jibes because you, yourself, know that they are untrue. You would find it much harder to defeat if you became what they would like you to be, and what they resent your not being."

He picked up his glass, and finished his drink. "I've said

more than I intended, but I hope that it will make you pause. Will you hold up your request, Harris?"

The young man stood up, and looking the Captain in the eye, said, "I'm sorry, sir, I would like it to go through."

The Captain nodded slowly. If he was perturbed by the futility of his speech, he gave no sign. "Very well, Harris. Make out a request chit and give it to Lieutenant Bowers."

Stoker Petty Officer James Collet stood in the middle of the Captain's cabin, wearing a slightly stained uniform, under which could be seen a woollen baseball sweater bearing across its front in diagonal script the words "Wentworth Taxi Company".

The evidence of Mr. Allison, the Chief E.R.A., and the quartermaster had been heard, and the First Lieutenant had produced his unsullied conduct record, and had spoken of his excellent character assessments, and the aggravation preceding the assault on Sub-Lieutenant Smith-Rawleigh.

"What have you to say on your own behalf, Collet?" asked the Captain.

"Nothing much, sir. I think that everything has been said about the fight last night. I was pretty drunk when I came aboard, and I heard about the subby—the Sub-Lieutenant—having the kid working in the wardroom, and I just went haywire, I guess. Nearly all the ratings aboard the ship have had trouble with the Sub-Lieutenant at one time or another. When a person looks down on you, sir, as he looked down on all of us, it makes you want to show him that you're as good as he is. In the Service the only way you can do that is fight him. I guess that's all I have to say, except that I've enjoyed serving on the *Riverford*, and I hold no grudge against any man."

The Captain cleared his throat, and shuffled the papers on the desk, before he spoke. "Stoker Petty Officer Collet, you admit that you struck your superior officer last night. I am fully cognizant of the aggravation preceding the assault, but I know that there was aggravation on your part as well. I also know that you were intoxicated when you came aboard. You realize that although the Service takes a lenient view of intoxication, it does not sanction it as an excuse for the striking of a superior. Because I am unable to take an impersonal position in this matter, I am forced to draft you ashore under close arrest to await trial by the Naval Officer In Charge, St. Johns, or by Court Martial, as is your privilege as a petty officer.

"I want you to know how much I regret this, personally, and I hope that you will have the guts to stand up to it, and make a successful come-back. Sub-Lieutenant Smith-Rawleigh has also been drafted ashore to face charges. I have been proud to have you as a member of this ship's company, and recommendations have been made that leave be granted as soon as possible."

"Thanks, sir," whispered Collet, staring at the deck.

The Captain nodded to the Coxswain, who shouted, "On caps, about turn, dismiss!"

When he and Bowers were alone again, the Captain said, "I've been wondering if there isn't something in the superstition about carrying a corpse. God knows, we've had nothing but bad luck so far."

"Some of the ratings were telling me that Powers—he's the chief necromancer of the seamen's mess, apparently—claims that bad luck will follow a ship for days, even after the body is disposed of."

"I don't believe it, but I'm keeping my fingers crossed."

"Me too," said Bowers, laughing.

"By the way, is the mail aboard yet?"

"I don't think so, sir." It was strange that the Captain was so concerned about mail; perhaps it was not the affairs aboard ship which had him worried after all.

CHAPTER 19

The funeral procession marched through the slush of the sun-softened streets, the naval band alternating between the "Dead March" and faster pieces of music, as the step was changed periodically from the slow march to the quick step. Behind the horse-drawn hearse marched the officers and men of the *Riverford*, having a strangely stereotyped appearance in full uniform, after the individuality of their sea-going dress. Behind them came the much smarter turn-out furnished by the naval barracks, the ranks properly sized, and marching like the Guards.

Small groups of people, attracted by the band, stood on the corners in the sunshine, and watched the *cortège* pass; while servicemen saluted the hearse carrying the remains of Knobby Clark.

It was not an imposing funeral procession. There were no crowds, as there might have been if the event had been publicized in advance. The band seemed too large for the small parade. The floral offerings were small, and they could not dispel the illusion that the affair had been arranged hastily, with a pick-up team. No real mourners were present, and the grim, bored faces of the marching men merely emphasized this fact. Everything seemed to say, with vulgar ostentation: "We are burying the body of a boy who had an unfortunate accident at sea, but we are only obeying protocol in a make-shift manner. Wait until one of our admirals die, then there'll be something real in the way of funerals, something worth walking down to the corner to see."

At the cemetery the Protestant padre read the burial service, and the buglers blew the "Last Post" and "Reveille". A squad fired a volley over the grave. When the body of Ordinary Seaman Clark had been placed again within the earth, the Captain and the Coxswain stepped forward and set their wreaths upon the clean, new mound which stood out stark against the melting snow.

"It's impressive, isn't it?" Manders asked of the man next to him in the ranks.

"I think it's all balls. I hope the next guy kicks off in the summer; my feet are soaking wet."

Pinchott looked to see who had spoken, before he said, "You haven't any right to talk like that. Be thankful you're alive."

"Oh, shut your bloody trap, Pinchott, or I'll bury *you* myself!" said the speaker.

"Some people haven't the common decency to know when to be reverent," Pinchott went on.

One of the stokers in the rear rank gave Pinchott a kick. McCaffrey, who was right-hand outside file in the front rank, spoke to the man next to him through the corner of his mouth. "Tell Pinchott to shut up, or I'll have him rattled as soon as we get back to the ship. Even the 'Bingo Bosun' is looking around to see who's skylarking."

McCaffrey felt the self-consciousness of a person whose family fight spills out to the front lawn. The shabby spectacle of Knobby's funeral assaulted his sensitivity as to what was right in the Navy. He looked around him at the dirty snow, then allowed his glance to slide along the set faces of the shore party, whom he regarded as interlopers. The officers could hardly hide their disinterest; even the padre seemed glad that his duties were over for the day.

McCaffrey sized up the padre as one of those young, modern churchmen who had visualized himself leading the crew of a sinking ship in the singing of "Rock Of Ages" while the water slowly rose to their necks. He would be willing to curse a very effeminate "Damn!" on occasion, and drink a glass of beer in the wet canteen, to show he "was one of the boys". "Probably looking forward to a hot rum toddy," said McCaffrey to himself.

When the funeral parade showed signs of getting ready to leave the cemetery, he was on pins and needles lest the *Riverford* party should make a blunder before the set, critical stares of the barracks contingent.

The band and shore party turned into the naval barracks, and left the small, untidy *Riverford* group to find its way back through the town alone. The Captain whispered to the First Lieutenant, before falling out, and making his way down a side street.

As the party passed one tavern after the other, there were mumblings in the ranks, causing the Coxswain to turn his head in a vain attempt to catch the offenders with his eye. Some drunken crew members from the *Milverton* appeared at the door of a hotel, and one of them shouted, "What's that? The *Riverford* short-arm parade!"

As they showed no sign of breaking off, the Coxswain ran up and fell into step beside the First Lieutenant. "Are we going back to the ship, sir?" he asked, hoping to get a negative answer.

"Yes, Cox'n."

"The men are grumbling, sir; some of them want to stop off for a drink."

"I know, but it's the Captain's orders."

"Very well, sir."

As he dropped back, the Coxswain told McCaffrey the bad news, and it spread among the men, who cursed the Captain, the ship, and all naval funerals.

By the time they reached the ship, their trouser legs were soaking wet, and they climbed aboard sullenly, their spirits almost as damp as their trousers. While they were changing their clothes, and envying the ones who had missed the funeral, the Coxswain and the Supply Assistant entered the seamens mess carrying a gallon jug of rum, and the tot measure. "Line up, funeral party!" cried the Coxswain, a happy gleam in his eye. "Tots for the funeral party, *only!*"

There were happy shouts as the news filtered into the other messes, and the erstwhile mourners lined up for their rum. "Who thought of this, Frank?" asked McCaffrey, shouldering his way into the queue, a cup in his hand.

"The Old Man told the Jimmy to break out a tot for each man in the party because their feet were wet."

"Good for the Old Man! I'll take Pinchott's tot too, because he's a Christian Scientist or something, and doesn't believe in medicine."

"I'm not a Christian Scientist, but I think it's terrible the way everything in this outfit ends with a drink," said Pinchott.

191

"Le' us drink a toast tae the dead, then," said Wright, hoisting his cup.

"Yeah, to Pinchott—he's dead, but he won't lie still!"

The Captain tried again to contact his wife by telephone, almost certain that he would find her home during the afternoon. Following a prolonged wait, the operator informed him that there was no answer. He hung up the receiver, drooping with a sudden fatigue, and made his way from the telephone booth.

He crossed the hotel rotunda to the telegraph office, and wrote out a message, with a hand that was trembling so much he could scarcely form the letters. "Get this off as quickly as you can, please," he said to the man behind the counter. He left the hotel, and walked up a residential street, torturing himself with his thoughts.

There had been no mail again today. If she would only write to him, or answer the telephone. It was not like her to act like this. No matter whether the news was bad or good, it would be better by far to hear it, than to live in this terrible vacuum, not knowing what had happened.

His concern for his wife was giving ground to a terrible anger against her. He no longer gave a damn about taking a civilized attitude toward the affair. As far as he was concerned, she could go to hell or Timbuctoo with her grounded airman, if only she would send him news about his son Ronnie. He had decided to stay ashore, rather than go aboard and carry on the pretence that everything was normal. As it was, Bowers was beginning to notice that all was not well.

He paused in his walk along the street, and crossed the road in the direction of the liquor store. He said to himself, "I can tell everyone else not to allow their personal problems to interfere with their job, but I don't take my own advice. Luckily, most wives write often, and only a few, like mine, fall in love with other men. If I don't hear from her tonight, I'm going to get as drunk as a skunk; and if I could meet Reggie, I'd act towards him exactly as Collet acted when he met Smith."

He bought a bottle of rum, not to help him spend a happy evening, but to imbibe as an analgesic.

CHAPTER 20

On march 14th, 1943, according to the B.B.C., the German Army was advancing over plains strewn with its own dead, against the Russian city of Kharkov. Allied bombers had strafed Field-Marshall Rommel's dug-in positions on the Mareth Line in North Africa. The U.S. had mounted an offensive to wipe out the Jap base on Kiska. Four submarines attacking a British convoy off the Portuguese coast, had been sunk, and their crews taken prisoner, according to a Lisbon report. The Italian Navy claimed that the *Empress Of Canada* had been sunk by an Italian submarine . . .

On a Canadian corvette lying in the harbour of St. Johns, Newfoundland, Leading Seaman Hector McCaffrey awakened to the sound of rain spattering on the decks; and a light wind carried the dreary wetness through the open scuttles into the hammocks slung nearby. The blackout screen was closed, and it swished wetly as the oilskinned figure of the quartermaster pushed his way beneath it. "Rise and shine, my sons! Wakey, wakey, wakey! Come on, my sons—you know what sons I mean!" There was an ear-splitting blast of the bosun's pipe, aimed first down the companion-way to the communications mess, then closer at hand as the sound was levelled below at the stokers. This was followed by a tremendous blast directly beneath McCaffrey's hammock.

"Listen, you silly bastard, we're not all deaf in here!" McCaffrey shouted, pushing his face between the hammocks.

Able Seaman Williams, the one responsible for all the noise, smiled the happy smile of one who has already

193

breakfasted, and is looking forward to turning in soon. "Sorry, *Mr.* McCaffrey, it's time to get up. Which paper do you wish to read, the *Province, Free Press, Gazette, Chronicle* or *Globe and Mail*?"

"Quiet, you son-of-a-bitch, there's a sick man over here!" cried a voice from forward, behind a wall of hammocks.

"I didn't know," Williams excused himself, his tone tinged with concern.

"Well, you know now!"

"Who's sick?"

"Me."

There was a titter of laughter. Two or three sets of feet appeared, feeling below them for the lockers or the mess-deck tables.

The quartermaster's muffled voice came from the stokers' mess. "Come on, my sons, rise and shine! Show a leg there, lads! Come on, you black bastards, rise and shine!"

A heavy object struck the stokers' ladder.

"Wakey, wakey, wakey!"

"What's the weather like, Williams?" asked a stoker.

"Beautiful. Get up before the sunshine burns your eyeballs!"

In the P.O.'s mess, Jimmy Collet sprang to full consciousness as soon as he heard the Bosun's pipe. It was odd to think that this was his last day aboard the *Riverford.* He tried to feel like a person awaiting sentence, but could not. The consensus of opinion in the mess was that he would lose his Good Conduct Badge, and one hook, being reduced to a leading stoker. He wished that it were possible to do fourteen days detention rather than lose his P.O.'s rate, and he glanced at his fore-and-aft rigged uniform, with its shiny brass buttons and arm badges on the left sleeve, and wondered how much longer he would wear it.

The Chief came out of his cabin, a towel slung over his bare shoulder, and a soap dish clutched against his naked paunch. "Hello, Jimmy," he said. "How do you feel this morning?"

"Pretty good, Chief. What all did we drink last night?"

"Take a look at the table," answered the Chief, laughing.

Jimmy glanced at the table, upon which were strewn in majestic disarray two dead soldiers of rye whiskey, one f Scotch, and the splintered wickerwork of a rum jar. "It must have been good," he said.

"It's not everybody who gets a send-off like that was. Take a look at Frank," the Chief said, and he opened the curtain in the doorway of the Coxswain's cabin, to disclose that worthy curled up in embryonic innocence, fully dressed, one corner of a blanket covering his shoulder, and his beard standing on end like a scared cat's tail.

"Thank God, there's one man who will feel worse than me when he wakes," said Jimmy.

Frenchy Turgeon set the tables in the mess, before going to the galley for the breakfast. He returned, carrying a large baking-dish full of sausages and eggs, a pound of butter held precariously between one thumb and forefinger, and two tins of Carnation stuck in the pit of each arm. He felt his way carefully down the forty-five degree angle of the steel ladder, and deposited his load on a bench.

"Wakey, wakey, wakey!" he cried, in imitation of the quartermaster's traditional call. "Come an' get eet!"

"Come an' get *eat!*" said Leading Stoker Dunderfield. "I'm gonna get eat later on today."

"What's the garbage this morning, Frenchy?" asked Wally Crabbe.

"*Les oeufs avec saucisse, monsieur,*" Frenchy replied.

"Never mind the hoofs, say it in Canadian."

"Heggs an' saus'ages."

"Saus'ages! Maybe you'd better stick to that frog language."

Dunderfield dropped from his hammock and pulled on his trousers. He shook the hammocks occupied by Sanderson and O'Brien. "Come on, you two, this is our last fling eggs until they let us out of chokey. For the next two or three weeks we'll be eating bread and molasses every morning, on the double."

"'ow can you mak' a joke on dat?" asked Frenchy.

"What do you want us to do, break into a sweat?" Sanderson asked, swinging himself down to the lockers.

"Shut up, Sanderson, if it hadn't been for you we wouldn't be in this fix," Dunderfield said, lacing his shoes. "I must ave been nuts listening to you talking about the dead kid."

"You didn't seem in no hurry to go into the stores yourself, anyway."

"I wish I *had* gone in. I'd stand a twenty-four hou
watch in there now to get out of this mess, so I could g
home on leave with the others."

"It would have been all right if everybody had've stuc
with us; the Old Man would've had to throw him over th
side," said O'Brien.

"Don't talk like a bloody fool. The Old Man would hav
taken the ship in himself, sooner than that."

Bodley awakened to the sound of breakfast coming fro
the communications table across the mess. He peered ove
the edge of his hammock at the open porthole, and sa
the drip of the rain gathering in beads, before it fell wi
a splash into the harbour. A few inches away was the o
stained camouflage of the *Port Dover's* side, bobbing gentl
to and fro in the slight harbour chop. The wintry sme
of the day before had been washed away by the rain, an
now the air had the odour of the sea—of the cold, rai
dripping North Atlantic.

He eased himself beneath the blankets, allowing his min
to race back to the night before. It had been a wonderf
night—well worth the effort of two evenings' dancing at th
U.S.O. He said her name over to himself: "Betty, litt
Betty from Cornerbrook."

They had walked, arms around each other, from th
U.S.O. canteen to the house on the edge of town whe
Betty was visiting with her aunt. They had stood togeth
at the door, surrounded by the darkened houses with the
offerings of empty milk bottles on the steps, and the creak
sound of new-born ice in the sagging eaves above the
heads. His hands had pressed her to him, their coats unbu
toned, and their bodies bowed against each other, so th
he could feel with his chest and belly the outlines of h
underthings. He had kissed her face and neck. His hands ha
explored her back, and down over the soft flesh of h
salient hips.

She had cried softly, "No, Ransome, no!" but had giv
the lie to her protestations with fervid little bites again
his cheek. Once, she had murmured, panic-stricken, "Som
body'll see us, Ransome, please!" Then later she had sai
"Come and sit in the car!" and they had felt their wa
through the snow to an old car parked beside the house .

196

He lay in his hammock, remembering every minute of the night before: the feel of her in his hand; soft flesh, the smooth contours of her breasts, the warmth of her cheek beneath his. The memory of her made him realize what Clark had missed by dying, and he felt a fleeting sorrow that young men should die. He thought that to the young, death should be a thing of tomorow, not today. "I'm a philosopher," he said, before forcing his thoughts back to dreams of Betty.

The voice of the Yeoman stirred him from his voluptuous dreams. "Get that tiffy up, somebody. He goes out tom-catting every night, and then sleeps away half the morn-ing!"

"Come on, get up, you chancre mechanic!" a voice cried in his ear, and his hammock began swinging wildly.

"Okay, okay, I'm awake!"

"Get up, then, your breakfast is getting cold."

"Throw it out, I'll eat later in the galley."

A signalman rushed down the steps to the mess. "The *Milverton* just got a signal to prepare to sail this after-noon!" he shouted.

"Good-O! Let's get out of this burg. Another day or two and we'll be home, boys!"

There was an increase in noise as they celebrated the good news. The record player gave vent to "She Had To Go And Lose It At The Astor", and somebody banged out an accompaniment with a pair of knives on the table top.

Bodley allowed the news to filter through him; letting it turn up the corners of his mouth into a smile. Poor Betty, she would not see him again that night, if ever. A picture came to mind of thousands of trusting little Betties in Montreal and Murmansk, Halifax, Nova Scotia and Hali-fax, Yorkshire, St. Johns and St. Kitts, Galveston and Gibraltar, all left like she was; their unborn children con-ceived on doorsteps, against the wall of the Guildhall in Londonderry, under a bridge outside Ponta Delgada in the Azores, on the loading platform behind the biscuit company in Cardiff . . .

"Come on, Tiffy, get up. Did you hear the news; we may be going home today!"

He pushed his concern for her to the back of his mind, salving his conscience with the thought that she would be all right—the Betties had a way of always being all right. Anyhow, there was nothing he could do now. "Coming, mother!" he shouted, in imitation of the radio voice of Henry Aldridge, and vaulted from his hammock to the deck.

The Captain sat in his cabin with the letter he had received, crumpled in his hand. They were all bad . . . there wasn't one of them who was decent . . . no, not even mothers . . . the only ones who thought mothers perfect were their sons . . . to know about them you should ask their daughters . . . or their husbands . . . ask a husband if his wife was perfect . . . ask *him* if *his* wife was perfect . . .

> *Dear Joe:*
> *By the time you receive this I will have gone away. I have left Ronald with Mrs. Dexter, and he will be well taken care of. Reggie has a posting to Calgary, and I have gone with him. I suppose you had better stop your allowance, and things of that sort. The furniture is in storage, and your insurance policies and other papers are at the Dexter's.*
> *Goodbye, Joe, and all the luck in the world. Take good care of Ronald.*
>
> *Joyce*

He tore the photograph from the bulkhead, and stared at it for a moment, before he took a pair of scissors from the drawer. As carefully as his palsied hands allowed, he sheared around the figure of his son, cutting his wife from his life forever. Then he placed the mutilated photograph on the bulkhead again, pressing the adhesive strips into place, where they had been before. With the shaking scissors he chopped the grinning picture of his wife into bits, and let them lay like a forgotten jig-saw upon the desk.

As he made his way into the wardroom, Bowers came forward with a young officer in tow. "Sir, I'd like you to meet Smith-Rawleigh's replacement — Sub-Lieutenant Harper. Lieutenant-Commander Frigsby."

"How are you, Harper? There's no hyphen in your name, is there?"

198

The young man made a tentative smile, looking from him to Bowers. "No, sir, just Harper—Thomas Harper. It's a pleasure to meet you, sir," he said, making a move to shake hands.

"Glad to have you aboard, Harper," the Captain said, grasping the half-proffered hand, and shaking it heartily.

"Are you ill, sir?" asked Bowers, staring at the Captain's drawn features.

"No. There's nothing wrong with me that a good drink won't cure."

"We've got that kind of medicine," Bowers said, walking to the wicket in the pantry bulkhead. "Three whiskeys, Roberts, ginger-ale with mine, water for the Captain, and ——" He turned to Harper, "How do you like yours?"

"Oh, I don't care; ginger-ale, I guess."

"And ginger-ale with the third."

When he turned from the wicket, he said, "I hope there wasn't any bad news in the telegram?"

"Telegram! Oh yes," the Captain answered, suddenly remembering the wire he had received shortly after the letter. He felt in his pocket, and pulled out the blue and yellow envelope, opening it quickly. His face was taut as he read it, the muscles around his nostrils stretching the skin. Gradually his face relaxed, and when he finished reading, his face was loose, and soft with pride. He looked up, and smiled. "It's from my son," he said. "It's from my boy Ronnie!"

"Good for him," said Bowers, the Captain's new-found happiness as contagious as a yawn. "He's getting to be quite the man."

"He sure is."

The drinks were passed around, and the Captain said, in a voice which had once more come to life, "Here's to your new berth, Harper, I hope you'll be happy aboard."

The quartermaster piped "Clear Lower Decks", and those aboard moved aft slowly, and took their positions on the quarter-deck. In the crowded stern, with its depth-charge rails and coils of lines, there was no room for barrack square precision. The ship's company fell into ragged ranks, seamen along the starboard side, stokers to port, miscellaneous and communications ratings forward of the stokers. The petty officers lined up along the after rail.

199

They were a heterogeneous picture, some in duffle coats, others in windbreakers or hockey sweaters, their head-gear half naval, half civilian wool caps. The cooks wore once-white summer drill trousers and blue denim shirts, and only the stewards were immaculate, in clean whites.

The prisoners, Dunderfield, Sanderson and O'Brien, stood with studied nonchalance in front of the members of the shore patrol who were there to escort them ashore. They stared ahead, trying to avoid the winks and smiles of encouragement from their friends. The shore patrol members were conscious of their spic-and-span appearance, and they were suddenly ashamed of it, separating them as it did from the sailors on the ship.

The officers came aft, and took up positions facing the assemblage. The Captain whispered to Lieutenant Bowers, who stepped forward, and brought the ship's company to attention. "Ship's Company, off caps!" There was the flurry of caps in the air, as seventy-five hands removed them from their heads. Without further preamble, the First Lieutenant called the name of Leading Stoker Dunderfield, who advanced one step, as his cap was wrenched from his head by the escort.

"Leading Stoker Dunderfield, you did, on the night of March 10th . . . wilful disobedience of a naval order . . . and did further . . . an act contrary to good order and naval discipline . . . it is the findings of this court . . . guilty as charged . . . the forfeiture of Ist. Good Conduct Badge . . ."

The Coxswain approached him, and, white-faced beneath his beard, grasped the badges on Dunderfield's left sleeve, and ripped them away in his hand.

". . . and be reduced to First Class Stoker . . . you shall also be detained . . . seven days . . ."

As his name was called, Sanderson took a forward step, which brought him into the open before the others. "First Class Stoker Sanderson. . . . an act contrary to good order and naval discipline . . . fourteen days detention . . ."

O'Brien took a sullen step, wearing on his face what he hoped was a devil-may-care grin. "First Class Stoker O'Brien . . . an act contrary to good order and naval discipline . . . fourteen days detention . . ."

There was a rustling of the sheets of paper in the First Lieutenant's hands. The assembly shuffled its feet, and turned to look at one another. "Ship's Company, on caps!"

Upon dismissal, the prisoners were marched forward to pick up their gear, while the remainder, conversing one with the other, followed the officers along the waist of the ship.

Frenchy Turgeon stayed behind, and followed Jimmy Collet below to the P.O.'s mess. He tapped him on the shoulder. " 'Ey, Jimmy."

"Hello, Frenchy."

"You go now, too?"

"That's right."

"'Ere, tak' dis," Frenchy said, handing him a bottle containing three inches of rum.

"I can't take it up to the cells, Frenchy."

"No, it is to drink—to 'elp your *courage*."

Jimmy laughed. "Frenchy, thanks a million," he said. "Where'd you steal this?"

"I 'ave been save it for t'ree day," answered Frenchy.

"Good boy. Well, here's looking up your kilt, Frenchy!" He upended the bottle, and allowed its contents to roll down his throat.

"You will feel good soon, Jimmy," Frenchy said, wearing a smile of satisfaction.

"I feel great now, you old Pea-Souper. You're all right, Frenchy; you're the real McCoy. You've always been a good man in the stokehold, and you're a good guy all 'round. *Tu comprenez pas?*"

"*Oui, Jimmy, merci . . . bonne chance, Jimmy!*"

The authoritative voice of the escort came down the ladder, "Get a move on down there!"

"Keep your shirt on, I've got to collect my gear."

Frenchy ran up the ladder, brushing past the shore patrol as roughly as he could, and walked forward along the starboard side, his face alight with an inner glow.

Before lunch, the Captain received a confidential signal, which he read in his cabin. He sent for the First Lieutenant. "Read this, Bowers," he said, handing him the flimsy.

"Oh good, suffering Christ!" exclaimed the First Lieutenant.

"It's a knockout, isn't it?"

"But—but we've all written home to say we're coming."

"I know. I need to go home more than anyone aboard," said the Captain, allowing his gaze to fall on the picture of his son on the bulkhead. Bowers glanced at the mutilated photograph, and a look of understanding passed between the two men.

Mollified now, Bowers asked, "How long will this mean, sir, do you know?"

"No, I'm sorry to say that I don't."

"One more trip?" he asked, hopefully.

"Perhaps. We may even refit on the other side."

"Oh no, not that. Half the men will cut their throats."

The Captain rose from his chair, and walked across the cabin. "Bad luck! I didn't believe it before, but I do now. It's bad luck to carry a corpse. If I sail until I'm ninety, I'll never do it again, for any reason."

"Can we write or telegraph, sir?"

"I'm afraid not. I'd like to myself, but I'll have to forbid it for security reasons."

"But—but——"

"I know. We'll be able to cable from 'Derry, that's the best I can do."

"And I felt sorry for Collet and the others," said Bowers, collapsing on the bunk.

"Get a signal ashore to rush down three experienced stokers and a stoker P.O. Send the Supply Assistant up here immediately," said the Captain.

"Yes, sir," answered Bowers, automatically. He made for the door.

"Oh, and Bowers, all leave is stopped, of course. That ordinary seaman, Jenkins, is it? Tell him to muster his gear. I was going to let him stay with us to Halifax, but I'll have to drop him off here. The drafting officer knows about him, they'll send another man."

The Supply Assistant knocked on the Captain's door.

"Come in, Walters. How many days' supplies have we on board?"

"Three or four, sir."

"I want you to telephone the Supply Depot, and have a full sea-stock order delivered before three o'clock."

"Yes, sir," answered the young man, his face wearing a woebegone expression.

"How is the rum?"

"We have about eleven gallons, sir."

"Get another keg."

"Yes, sir."

"Is the survivors' gear intact? Plenty of blankets?"

"Oh yes, sir it's all there."

"Good. Tell them three o'clock for sure. We are sailing at four."

Walters wanted to ask where they were going, but he thought better of it, and left the cabin.

Butch Jenkins packed his things in the seamen's mess. Already there was an invisible barrier erected between himself and the men who were staying aboard. They envied him, and yet there was an undertone of contempt for one who was destined not to share their bad luck, and the dangers of another trip. He felt a nostalgia now for the things he had hated such a short time before, but he hurried his preparations in order to retreat from their condescending flippancy.

"How do you get so lucky?" asked McCaffrey. "You'd fall in a sewer, and come up covered with diamonds."

"I don't want to leave. I'd be all right now that Knobby's gone."

"Don't be a sap, take the opportunity when it's offered. With our luck, we'll be fished for sure this trip."

McCaffrey turned the dial of the P.A. speaker, and the mess was flooded with the story of a young woman's loss of something at the Astor. McCaffrey said, "She's been losing that thing for over a month now; maybe she's a perpetual virgin." Then, as though amazed at the sharpness of his humour, he began to laugh.

There was a sudden crash from the loud-speaker, and the young woman's woes were terminated in a whining cacophony of sound. "She's had her time, I guess," he said.

Pearson entered the mess. "Thank God that's finished. The Yeoman just now broke the 'Astor' record with a well-aimed teapot. This trip won't be so bad now."

There followed a reluctant scratching from the loud-speaker, then a honeyed voice began: *"She said no—I said please——"*

Lieutenant Harris caught the Captain as he emerged from the wardroom. "May I have a word with you, sir?" he asked.

"Of course, Harris. Is it about your draft? Were you wondering when you could get ashore?"

"It is about my draft, sir. I hope that I'm not too late to reconsider?"

The Captain's face broke into an easy smile. He appeared much younger than he had earlier in the day. "I'm glad that you said that, Harris. What changed your mind?"

"I've been thinking it over. It would be all right if we were going in for a refit, but it would look bad if I asked for it now."

"Yes, it would."

"Do you mind telling me what all the rush is about, sir?"

The captain led him away from the pantry, and the wide-open ears of the stewards. "An east-bound convoy is under heavy attack three hundred miles from here. The R.N. escort have already lost a destroyer and two corvettes. Apparently Jerry has begun to use his new sonic torpedo. We are going—because we are still relatively seaworthy— along with the *Milverton* and an R.N. destroyer, to take the place of the torpedoed ships."

"I see, sir."

"Do you still want to go?" the Captain asked, smiling broadly.

"Sure, sir."

"As it happens, you wouldn't have been drafted today, in any case." He searched in an inside pocket for a moment, before his hand reappeared with the request chit. "Here, Harris, keep this for a souvenir," he said.

Through the espial grapevine of the Navy's signalmen, Cowboy Henderson received a phone call at the hospital from a friend of his in one of the nearby signal stations, who informed him that the *Riverford* was due to sail that afternoon. As soon as he received the message, he saw the medical officer, to whom he poured out a heart-rending story about the imperativeness of his getting home without delay.

This gentleman, after consulting Cowboy's chart and admittance records, wrote out a release, but not before pausing several times in obvious, and heart-stopping, indecision.

"Thank you, sir," gushed Cowboy, when the release was filled out. "You see, I've got to get aboard or I'm stuck here for weeks, and my mother may not last that long. As soon as we get to Halifax, I can leave for Toronto."

"Ye-es," hedged the doctor, torn between the twin oaths to Hippocrates and King George the Sixth. "You should stay another couple of days, you know, so that we may be sure your infection is really cleaned up."

"I know that, sir," answered Cowboy, with the forthright sincerity of a vacuum-cleaner salesman. "I requested to come here in the first place. I'm as anxious to get cured as the next man, sir. Can't you give me some pills to take on the way?"

"I don't think that will be necessary. You say your mother is at death's door?"

"Yes, sir," answered Cowboy. He said to himself, "She's even closer than that!"

"From what is your mother suffering?" asked the doctor, holding the release in his hand.

Cowboy thought fast. He was going to say cancer, but decided on something less obvious; something reeking of fatality: "Gingivitis, sir," he answered, solemnly.

The doctor stifled an exclamation. He thought, this will be something to use as an opener when speaking before the C.M.A. after the war. If I withold the release, I'll spoil the gag. Keeping a straight face, he said, "All right, Henderson, you can go. God speed you on your lying way."

"What, sir?"

"You can go—blow—scram!"

"Yes, sir, thank you, sir."

By the time he reached the lower end of town he saw that the *Riverford* was slipping her lines. He had the cab drive down to the wharf, and stepped aboard a water-taxi. "Skipper, get me aboard that ship coming out from the jetty!" he cried, out of breath with haste and excitement.

The small motor launch cut across the *Riverford's* bows, while the figure of Cowboy stood in the stern, and semaphored with his arms. The corvette's engines stopped, then began churning up the water as they were thrown to half speed astern. The taxi swung along the bigger ship's flank, and a ladder was lowered over the rail.

"It's that screwball Cowboy," the Yeoman remarked, leaning over the wing of the bridge.

The Captain took a position beside him, and peered down as Cowboy's gear was thrown aboard. "What a surprise he's going to get," he said, unbending from his usual reserve while on the bridge. He nodded to Allison, who ordered a resumption of half speed ahead.

"Hello, boys," Cowboy shouted, in greeting to the seamen who were stowing the ladder inboard again.

"What are you so happy about?" asked one.

"Didn't you see me just make the ship? Boy, I thought I was going to be stuck in Newfy. Well, let 'er rip—Toronto, here I come!"

"After a slight detour."

"What do you mean?"

Another seaman said, "He means that we're going back across the drink."

Cowboy stared in disbelief. "You're crazy! We're going to Canada for a refit."

"Do you hear anybody cheering?"

Cowboy looked from one to the other. Then, quickly, he climbed the ladder to the boat deck, and asked the stokers there if what he had heard was true.

"Sure it's true. We're not going home, mate."

"And I gave that taxi-bandit a dollar!"

"We go to play wit' de *sous-marine*," said Frenchy, illustrating a wriggling fish with his hand.

"I'd go back to that nice clean hospital bed if I were you," said Wally Crabbe. "All you need to do is put on your Jesus boots and walk to shore."

"Where are we going, 'Derry?"

"I guess so."

Cowboy's face underwent a metamorphosis, and he began to laugh, like a man reading his own obituary.

"Well, of all the——!" Then, remembering something, "As soon as we get there I'm going to get a forty-eight hour pass, and go to Belfast. If you guys think the Battle of the Atlantic is big, wait until you hear about the Battle of the Silver Harp!"

After sending his hammock and sea-bag to the barracks, in the naval truck which brought the newly drafted men, Butch Jenkins made his way through the town on foot. He climbed a hilly street in the gathering murk, and stopped, when from below him in the harbour came the rising whoo-oo-oot—whoo-oo-oot of a destroyer's siren. Looking back, he could see the sleek form of the ship passing through the harbour gates, her company standing in rigid attention along the upper decks. Behind her, but farther down the harbour, waddled the stubby, oil-smeared forms of two corvettes. On the bow of the last one, he could read the *Riverford's* number.

He let his gaze flow from the line of men on the fo'castle, over the bridge, with its bundled figures, and along the green-and-white camouflaged side, to the stern party standing on the quarter-deck. They don't look like a naval crew does in the movies, he thought. They're not as smart-looking as the men on a destroyer, or a cruiser. Look at Scotty Wright wearing the yellow sweater Manders gave him. And McCaffrey, cap resting on the bridge of his nose, and wearing those turned-down hip-boots.

Newfy Powers was coiling a line, but stopped to shake his fist at someone ashore. The Supply Assistant and his party were passing bags of sugar down the hatch to the after stores. On the bandstand, Able Seaman Williams had taken the covers from the machine guns, and now he was swivelling them around on their posts, like a fighter flexing his shoulder muscles on the corner ropes of a ring. Abaft the funnel, a small group of loungers were pointing to the torpedo hole in the bow of a merchant ship. A signalman lowered the clean White Ensign on the gaff, and changed it for the tattered, soot-blackened one which the ship wore at sea. There was a puff of black smoke from the funnel, as the stokers flashed another boiler.

Butch thought, if you didn't know them, you'd laugh to see them going out to fight. There's nothing dramatic about them, and I've never heard one of them say he wanted to go. They have no slogans or war cries, except perhaps an oath or two. If you played "God Save The

King" on the P.A. system, they'd turn it off. But they're good, and in two or three days' time they'll be showing it again. When it's dark and wet and lonely, and their nerves are jumping with expectation, and the icy wind is blowing through the halyards, they'll be there, and they know what to do.

As the corvette swung her wide backside at the town, making the turn for the gates, Lieutenant Harris dismissed the party at the stern, and the men ran forward towards the mess, while the cook shut the door to the galley.

Butch watched her slipping past the fishing shanties, an ugly little banana boat, going out there into the cold and danger, with no more concern than a chippy going to a corn-roast. He wiped the wetness from his cheeks, and said aloud, as though in answer to a question: "I'm lonely, that's all. I feel lonely as hell, that's why my eyes are running."